addicted

DARK ROAD SERIES

KRYS FENNER

addicted

DARK ROAD SERIES #1

Published by
TWO REALMS PUBLISHING LLC
HTTPS://TWO-REALMS-PUBLISHING-LLC.COM/

Cover and Interior Design: We Got You Covered Book Design
Editor: Jamie Morris

Printed in the United States of America

"For I am not ashamed of the gospel of Christ: for it is the power of God unto salvation to every one that believeth; to the Jew first, and also to the Greek."

– Romans 1:16, King James Bible

"SEASONS"

Things have changed;
My life is no longer the same.
Once, I walked strong;
But now, those days are gone.

I don't know how to let go;
The smile I wear is all for show.
A nightmare I'd like to escape;
Hopefully, it's not too late.

You are not alone.

prologue

Gervasio's hand wrapped around the base of the beer bottle as he eyed the dark-haired beauty from the corner of the room. These parties served as good hunting grounds. On occasion, he'd locate a victim no one would miss. A lonely girl starved for attention. But this one, she was different. She'd spent the last hour tucked against a wall, much as he'd done. However, her inability to socialize and interact with her peers hadn't been what caught his attention.

Long, midnight black hair. High cheekbones. Structured like that of a goddess. Mocha-colored skin. A richer chocolate than his own. Compared to her, his skin would be fair. Other features convinced him she looked familiar, though he hadn't entirely placed the face. In the recesses of his mind, he'd become certain he knew this young woman.

Only one way he'd discover the truth. He drained the last of his beer, set the empty bottle down on the nearest table, and strode across the room. The Fourth of July party was in full swing. Writhing bodies parted as he cut through the middle of the dance floor. No one dared to grumble or get in his way. Good thing too. Disposing of a body because some idiot crossed paths with him hadn't been in the cards tonight. No. This evening was about pleasure.

His pleasure.

Gervasio sidled up to his dark-haired beauty. Her midnight tresses were loosely braided and ended near her nice, round ass. She fidgeted with the hem of her white lace top. It worked well with the short, denim skirt. His eyes travelled along the curve of her hips, continued down the length of her smooth legs, and paused at the brown ankle boots. Certainly, one of a kind. A grin tugged at the corner of his lips as his gaze returned to her face. Soft hazel eyes touched with flecks of green.

Of course. Why hadn't he seen it sooner? She had her mother's eyes and cheekbones. No wonder she looked so familiar. That woman had been his favorite. Hmm, her presence at this party presented him with the opportunity he'd been in search of all these years. A way to get someone out of hiding and get everything he deserved. Indeed. It was time to play ball. He smiled at the teenage girl beside him. "You not like party?"

"Huh? What? Oh, no. I'm having a great time."

"How this possible? Pretty girl like you stand here alone. Cannot be fun."

"Am I that obvious?" She raised an eyebrow at him.

He nodded and offered her his hand. Normally, he took what he wanted, but he had special plans for this one. For a short time, he could play the part of a nice host. One who simply welcomed everyone into his home, even if the house didn't belong to him. He just provided the party favors. And no one had ever been wiser as to what he truly used them for. "*Sí*. I am Jorge. Tell me, you have drink?"

"Bella. And, no. I'm not really big into alcohol." A warm smile crept onto her mouth as she gently placed her hand in his for a polite handshake.

"This okay. I get you something. You like orange juice?"

"Oh. That's not necessary. Really, I'm fine."

Not for what he intended. She'd be the type to fight back. While he'd get there eventually, now he wanted quiet. He'd break her, but not like he'd done with his other girls. All he'd have to do, spike her drink. The drugs he had with him would be tasteless in orange juice. His own special concoction. "Plain orange juice. No alcohol. I promise."

"Well, all right. I am kind of thirsty."

"Okay. I be back." Gervasio pushed off the wall and trekked down the hall into the kitchen. He'd been to this house enough times to know its layout by heart. Never before had he taken a girl at the party. He had to be sure the attacks couldn't be linked to his hunting grounds. Otherwise, he'd lose his favorite pastime.

However, for Bella, he'd make an exception.

He scanned the empty kitchen. Must be his lucky night. Without a second to waste, he collected a couple of glasses and made two drinks, one laced orange juice and one plain Coke. No more alcohol for him. For the rest of the night to go according to plan, he needed a clear head. Returning to the spot on the wall where Bella awaited, he smiled brightly, handed the juice to his dark-haired beauty, and held his glass toward hers for a toast. "To fun for rest of night."

"I can drink to that."

They clinked glasses, and she swallowed a couple of big gulps from his offering.

Exactly what he wanted. Soon she'd feel the effects, and he'd gently escort her up the stairs, where he'd do anything he desired. His gaze held to her face. Her eyes wandered around the room. One hand dropped to the hem of that blouse again. Nervous ticks worked in his favor. Would she be as good as her mother? No. She'd be better. The teenage girl who stood before him, she still had her virtue. And he'd enjoy ripping it from her and leaving a part of himself with her. In due time.

Another smile pulled at the corners of his lips. "I not see you at parties before."

"Yeah. I don't usually go. My friend dragged me to this one tonight."

"But friend not here?" A friend could complicate things. Especially a regular partygoer. No way he'd be able to disappear both girls.

"Well, no, she's around."

His brain tumbled over a few ideas, then Gervasio set his half-empty glass of Coke down and offered Bella his hand. "Come to dance floor. Maybe you see her there." And then he'd know more about the possible complication.

"Um, okay." She set her half-full glass down, took his hand, stepped off the wall—and stopped. Blinking a few times, she pinched the bridge of her nose and rubbed at her forehead.

"Okay?"

Bella nodded. "Yeah. Guess I've just been standing there too long. Come on, let's go." As if nothing had happened, the two headed onto the dance floor hand in hand. They made their way to the center of the throng of bodies as the music softened.

Perfect. He gave her one quick spin out, then spun her back in until she was flush against his body. Precisely where he longed to have her. Dropping one hand to her low back, he kept her pressed in tight and, slowly, they moved to the music. A slight tinge of pink touched those dark cheeks of hers and her body warmed beneath his touch.

No woman had ever been attracted to his mangled face. Bella's must be responding to the male attention—or the power of his body. He'd bulked up over the last few years. His brute strength alone was now a force of nature and aided in his favorite pastime. And women found it nice. But no way any woman could ever see past the scar on his face. The one he'd been left with as a parting gift from Bella's father. Bastard would get what was coming. And Gervasio would use the man's daughter to do it.

"B! Hey, B!" A girl with stringy, dirty blonde hair shoved through the crowd, dragging some guy behind her. The girl was tall and lanky, much like the young man she'd brought along for the ride.

"Alex! Where have you been?" Bella's eyes narrowed, perhaps in concern, at the girl Gervasio presumed to be the missing friend.

"Sorry. Joe and I had some stuff to do, but you look like you're doing okay." The lanky girl shifted her attention from Bella to Gervasio. "I'm Alex."

Upon closer inspection, Gervasio recognized the girl's wide, bloodshot eyes. He knew the teenager. She frequented one of his men. For the same tasty morsel that had her stoned out of her mind. Gervasio grinned. His Bella could've selected better friends. "Jorge. And no worry. Friend in good hands."

"I'm sure. B. You okay?"

"Yeah. Go do what you want. I'm okay." Bella nodded.

Alex shrugged and eyed Gervasio. "Take good care of her. I'll leave you guys to it." Briefly she squeezed Bella's arm and shuffled back through the crowd with the guy she'd called Joe. He was glad not to have had to respond. That was just the way he liked it. As little conversation as possible. His dark-haired beauty wouldn't remember the night. And based on the amount of orange juice she'd drunken, the drugs would take effect any moment now. "Good friend?"

"Yeah. My best friend, actually. Probably why I joined her tonight."

"Always hard to say no to best friend."

"Yeah." Bella mumbled the single-word response. Her eyelids dropped to half-mast, and she curled her head against Gervasio's chest. Sagging a bit in his arms, she rubbed her forehead again. "Room's spinning."

Perfect. He leaned down and whispered in her ear. "No worry. I take you upstairs. *¿Si?*"

"Um ... yeah ..." The words barely tumbled out of her mouth before she slumped further against his body.

Though she was thicker than most girls he'd taken, he carried her weight with ease as he escorted her off the dance floor. To most, it would simply appear that she had a tad too much to drink. Gervasio snagged her half-empty glass of orange juice along the way. Without any resistance, he urged her up the stairs and toward the master bedroom, the one room that always remained unoccupied. It also happened to be the only one with a lock on the inside of the door.

Like at most parties, the room usually served as a coat rack. Gervasio set the glass down and escorted Bella over to the four-poster he'd make damn good use of for the next hour. The jackets covering the comforter could end up as evidence, but only if he left his DNA behind.

She sagged further. She was close to passing out. Shooting a glance over his shoulder, he confirmed their privacy and laid her beside the stack of coats, then pressed a chaste kiss to her lips. "Be good girl, honey bear."

"I ..."

"Shh. No worry. I take good care of you." Gervasio crossed to the door in two strides, closed it, and locked it. Pulling his shirt over his head, he returned to the bed, shoved the coats to the floor, and scooted Bella to the middle of the bed. Less room for her to struggle. Then he climbed on top of her and straddled her hips. A grin tugged on the corners of his lips, like the Cheshire Cat who ate the canary, as her eyelids drifted shut and she passed out.

Tonight, he'd touch the unmarred skin of purity and destroy it. His well-used hands would cover her body from head to toe; not that she'd remember any of it. He'd break her, but not in the same way he'd done his whores.

She was different.

She deserved different.

Bella was special.

With her he'd take his time. It would be worth the wait once he finally had her completely. For now, only his hands and lips would devour her sweetness.

one

"First day of school and already I want a redo." Bella's junior year could've started off a little better. Hell. A *lot* better. She strode beside Alex as they walked toward her locker. Her shorter stature made for smaller strides, but she always managed to keep up with her best friend.

Alex rolled her eyes. "Come on. Vick's ultimatum isn't that bad."

"Says you." She wasn't sure she had the courage to do what her brother had demanded. "But I guess I don't have a choice," Bella said with a shrug.

"All I have to say is, I wanna be there when you tell Heather off." Alex tucked a piece of her dirty blonde hair behind her ear.

"I don't know when I'm going to do it, you know."

"Oh, come on. I've never seen anyone have the guts to tell Heather Warren off."

Bella laughed. "All right. I'll do my best to wait until you're around."

"Thank you." Alex's smile revealed her slightly crooked teeth. Usually, she hid behind a close-mouthed grin, but things had changed over the past few months—and Bella never questioned why.

"Don't mention it."

As they rounded the corner of the hallway, they both stopped. Bella groaned and pulled her books to her chest. Evidently, the day could get worse. Then again, David had appeared at her locker every day for the past two years. Why should the first day of this new year be any different?

"Do you need me to stick around?" Alex asked.

"No. I'll have to deal with him sooner or later. Might as well be now."

"Okay. But he's a glutton for punishment."

Bella rolled her eyes. Nothing yet had ever persuaded David to stop pursuing her. "I don't think it's necessarily punishment," she said. "Somehow, he got the idea he could eventually wear me down."

"I still don't get why you won't go out with him. I mean, he's David Warren."

"If his sister didn't make my life miserable, I'd consider it."

"So, you'll say 'yes' after you tell her off?" Alex waggled her brows.

"No."

"But why? He's so fine. I could just eat him up."

Bella had never denied David looked good. He was also the most popular guy in school and captain of the soccer team. But sometimes bad things appear in pretty packages. "Yes, he's gorgeous, but my parents won't let me date. And even if they did, they wouldn't let me date him. And I don't even know why he wants to go out with me!"

"In other words, you're too chicken to ask your parents for permission, or to ask him why. Gotcha."

"Have you met my parents? As for him, part of me wanted to know—until all those gifts started showing up. Now, I just want it to stop."

Alex paused. "I thought you were going to talk to him about that."

"Never had his number."

Shaking her head, Alex slowly backed away. "Guess now's your chance."

"Fantastic," Bella mumbled as her best friend disappeared. Left to face the inevitable, Bella turned her attention to the guy leaning against the lockers. Was she insane for saying no? On an attractiveness scale, David was a nine: six feet tall, perfectly defined musculature, not to mention all that luscious, blue-black, wavy hair. And he had a smile that could charm its way into almost any girl's world. Except hers. She loved his smile, but had yet to be sucked in by it. And if anything could ever convince her to go out with him, it would be those piercing blue eyes.

"Hey, Bella."

"Hi, David. Have you been waiting long?" Averting her eyes, Bella focused on opening her locker, suddenly aware of her curves and that she stood nearly a foot shorter than him. What did he see in her?

"No."

"Good. What's up?"

"I heard you're head tutor. I wanted to come by and— Hey, you okay?"

Bella's gaze narrowed on the bouquet of orange roses neatly propped atop her books. When was the last time she'd been in her locker? After lunch? She glanced to the two books in her hands. Yeah. She had collected what had been necessary for her last two classes of the day. With a deep sigh, Bella reached forward and removed the bouquet. "David, this has got to stop."

"What are you ..." His eyes paused on the roses in her hand. "Where did those come from?"

"From my locker. Where you put them."

"Me?" David's eyes widened. "Wait. You think I put them there?"

"Along with all the other gifts I've been getting all summer." There were various items that had turned up on her doorstep over the last month or so.

"What gifts? I haven't given you anything."

Bella just stared at him. David folded his arms across his chest and stared right back.

"Chocolates, the Mexican coffee beans, earrings, the necklace. And now these. Don't you think it's enough?"

"Has there been a card with any of these gifts?"

"Well, no." But who else could it be?

"One," David held up a finger, "I wouldn't give you roses. Two, if I gave you anything, I sure as hell wouldn't hide that it was from me." He sighed and unfolded his arms. "You said there haven't been cards with the other gifts, but why don't you check this one."

Narrowing her eyes, Bella held her books out for him to hold. Then she searched the bouquet of roses—and blinked. There was a card. But it wasn't signed.

Instead, there was just one word written on it: *Soon.*

"And?"

"It says, 'soon.'" She flipped the card around and showed it to him. "I don't get it. Soon, what?"

David took the card from her and checked out both sides. He raised an eyebrow and handed it back. "You're sure there wasn't a card with any of the other things?"

"No. I even checked the boxes the jewelry came in for a store name. Nothing." She chucked the card back in the bouquet and glanced at David. "I have no idea who could be leaving me these things."

"Maybe it's a secret admirer and 'soon' just means they're ready to reveal their identity."

"Maybe." Shaking her head, Bella returned to the beginning of their conversation. Before she'd noticed the roses, he had ... crap. How the hell had he found out about her being made head tutor? It didn't matter. He had. She reached out and took her books back. She'd handle the flowers the same way she'd dealt with the chocolate and coffee. "Anyway, you were talking about tutoring. I'm guessing you want to make sure I can still tutor you."

"Um, yeah." David gripped the back of his neck. "The principal said you might be too busy with the new position, but to check with you about it."

Turning to her locker, she collected her backpack and grabbed the books she needed for homework. Bella had started tutoring David her freshman year. They'd worked together for two years. Except for that one time she'd tried to have him reassigned. After she brutally rejected him in front of the entire school, their tutoring sessions had gotten awkward. But he'd yelled at the head tutor and refused to have anyone except Bella tutor him.

"I get it if you really are too busy, but please don't say you are just to get rid of me."

There seemed to be no plausible reason to deny him her tutoring skills. If things got weird again, she could always reassign him. Bella smiled at David. "I'll still have time."

"Cool. When do we get together for our first session?"

"How about Wednesday after school?"

"Perfect. I'll see you then." Bella saw David eye the flowers one last time before he left.

Inhaling deeply, she tugged the backpack over her shoulders, snagged the bouquet of roses, and shut her locker. Another gift was too much to deal with at the moment. An escape would be nice. And what better way than a new book from her favorite author. She'd head downtown and hit the mall. Only bookstore in all of Rescate County, New Mexico.

Nibbling on her bottom lip, she meandered through the throng of students still gathered in the hallway, slipping out the doors and stopping by the trash can outside. Her intention had been to toss the roses. Instead, she spotted a familiar face. "Petar?"

"Hey, B. How're you doing?" He hugged her.

Briefly, she returned Petar's warm squeeze. The guy neared six foot, but had fallen a couple inches shy of it. Still, he'd always towered over her five-foot-two-inch frame. Had he bulked up? Bella stepped back. Same dark blonde hair and soft brown eyes, but he'd definitely put on some weight. The muscular kind. Even the scar on his face was less noticeable. "You look good. I guess college has done you well, but what are you doing here?"

"I came by to pick up a few things for school." A smile pulled on the corners of his lips, and he fidgeted with the folded papers in his hands.

Oh. She nodded, more to herself than in response to him. "Principal Owen asked you to talk to me, didn't he?"

"And here I thought I was doing an excellent job of hiding my ulterior motives."

Petar had been head tutor last year. He'd been in charge. All their work in the tutor group had pushed them together. Forced them to get close. Close enough, he'd almost been her first kiss. A tiny secret she'd kept from her best friend. And she'd learned his nervous tics. "If it were anyone else, I'm sure I wouldn't have noticed."

"The principal thinks I can give you some pointers. Come on. A little help never hurts."

"Fine, but not today. I'm on my way to the bookstore." No way he'd stop her from delving into her fantasy world. But he'd done an excellent job last year. Probably no one better qualified to offer advice.

"Tell you what," Petar said. "Let's kill two birds. Let me drive you to the store. We can talk on the way and get dinner after."

Her lips tightened. Usually she walked everywhere, but if he was going to meet her at the mall, anyway, it made more sense to go with him. And they had become friends. Because she only had room in her life for one botched first kiss. Bella nodded. "Okay, but it's not a date."

"You drive a hard bargain, but I'll concede."

"Glad we're on the same page." She smiled and tossed the flowers in the garbage.

Petar raised an eyebrow. "I'm assuming they did something to you, and that's why they deserved to be thrown out."

"Not really. I just don't keep strange gifts." That was a bit of a lie. She'd kept the jewelry, but only because it seemed wrong to throw it away. Instead, she'd placed those pieces in a drawer full of junk.

Shoving his hands in his pockets of his slacks, Petar nodded. "Duly noted. Shall we?"

Bella rubbed her eyes. What was her first class again? She hadn't gotten much sleep. That nightmare had returned. Why? She hadn't dreamt of that day in months. It had to be the stress. Yesterday, the tutoring requests had begun to come in, more than she had anticipated for the first day of school. There was so much organization required. And her parents hadn't helped. All night long they'd talked about how it would look on college applications. Graduation was still two long years away. College wasn't even a top priority at the moment. Surviving her junior year was the most important thing. Her brain was clogged like a hair-filled pipe. Not even Drano could unclog this mess.

"Did you roll in a pigsty before you came in? Or is that just your natural stench?" Heather Warren jeered as she paused behind Bella. Heather's tag-a-longs took up a spot on either side of her and cornered Bella against her locker.

"I think it's her clothes. She probably got them at the same place as the local white trash. I mean, we are close to Carlsbad."

Bella's lips pressed together. That from stupid Missy Watkins, a prickly blonde witch, who was on the cheerleading squad. Bella turned back to her books. Yes, she'd agreed with Alex that this year, she would deal with their insults, but it would be on her time.

"You're probably right. She does smell a little like gas and manure." Heather waved a hand in front of her face as if she were attempting to fan fumes away.

"Nah. It's her B.O. She's just gotten so used to the smell from her cage, she doesn't even notice." Cassie Shows giggled. She was an uptight redhead, a third wheel in their little clique, and the only one not a cheerleader. She just had money. These girls had been tethered together from the moment they met.

Their comments about Bella's clothes and her imaginary stench weren't out of the norm—and they weren't based on reality. She always washed. And she didn't have on anything unusual. A dark denim skirt, a short-sleeve, turquoise button-up trimmed with lace, and brown flats. Like always, her hair was braided and hung down her back. But the three of them barely had one brain together, which was probably why their retorts never changed. Bella dug around in her locker. What was she looking for?

"You know, I'm curious what your brother sees in her. She's barely human." Missy crossed her arms and popped a hip out.

Heather lifted her chin. "That's easy. He feels sorry for her."

They could make fun of her clothes or call her names, but Bella would be damned if they would use what someone might feel for her as an insult. Her hand tightened around a book. She could easily smack Heather upside the head with it. The bitch would never see it coming. Too bad she'd get suspended if she followed through. Taking a deep breath, instead, Bella slammed her locker shut and spun on her heel. "I'm shocked you guys can't come up with anything better. I mean, the three of you hardly use your brains. It's like they're brand new. Oh, I guess that's the problem. If you actually used them, they might explode. One-time thing, then. I get it. Originality would literally hurt."

"Excuse—"

"Nope. I didn't say you could talk, Heather. You have to let me finish. I know it's tough, but try to keep up. Once your looks are gone, all that's going to be left is an insecure little girl. And no guy wants that. So, get your heads out of your asses and stop trying to belittle everything about me. I have morals, and I'm proud of that. Nothing you could do or say can ever change that. What I stand for is worth far more than any crown you'll ever get."

"Why you little …" Heather spluttered. But Bella wasn't done.

"Maybe I wasn't clear enough. You're nothing but tainted sludge. I suggest you get used to the gutter. It's where you and your cronies belong." Bella shoved the three girls aside as if they were annoying flies. She hadn't even noticed the small crowd of students that had gathered nearby, all of whom clapped as she broke through. Her cheeks flushed. Inhaling deeply, she made her way through the assembled students. Several patted her on the shoulder and others offered congratulations. An arm hooked into hers, and she jumped. Alex, it was just Alex.

A breath escaped her lips, and her temperature started to come down.

"That was awesome!" Alex beamed a wide smile.

"So, you heard."

"Dude, a whole bunch of people heard. I bet by lunchtime the cafeteria will be buzzing. It isn't everyday Heather Warren gets put in her place."

She didn't share her friend's enthusiasm. And this could be all over school by lunch? She hugged her books as if they were a lifeline. Her skin prickled. What was the matter with her? She couldn't have picked a better time to go off on Heather? Like when no one was around?

"Hey. You okay?"

"Huh? Oh, yeah. I'm fine. Just thinking how huge a deal this will be, because it was someone like me who told Heather off. Not like if Missy and Cassie got into a fight with her or something."

Alex squeezed Bella's arm. "Come on, it isn't going to matter." Then she paused. "Okay, maybe you're right. It *is* a big deal because it was you."

"Yeah. Now, can we stop talking about it? Otherwise, I think I might throw up."

"Don't ruin it."

Amanda lifted her eyes to the female standing on the other side of the table. Had to be Queen Bitch. Somehow, she always crossed paths with them at every school she attended. Why should her senior year be any different? And of course, the queen had subjects. Right. Amanda smirked. "If I were wearing an outfit like that, I'd excuse myself too. A little advice honey? Just because the mannequin pulled it off doesn't mean you can."

The bitch stared, then gestured to herself and her friends. "You're new here, so I'll give you a freebie. Maybe you aren't aware of the social order. We run this school. And *this* is our table."

Leaning her chin on her hand, Amanda homed in on their hair. A raven-haired chick, a red-head, and a blonde. Sounded like the beginning of a bad joke. But something about the three of them looked familiar. She blinked. Oh, right. "Wait. I'm sorry. Did you say you run this school?"

"Yeah. As in the top of the pyramid."

"Gee, that's got to be embarrassing then." Knocking this girl off her pedestal would be easy. A little bit of fun never hurt anyone. And she deserved it. Amanda glanced past Queen Bitch and noted the group of guys headed in their general direction. Could prove interesting.

"What does?" the queen huffed.

"That you got your ass handed to you by none other than the school nerd." Amanda snickered. She'd spotted the scene on her way out of the administrative office—and then heard people talking about it in the hall. The whole thing had been laughable. "Don't get me wrong, but if you were really at the top, you wouldn't have let anyone underneath you walk all over you like that. Then again, maybe it's just the outfit. You do look like a doormat."

One of the guys paused at the table, with the rest of them hanging behind him. He glanced from Amanda to Queen Bitch. "What's going on?"

"She won't move," the girl said.

"Okay. How about you just let her join us?"

"Because this is our table." The bitch straightened her back and jutted her chin. "Mike, make her move."

Rolling her eyes, Amanda shook her head. Was this chick for real? Wow. Her family left California for this shit? Whatever. If she didn't move at the first demand, what the hell made the whore think she'd move for her jock boyfriend? Entwining her fingers together, Amanda leaned forward on her elbows. "Yes, Mike. Make me move."

"Heather, come on. You're being ridiculous." Mike glanced over his shoulder to his friends. As if to prove a point, they all put their trays down and started to sit.

"You would choose some monkey over me, your girlfriend?"

Mike crossed his arms. "You mean ex-girlfriend. I'm done. Now walk away before you make an even bigger ass of yourself."

Amanda covered her mouth and stifled a chuckle. Causing the two to break up was an unexpected bonus. And it sure as hell was funny to witness.

Heather's brother bellowed in laughter. Heather knew that rumors had flown around all morning about her altercation with Saint Bella—and then her run-in with that new chick at lunch. Some of the stories were ludicrous. The worst part was that someone had caught the festivities on video and uploaded unflatteringly creative versions of them online. And now her fraternal twin walked down the hall beside her, staring at his phone and yukking it up. How humiliating. "Are you quite finished?"

"Oh, come on, Sis. This is some real handiwork here. I feel like I need to go congratulate Bella on her epic win."

"I wouldn't rush to judgment. She may have won the battle, but I'll be the one to win the war." Things had already been put into motion. It wouldn't take much more to exact her revenge.

"Really? Don't you think enough is enough?"

She clenched her jaw. "No, I don't. We're Warrens. We have a reputation to protect. What would mother and father think?"

"I don't care what they think. Their opinions are overrated. But I know you're going to do what you want, anyway." David frowned and shook his head.

Heather had to admit he had a valid point about their parents. As long as they stayed in whatever country they'd traveled to this time, she shared her brother's sentiments. But when they were around, their opinions mattered. Still, she had to get her brother back for laughing. Of all people, he should know better. A slow smile crept onto her face. The corkboard ahead should have all kinds of goodies she could have fun with. "You're right. The only opinion that matters is yours. And you know, considering how much you enjoyed my humiliation, it seems imperative I return the favor."

"Oh? And how do you plan to do that?"

"By signing you up to audition for the school play." Heather stepped to the bulletin board, pulled out a pen, and began to scrawl her brother's name across the signup sheet.

David snatched the pen out of her hand. "Oh, no you don't! I'm not auditioning."

"What's the matter *big brother*? Scared of a little competition? Or of making a complete fool of yourself? Or maybe, just maybe, you don't want people to know your little secret."

Heather delighted in the fact that the big bad captain of the soccer team also played piano and sang. The guy had a voice like John Legend—but he only allowed people at school to think of him as a jock.

"You said you'd keep that bit of information to yourself."

Tilting her head, her lips twisted in a sneer. She relished the idea of torturing him just a little. It wasn't much, but it certainly made her feel better. It even made the day seem a little less bleak. "Maybe I will, but only IF you sign up for auditions. In fact, I dare you to sign up."

David hated his sister. His twin had always been a major pain in his ass. Daring him to do things he hadn't been interested in was at the top of her list of ways to annoy him. His eyebrows lowered. Heather just grinned and flipped her raven-colored hair over her shoulder. One of the many things they had in common.

"You can't be—" he started, but before he could finish, some guy stepped right between him and Heather and stared at the audition signup sheet. Who the hell was this guy? David had never seen him before. "Excuse you. Can't you see we're having a conversation?" David huffed.

"Dude, didn't sound like much of a conversation. More like her daring you, and you trying to come up with some lame-ass response. I mean, I'm signing up because I'm interested, not because I got dared." The guy pulled a pen out of his back pocket.

What nerve. For David and Heather, bickering had always been considered conversation. Not that he had to explain anything to this douche-bag. "You don't even know me. How do you know whether or not I actually *am* interested?"

"No offense, but if she had to dare you, I'm going to say it's safe to assume you aren't. But by all means, if you really want to sign up, I'll be right out of your way." Completing his name, the new guy flashed the two of them a quick smile and backed away from the board.

David glanced at the name scribbled on the fourth line. "Jeremiah Detrone, is it?"

"Yeah, that's me. The name may not mean much now, but give it time." He cracked one last smile and walked away.

Hand to her mouth, Heather stifled a giggle. "I know I shouldn't laugh, but I feel like you just got schooled."

Narrowing his eyes at his twin, David growled and tightened his grip on the pen. Before he snapped the damn thing, he scrawled his name in big block letters on the audition sheet.

t w o

Bella ran down the hallway, hooked the corner, and threw open the door to the administrative office. Mrs. Brown wasn't at her desk, but the principal's office door was partially open. Might not be a good sign. She knocked on the door and cracked it a little further. "Sorry I'm late."

"That's okay. Come on in." The principal waved her forward.

Her lungs constricted as she struggled to catch her breath. She had gotten so caught up in hiding, she had lost track of time, but now, here she was. As she slipped inside, Bella stopped, and her jaw slackened. A guy with the prettiest emerald green eyes stood opposite her, and those eyes lit up like lights on a Christmas tree. Holy crap, he was gorgeous. She brushed a hand down her skirt and looked at the floor.

Principal Owen stood to introduce them. "Jeremiah, this is your student buddy, Maylin Kynaston. Miss Kynaston, this is Jeremiah Detrone."

Playing with the ends of her hair, Bella forced herself to focus. "I'm sorry, what?"

"Miss Kynaston, why don't you show Jeremiah the library on your way to the meeting."

"Meeting?" What meeting? Was she supposed to be going to a meeting? Bella tilted her head.

"The tutor meeting."

"Oh. Right. Yeah, sure I can do that." Chewing on the inside of her cheek, she smiled. The principal might've said something else as they left, but her attention was on the gorgeous guy beside her. As they left the office and headed down the hall, Bella dared not look at him again. But she couldn't help herself and snuck a peek from the corner of her eyes. He was taller than she and had light skin, a color somewhere between her father's tan and Alex's white. And that dark brown hair. Its buzz cut was made to have fingers running across it.

Jeremiah broke the silence. "Maylin. That's an interesting name."

"Huh?" Bella blinked. "Oh. um, Bella. I go by Bella."

"How do you get Bella out of Maylin?"

She bit her bottom lip hard and squashed a giggle. "Um, you don't. Maylin Nadalia Christabel Kynaston. My full name."

"I see. Bella from Christabel. So, it isn't some nickname your parents stuck you with."

"No. When I was little my parents went back and forth between Lin Lin and Dalia. But when I was four or five, they told me to pick. I picked Bella. My friends sometimes call me 'B' though." There was another nickname she failed to mention. But her father hadn't called her Cinderella in such a long time.

"I like the whole one letter thing, but I'd rather call you Bell. I like that better. It's more fitting."

Bella canted her head. There was something going on she couldn't quite put her finger on. Her whole body softened like goo, and her mind had quieted. A slow smile spread to her lips and her cheeks warmed. "Okay, but on one condition."

"Name it."

"You let me come up with a nickname for you."

Jeremiah bopped his head as he contemplated her request. "Not anything weird, right?"

"No." Bella giggled.

"Nothing like Frankenfirth or Tronebot, right?"

"I promise."

"Deal." Jeremiah stopped and offered his hand.

Bella paused. As she removed one hand from her notebooks and placed it within his, her gaze shifted from their hands to his eyes. A shock of electricity flowed between them. She gasped, yanked her hand back, swallowed and started forward again. *Say something dumdum.*

Bella kept her mouth shut a moment longer. What a strange day—and one of the best. "Miah. I like Miah." No truer words had ever been uttered from her lips.

Jeremiah gripped the straps of his backpack. "I like that, too."

The library was just around the corner. How could she drag this out? "Where did you transfer from?"

"Los Angeles."

"I bet Rescate County is nothing like that."

Jeremiah shrugged. "No. But I haven't had much time to explore. Maybe you can tell me what there is to do around here."

"Mostly we have downtown. And our churches have functions."

"I didn't think this place was big enough for more than one church."

"Sure, it is. Three towns make up Rescate County. We're in Nautica Valley, and then there's Desemper Ridge and Amorte Cliffstone. Each town has their own church. Ours is United under Christ, or UC Baptist. That's where I go. Desemper Ridge has Desemper Fellowship, and Amorte Cliffstone has Cliffstone Catholic Church." Hopefully, she didn't sound like some tacky website advertisement attempting to show the world how wonderful Rescate County had become.

Jeremiah rubbed his chin. "What's your church like?"

"It's the second-largest, and is really involved with the community. We put on a huge production every October in place of Halloween."

"Sounds interesting. What about downtown?"

"There are a few—"

Whatever Miah was going to ask was interrupted when Vick rounded the corner and skidded to a halt beside Bella. "B, where have you been? I've been looking everywhere for you."

Vick gave Bella a big hug, then Bella glanced at her watch. How long had she and Miah stood there? "Um, sorry. I guess I lost track of time. Go on in. I'll be there in a second."

"We'll go in together," Vick said firmly, leaning back against a locker and crossing his arms.

Then a female voice called out, "Jeremiah. Come on, we gotta go."

The girl who approached had wavy mahogany hair and eyes as bright green as Miah's. She was the one who'd caused the scene with Heather in the lunchroom.

Why'd she have to be pretty?

Jeremiah looked past Bella. "I'll be there in a second, Mandy."

"Now." The girl, said, then turned and stomped away, as if expecting Miah to follow immediately.

Instead, Jeremiah returned his attention to Bella. "Thanks for all the information. Think I could see you again?"

"Um, I'm your student buddy," she replied. "If you want, we could meet tomorrow morning before classes, around eight o'clock, and I can show you around." Bella brushed her hand over her ear, tucking back a loose strand of hair.

"What about outside of school?"

"Um, I … we … um … Tuesday nights. We have a teen Bible study session. The address and stuff is on the UC website."

"Cool. I'll check it out. See you later, Bell."

Bella clutched her notebooks and smiled brightly. "Bye, Miah."

Jeremiah bustled down the hallway after the girl he'd called Mandy. Then Vick looped his arm through hers and dragged her inside the library door.

"Finally. I couldn't stand watching you two flirt any longer," he said, with a groan, and continued to the room where the tutor group waited.

"Flirt? Me? What?" Bella said to Vick's retreating back. Then she hurried to catch up with him.

Jeremiah peered over his shoulder in time to see Vick pull Bella into the library. That guy acted way too possessive with her. Too much like a— Shoving his hands in his pockets, his brows creased. Who was he kidding? Of course, she had a boyfriend. But she had flirted back. Maybe the guy was just a close friend. Good thing he'd grabbed last year's yearbook. Research had always been his strong suit.

"Christ. What the hell took so long?" Amanda asked, when he caught up with her.

"That girl? By the library?" Jeremiah felt his grin stretch like he'd just completed an air flare for the first time.

"What about her?" Amanda raised her eyebrows.

"I like her."

"Oh, God. We haven't even been at school one day and already you met someone? How's that even possible?"

It had to be fate or divine intervention, Jeremiah thought. Yeah, God's will. He and Bell were supposed to cross paths. Hard to say why, but he had a good feeling. But all he said to his sister was, "Because I accepted this could be a good move, Mandy."

Amanda hooked her fingers in the belt loops of her jeans. "Only in your mind. I hope everything blows up so we can move back to California."

"You can't really be this selfish."

"If you only knew, little brother."

Jeremiah gripped the straps of his backpack. Oh, he knew all right. More than he'd ever let on to their parents. Eventually they'd catch her, though, and she'd get punished in the worse way possible. But that was for another day.

"You know, you might actually like it here, if you just give it a chance," he told her.

"Says you. This has been a pretty shitty day."

"It can't really have been that bad."

Pressing her lips together, his sister frowned slightly. "Maybe not. I mean, I did get to tell that bitchy girl off. Heather's her name. And I watched her boyfriend dump her. That was fun."

"I really don't know about you sometimes. Now, as long as Mom and Dad don't find out about your change of clothes, your day will be complete."

Amanda looked away. "I've no idea what you're talking about."

"Sure. Keep telling yourself that." Jeremiah pushed the door open and headed outside to the parked van where their mother waited. He opened the front passenger side door and glanced once more back at the school. Definitely worth the move.

Jeremiah glanced at the time on his watch. Five past eight. He'd arrived about ten minutes ago. A little early for the meeting with his student buddy, but he had to be fully prepared. The school wasn't huge. Wouldn't take long to learn the layout. Hell, he could've used a map for the next week for all he cared. This hadn't been about a tour. Not at all. He waited because his student buddy had turned out to be the most gorgeous girl he'd ever seen. A beautiful angel he'd been destined to meet. All he had to do was find out every detail he could about her.

Last night, he searched her church website. It provided useful insights into her life. Her father was one of the youth pastors. He worked as a counselor at the local juvie center, too. Unfortunately, there hadn't been much more information. He'd checked multiple social media sites and found nothing. Almost like she was imaginary. Or lived in the dark ages. Either way, it seemed a little peculiar.

But not everyone could strive to be on social media every day, like his mother and sister. Of course, his mother had a valid excuse. Her work thrived because of what she posted online every day. His older sister, on the other hand … She'd demanded a cell phone when she turned fourteen. Not that she'd gotten what she so desperately wanted. Their parents had provided cell phones when they each turned fifteen. Him a year after her. It had become more useful about four months ago on his sixteenth birthday. The day he officially obtained his driver's license. He and his sister shared responsibility when it came to the car. Of course, she used it more often than he did.

He sighed and glanced to his watch again. Eight-fifteen. Where was she? Maybe she forgot all about the offer. Maybe he hadn't made an impression on her, after all. He'd check the parking lot once last time. If she wasn't there, then he could self-guide it. Jeremiah stepped out the doors as his angel rounded the corner of the building.

Bell stopped before they toppled right into one another. "I'm sorry. I know I'm late. I just got caught up on tutor assignments this morning."

"I get it. Not hard to get lost in your head sometimes." Jeremiah smiled. She had shown up. Right now, it was enough. "So, you tutor?"

"Well, yes, but I'm also the head tutor. Turning out to be a bit more organization than I expected, but I guess I like it. Enough about that. You're here for a tour. Shall we?" Bella gestured to the double doors.

"Can we talk and walk at the same time?"

She tugged on the hem of her blouse and raised an eyebrow. "You don't really care about a tour, do you?"

Man, she was cute, scrutinizing him the way she was. And right on point. Jeremiah smiled. "I would've agreed to a baseball game if it meant I could spend more time with you."

"Not necessary." Without uttering another word, Bell strode past him, opened the door and paused, then batted her eyelashes. "You coming?"

Who the hell was she? Where the hell had all this come from? It had to be this guy—Miah. He did something to her. Twisted her mind. Or maybe it had been twisted all along, and he simply brought it out. Bella eyed Jeremiah from head to toe. He just stood there, running a hand across the top of his hair. Would the hairs tickle the palm of her hand if she touched his head? He said something. What did he say? Crap.

"Mind if we put our stuff in our lockers first?" Bella asked, to bring herself back to the moment.

A small grin tugged on the corner of his lips. "Yeah, that's okay with me," he said.

"You just suggested that, didn't you?" Bella blushed. Way to look like an idiot. Shaking her head at herself, she giggled. "I'm not sure what's worse. Repeating what you already said or boring you to death with unnecessary history about the school."

"History, definitely history." Jeremiah moved closer so they walked in step. "Do you really have to give new students the school's history?"

"Every student buddy is asked to recite it, but I can't say that most do. Unless, of course, we spot the principal. If I jump off onto some historical tangent, that's why."

"Are there any other informational bytes you're supposed to share?"

Bella input her combination and opened her locker. "Aside from making sure you know where everything is, I'm responsible for telling you about all the different clubs we have."

"So, basically, it's your job to hold my hand?"

Bella laughed, hung her backpack in her locker, and closed it. "You know, I never thought about it like that, but I guess so. I think the idea is to make the transition as easy as possible. Not that the layout of the school is hard to learn."

"I kind of noticed. One big square."

"And yet, you'd be surprised how many people are late for class. All right. Where's your locker?" She studied his features as he pointed toward it. Soft green eyes. Tall. His strides were way longer than hers, but he slowed his pace so they walked side by side. He was a little lanky, but muscular. Absolutely gorgeous. When they stopped at his locker, she asked, "What brought your family here from California?"

"My dad's job. He's in the service, so we tend to move a lot. I usually take our moves in stride. Try to see them as opportunities. Not all of my siblings share my outlook."

"How many do you have?" Though she called Vick her brother, they weren't related. She was an only child.

Miah shoved his locker closed on his backpack. "Six, soon-to-be seven."

Her eyes widened. Did he honestly say he had almost seven siblings? Wow. That had to be one busy, noisy house. "Six? Really?"

"Yeah. My parents always joke they want their own football team." He chuckled. "And now they're well on their way. I'm the second oldest. My sister, Amanda, she's the oldest. After me there's Connor, Owen, Jake, and Nat. What about you? Any sisters or brothers?"

"Do overbearing best friends who act like brothers count?"

Shoving his hands into the front pockets of his jeans, Jeremiah snickered. "Maybe as family, but not blood related."

Guess that excluded Vick. Bella snapped her fingers. "Then, no. Just me. Unless my parents have some secret love child I don't know anything about."

"I've never met your parents, so I can't comment."

"Think Wilma and Fred Flintstone." She frowned. Her parents weren't that bad. A little in the dark ages, but mostly when it came to technology. They had a TV, but no cable. Plus, a DVD player they hardly used. The only computer was in her father's office. And none of them had cell phones.

"Then I'm gonna go with no love child."

Rounding the corner of the hallway, Bella folded her hands behind her back. "What about your parents? What are they like?"

"Think the Bakers from *Cheaper by the Dozen*. Well, maybe my mom. My dad is more like Tom Baker meets Jason Bourne meets Black Panther."

She blinked and stared at the floor. She'd seen *Cheaper by the Dozen* and read *The Bourne* book series, but Black Panther? Who was that? She felt herself frowning.

"You look confused."

"Am I that easy to read?"

Using his thumb, Jeremiah brushed along the top arc of her eyebrow. "You have this adorable crease here. Like you're thinking a little too hard."

Her breath caught in her throat. She swallowed a bit of saliva and attempted to breathe. He was touching her. It was gentle and amazing. Bella swallowed again. "Um, Black Panther. I don't know who that is."

"What? He is one of the best, most important comic-book superheroes of all time. I have the first issue. You have to read it. Then you'll understand my dad perfectly."

"Okay." Comic books weren't really her thing, but for him, she'd read almost anything. "You know, you should join my friends and me for lunch. I think you and Vick would get along great."

"Yeah. Hey, can I ask you a question?"

Pivoting on her heel, Bella stifled a giggle. "That *is* a question, but shoot."

"When I saw you come up this morning, you were walking. Do you walk to and from school?"

"Every day. Why?" Her parents had cars, but they both worked in a different direction from her school. Walking to school was her way to make things easier day-to-day. Plus, it kept her healthy. Two birds, one stone.

"Would you mind if I walked you home this afternoon?"

Only one guy had ever walked her home before. And he was like a brother. She gave Jeremiah—Miah—a sidelong glance. "Yeah ... that would be okay."

Maybe he should've reconsidered this walking her home thing. Talking to Bell was great, but damn, this heat. It was much dryer here in New Mexico than in L.A. There, they'd lived by the ocean, so there was almost always a breeze to help cool him down. Here, no breeze, no water. Jeremiah eyed the sidewalk in front of them. "How much farther?"

"About four or five blocks. Is the heat getting to you?"

"You a mind reader?" No way he was sweating that much. He hoped. He touched his forehead. Maybe he was glistening.

Bell chuckled. "No. It gets all newcomers. Unless you've lived someplace like Texas." She stopped, dug a bottle of water out of her backpack and held it out to him.

Cracking it open, he chugged half the water back. "You always this prepared?"

"I was born here. So, yes." She slipped her backpack over her shoulders and continued forward. "Don't worry. Stay here long enough and you'll get used to it."

"Guess I'm a little spoiled, having lived by the ocean and all." Stay here long enough? Heck at this rate, he was planning on dying here. Unless by some chance, Bell decided she wanted to live somewhere else. The world was enormous.

"I bet that was wonderful, though." She half-glanced at him. "I've never seen the ocean."

Really? That was something to keep in mind. "Haven't you ever gone anywhere?"

"Only if Carlsbad and Roswell count."

No family vacation? No summer adventure? No spring break? Wow. She mentioned her parents were technophobes, but that seemed a bit extreme. "Is all your family here then? In New Mexico, I mean."

"Nope. Just us. My mom's parents live in Brazil. They've never left, and we've never visited. My dad's mom, she lives in China, but she comes here every few years. Always has the best stories. Usually about her and my grandfather, before he passed." Bell shrugged as if it were no big deal. Something she had grown accustomed to.

"I'm sorry to hear about your grandfather," Jeremiah said. Wow, he thought. No siblings. No aunts or uncles. Grandparents she didn't even speak to on a regular basis, let alone spend much time with. It was like this girl had been cut off from the world. On the spectrum of family togetherness, he and she were at opposite ends. He had almost a football team of brothers and sisters. Countless cousins. Several aunts and uncles, mostly on his father's side. They were so different. His world was loud and sometimes obnoxious. Hers?

Jeremiah glanced at Bell. "It must be so quiet for you."

"Honestly …" She paused and looked from the ground to him, "It's deafening. If it weren't for my *nǎinai*, my dad's mom, I think I'd go crazy. It's strange. You'd think being an only grandchild, I'd be … more connected to my grandparents somehow." Bell sighed. "There's so much heritage to learn, but it's almost like they don't care to teach me anything about my history. Doesn't matter if I speak the language. The rest, if I want to learn, it's up to me."

"Sounds lonely." He stopped. Open mouth and insert foot. "What I mean is—"

"You're right. So, I just do what I can. Hopefully, one day, it'll be enough." Bell stopped in front of a mailbox. "Anyway, we're here. Shall we?" She gestured toward the front porch and headed up the walkway.

Following after her, he eyed the pale yellow, one-story house. Half-way up the walk, he peered through the large bay window beside the open front porch. Looked pretty nice inside. Warm and welcoming. In front of him on the walk, Bell bent down to pick up something.

"What's that?"

"It's— Ow!" Bell dropped a single red rose on the ground.

Jeremiah glanced at the flower. Then, grabbing her hand, he lifted her finger up for inspection. "Doesn't look too bad. Probably just got caught on a thorn. You have peroxide and Band-Aids inside?"

Who the hell was the black piece of shit with his girl? Gervasio glared through the passenger side window. She'd always walked home alone. Her path hadn't altered one bit since the Fourth of July party. Had he known about the unexpected addition to her life, he certainly would've planned for a much better gift. A single rose wasn't as nice as a bouquet of roses, but she had tossed his bouquet in the trash. Maybe she just didn't like flowers in general. He leaned across the seat and stared at the ongoing situation on the front porch.

That thing had a hold of his girl's hand. What was he going to do? Kiss her fucking boo-boo and make it all better? Growling, Gervasio slammed his hands on the steering wheel. Not fucking happening. No white-washed piece of dung would interfere with his plans or steal his girl. She belonged to him! And no one else.

Not even her father could stop what was coming.

But he had to be patient. The last six weeks hadn't been for nothing. The moment had to be timed perfectly. Otherwise everything he desired would slip through his fingers. As for the piece of shit with his girl, he had to know more. Releasing his hold on the wheel, Gervasio dug his cell phone out of his jeans. This was a job for the messenger. "Tengo un trabajo para ti."

"Sí jefe."

"Te estoy enviando una foto. Averigua quién es. ¿Comprende?"

The guy had a knack for computers. Using a photo to find out who this thing was would be easy. It was one of the few things he trusted the messenger to accomplish.

"Sí jefe."

Gervasio had snapped a few photos when the two initially approached the house. Now, he sent them off to the messenger and to a few others who spied on his girl for him. Knowing who this thing was, that was only half the battle. How long had the piece of shit been around? How much time did the thing spend with his girl? All of these pieces of intel mattered. After all, he couldn't go on with his plan if she wasn't alone. And time was of the essence. Gervasio smiled. He hadn't waited six weeks to get caught now.

He would have her completely.

Soon.

Soon, she would forever be his.

This rose is another gift, Bella thought. This one had a card with it too. Same as the bouquet from the day before—no name, no greeting. Just one word. "Soon." The hairs on the back of her neck stood up. Was she being watched? Bella scanned the street. No cars out of the ordinary. It all looked the same as usual.

"Do you?"

She blinked. Did she what? He still had a hold of her hand. Her finger was bleeding. Right. First aid. "Um, yeah. We have Band-Aids." She spun on her heel and opened the front door. "The den's right there. Make yourself comfortable."

"Okay, sure."

Bella hurried down the hall into the bathroom. Turning the water on, she thrust her hand under the faucet and let the water wash out the wound.

"¿Quem é o menino na nossa sala de estar?"

Bella jumped. Holy mother of God. Wasn't the first time her mother had snuck up on her. With a quiet exhale, she yanked the hand towel off the rack and wrapped it around her finger. Who is the boy in our living room? How to answer that? The simplest explanation possible. A friend from school. No need to tell her mother she secretly hoped for more.

"Ele é amigo da escola."

"Então ele é novo. ¿Quando vocês se conheceram?" Her mother half-phrased it as a question.

The woman knew all of her friends. Obviously, he was new. Bella crouched down and dug around the cabinet for the Band-Aids. As for when they met? Physically, yesterday. Emotionally, it seemed like she'd known him all her life. Given she practically poured her heart out to him. Or at least revealed secrets she hadn't shared with anyone. Not even her best friend. Collecting a Band-Aid, Bella stood and lowered her voice. "Mãe, can you please not make a big deal out of this?"

A slow smile crept across her mother's face. "¿Você gosta dele?"

"Mãe." Did she like him? Had her mother really asked her that?

Bella rolled her eyes. Her mother's arms wrapped around her shoulders.

"Come now. This does not occur every day."

Okay. That was enough. Bella pulled out of the hug. "You're embarrassing me."

"Such is a mother's duty. Now, please explain the reason for your first aid."

Great. Onto something new. If only the new topic was any better than the original. "I cut myself on a rose thorn."

"How did this occur?" Her mother folded her hands behind her back and narrowed her eyes at Bella.

And that was where it got complicated. She hadn't told her parents about any of the other gifts. It seemed unnecessary to mention the items. Too bad she had no choice with this one. "It was on the front porch." Bella walked by her mother and past the den to the front door. Careful of the thorns, she picked up the rose, slipping the card into the back pocket of her denim skirt before showing the flower to her mother. "Probably left here by mistake. It's nothing to worry about."

"Are you certain?"

Her mother had every right to question the statement. Yeah, Bella had lied, but what David Warren had said about a secret admirer made sense. Not that she had any clue who the secret admirer could be. Still, nothing about the gifts screamed danger. No need to blow anything out of proportion.

Bella nodded. "Sim Mãe."

Her mother stared at Bella. It was that motherly look. The one that clearly expressed disbelief—combined with patience. "Very well. Come. I would like to meet your young man."

That had a nice sound. Her young man. The corners of her lips pulled into a bright smile. She could certainly bring them together. "All right."

three

There hadn't been much time, last night, to discuss the behind-closed-doors meeting Jeremiah had with their respective fathers, before he left. Good thing they got together this morning. The hush-hush tones between her parents suddenly made much more sense. And it was the exact reason she had come up with a plan of her own.

Bella peered over her shoulder—again—as she approached the main doors to Rescate County Juvenile Detention Center. Though she could've sworn someone followed her, at no point had she seen anyone behind her. At first, she figured Miah had chased after her, despite her insistence on going alone. If he had tagged along, she wouldn't be able to talk openly about him. So, she'd had made the trip to her father's job on her own. Except for that feeling of eyes on her.

Pushing the door open, she slipped inside. "Hey Josh."

"Hi, Bella. How're you doing?"

"I'm good. What about you? How's the wife?"

"Wonderful. We're pregnant again."

"Oh, wow. Congratulations. This is what? Baby number three?"

Josh blushed. "Yeah."

"I'll pray you have a boy this time." Bella grinned.

Josh grinned back. "Go on," he said. "I don't think he has anybody with him."

"Thanks." She headed down the hallway toward her father's office.

The door opened and a young man, no older than she, stepped out as the door clapped behind him. Bella and the young man bumped into one another and immediately jumped back.

"Sorry," the two apologized, simultaneously.

Bella gripped the straps of her backpack. "It's okay. Completely my fault. I didn't think anyone was in there."

"No. I should have looked before I left."

The office door creaked open, and her father poked his head out. "Bella? Why are you here?"

"Hi, Bàba. I was hoping you had a second to talk about Miah."

"Yes, of course. Come in." Bella's father backed up to give her room to enter. He paused before shutting the door, then, looking at the young man still standing there, "Cristobal, do you not have chores to attend to?"

"I do. I'm going."

"Good," Bella's father said, and closed the door.

Bella sat in one of the two chairs in front of her father's desk, while he took the other one. "Before you say anything, Mãe told me you don't think it's a good idea for Miah and me to date."

"This is true. You are where you should be in school. If I allow you to see one another, I fear that pattern will break."

"Bàba, you can't really think a boy will change the importance of school." There had to be more to his reasoning. Unless he didn't trust her. Or Jeremiah.

"It may not appear to do so in the beginning, but it always starts slow. First, you forget a homework assignment. Then you procrastinate so you can go out with this boy. Before long, the boy is all you care about." Her father crossed one leg over the other, as if to finalize his argument.

The last thing Bella wanted to do was laugh at her father, but the scenario he'd just described was highly implausible. Where had he gotten the idea? An outdated movie?

Right. Start simple. Let her father know her feelings for Miah. Bella spit it out. "Bàba, wǒ xǐhuan tā."

"Wèishénme?"

"He's kind, smart, and has strong values. He has big dreams and the focus to make them happen. Jeremiah is wonderful. I like being around him. How many teenage boys do you know would ask you first if he could go out with me?" Bella folded her hands in her lap. It wasn't her strongest argument, but she saved the best for last.

"This is true. It has become an archaic practice. Unless the child is taught by the mother and father."

Okay. Not quite what she was going for. They weren't children—and she wasn't his baby girl any longer. Maybe she wasn't a full-grown adult, but she was definitely old enough to know what she wanted. "Fùqīn, wǒ shíliù suì."

Her father winced. "Shì, wǒ zhīdào."

Bella stood and walked to the bookcase. She glanced at the titles, then, turning back to her father, she laid it on the line. "Do you? You say you know I'm sixteen, but you act as if I'm still that little girl who needs protecting. Bàba, it's time I start making my own decisions. My own mistakes. Have faith in everything you've taught me."

"Bella, you will always be my little girl. Though I do suppose you are at an age when I should trust your instinct."

"Really?"

"Yes. I have seen the respect this young man shows for you. Your mother has also advised me he plans to join us on Tuesday evenings and at church." Her father sighed. "You truly care about this young man?"

"I do, Bàba. I do." Bella's eyes widened. Was her father really agreeing to let them date? Had their entire conversation actually gone according to plan?

"Then I will allow you to spend time with him outside of school. However, if your grades should fall, your focus will return to your studies. Am I understood?"

"Shìde Bàba. Xièxie." Bella hugged her father tightly. "You won't regret this."

It wasn't outside of town, like Gervasio's other holdings, but it still remained well hidden. Mostly, because he had several government officials on his payroll. Hard to believe there could be so much corruption in one county, but he understood the art of persuasion. And blackmail. Amazing what secrets people tried so hard to hide. But things always had a way of coming out—when he deemed it appropriate.

His phone vibrated. Gervasio dug the burner out of his pocket and flipped it open and read the text message.

His baby brother had a visitor. Interesting. What could the two of them have discussed? He eyed the time. Swifty stopped by the warehouse every evening on his way home. A check in. Tonight, it would be useful. The messenger would be required to recreate the conversation he'd held with the teenager he once called brother—until Cristobal had proven disloyal, that is. Gervasio stroked his chin. Something had to be done about this outreach. This presented an excellent opportunity. He'd handle the situation with his messenger directly. As for his blood brother, he'd allow Bronco to deal with him.

Tucking his phone away, Gervasio leaned against the wall by the staircase. Voices echoed from upstairs. Not the whole crew, but enough. They would serve as witnesses. Word of his actions often spread quickly.

The door opened. His eyes never left the floor. He didn't need to look to know who had come in. "Tell me, talk with *mi hermano*, it go well?"

"Boss? What are you talking about?"

"Do not lie! I know where you go." Wide, hazel-colored eyes with flecks of green stared back at him. The messenger was good at many things, but not at hiding the truth. His face always gave him away. Swifty was as gullible as the other members. No one knew how deep his connections reached. He had eyes all over this county.

Gervasio narrowed his own eyes and hissed.

"Okay, yeah. Cristobal called and I went."

Pushing off the wall, Gervasio stepped forward. This lesson wouldn't go well for the young man who stood before him. Swifty had been with him a few years now. Slowly he climbed the ladder. His knack for invisibility made him a good messenger, but it also meant the man had access to certain information he preferred be kept secret.

"What he ask?"

"About you mostly. That you were well."

Trust no one. A valuable lesson his father instilled in him at a young age. One that had paid off over the years. By this point, some of his crew members had gathered by the top of the staircase. He had an audience. Perfect. Hooking a right punch, he knocked Swifty square in the jaw and flat on his ass. Blood trickled from his nose. Gervasio crouched down on his haunches and shoved a finger in the messenger's face. "Lie again and I give you to *verdugo*."

"The girl. He wanted to know about your intentions for her."

Aggression radiated from Gervasio's body. Satisfied he'd received an honest answer, he rose to his full height and turned toward the onlookers. Having his messenger killed would've been a bit much. But a threat to have him handed over to the executioner worked rather well. "Cristobal disloyal. He turn his back on his *familia*. This no good. You speak to him, I kill you."

Silence. Best response. No need to ask if they understood the message. If they didn't, well, he'd find out soon enough.

Gervasio glanced at Swifty. "Get clean. Work to do." He didn't wait to see what any of his members did or if the messenger bothered to move. The message had been delivered. And he had more important matters to attend to. Striding across the floor, Gervasio pulled his phone out again and typed, *Have job for you.*

His plan wasn't just about getting what he deserved. It was about getting his girl's father out of hiding.

After cramming a book in his locker, Jeremiah stared at Bell. Her father agreed? Had she said that? Her father agreed. Yeah. Amazing. It worked. He'd never sought permission before. Then again, he hadn't wanted more than friendship with anyone before, either. Old school had definitely been the way to go.

He blinked. "Sorry, I don't mean to stare. I'm just surprised."

"Really? I thought you'd be happy," Bell said with a wince.

Crap! That didn't come out right at all. Jeremiah grabbed Bell's hands and squeezed. "It does make me happy. I'm grateful he gave his permission. I guess I just expected to have to prove myself to him. And I was prepared to do so."

Lifting her eyes to his, he saw a faint smile tug at the corners of her lips. "Really?"

Jeremiah gazed into those bright, beautiful, hazel-brown eyes. She had no clue how gorgeous she truly was to him. "Absolutely. Now, why don't we head toward the cafeteria for lunch, and we can discuss plans for Saturday?"

"'Saturday,' as in tomorrow Saturday?"

"Yeah." Keeping hold of one of her hands, Jeremiah turned for the lunchroom. Maybe it was a little soon, but he had no intention of letting her go. "Unless you prefer Sunday. But I figured it might cut it a bit tight, with church and all."

"Um, no, tomorrow's fine." Bell's eyes flicked to their interlocked hands and back to him. "Yeah, tomorrow's good."

Tiny beads of sweat on her forehead told him she was nervous. Jeremiah gripped the base of his neck with his free hand. Made two of them. He had no clue what he was doing, but holding hands, it felt right. His heart and gut were in control. He opened the cafeteria door, still holding her hand. "Okay. How about I pick you up around eleven, and we can go somewhere for lunch, then a tour of downtown?"

Bell grinned and nodded, just as Vick approached them.

"Hey Bella," Vick called out. "Can we talk for a second?"

Jeremiah looked at Bell, who gestured to the table where Alex waited. "Why don't you head over, and I'll be along in a minute."

"Sure." He released her hand. Guessed whatever Vick, the guy she called brother, had to say must be important. Either that, or he wanted to break them up before they even got started.

Bella offered a tender smile to Miah as he walked away. This was the second time her brother had interrupted her interaction with this guy she liked. It had better be worthwhile, otherwise she might actually slap him. She shifted her attention to Vick. "What's going on?"

"I was going to ask you the same thing." He snagged hold of her elbow and pulled her off to the side. "I look up and see the two of you not only walking in together, but holding hands."

"I don't see how that is any of your business." Removing her elbow from his grip, Bella frowned. Where the hell did he get off? She had already obtained the permission of the people from whom she needed it—her parents. And they hadn't set limits on what she and Miah could and could not do. They trusted her to make the right decisions.

"You're my baby sister. Of course, it's my business. Did you even discuss this with Mom and Dad?"

Her jaw dropped. Her *brother* was certainly laying it on thick! Calling her parents Mom and Dad. Vick hadn't even been to Bella's house in over a year. His family had moved out of the city three summers ago, but even then, he and Bella had still hung out—until last year. Then things had happened, and their lives had gone in different directions.

Of course. So, his problems gave him the right to play protector? Not on her watch.

"Yes, in fact, I did. They both gave the okay. Last I checked, I don't need your permission. Just because you can't get control of your life doesn't give you the right to take charge of mine."

"B, this has nothing to do with my mistakes. I've done everything I can to keep you safe since we were kids. I'm not doing my job if I'm not looking out for you."

Bella crossed her arms and shook her head. His statement was only partly true. There had been times he had left her to her own volition. And it wasn't as if she expected him to watch over her twenty-four hours a day. He was a year older and had his own life to live.

"We aren't kids, anymore," Bella said. "I don't need you to protect me. I can take care of myself."

"Is that what you've been doing for the past year? Because until a few days ago, it sure didn't look like it to me," Vick retorted.

"Screw you." Bella pivoted on the ball of her foot, shoved through the cafeteria door, and stormed down the hall. How dare he bring up the crap Heather had put her through! So, what if she had done nothing about the bullying. It was her choice to turn the other cheek. It wasn't as if she stood by while the girl had bullied someone else. Douche-bag. Nearly bumping into David, she halted and stumbled back a couple steps.

"Hey, I was hoping to run into you. Can we—"

"No. We cannot. If you'll excuse me." Without giving him the chance to finish his sentence, Bella side-stepped him and stomped on down the hall.

Out of the corner of his eye, Jeremiah watched the conversation between his angel and Vick. It wasn't hard to tell Bell was annoyed. Should he step in? That was a last resort. He rubbed the top of his head and eyed Alex, who sat across from him at the lunchroom table.

"Bell tells me you're into old-time movies."

"Into is a bit of an understatement. If I could've lived *Casablanca*, I so would have. I've even heard there are places to cosplay *Casablanca*. Something I'm looking forward to." Alex waggled her eyebrows.

Shaking his head, Jeremiah chuckled. "I can see she might've underplayed your dedication a little." He was glad he liked Bell's girlfriend, whom, Bell mentioned, she'd met their freshman year.

Jeremiah nodded in the direction of Vick and Bella. "What's his deal?"

Alex shrugged. "I think he's just worried. He's looked out for her since they were kids. I mean, he's nice guy, don't me wrong. His assessments are usually spot on, but he can be a little overprotective at times."

Suddenly, the cafeteria door banged open and Jeremiah caught a glimpse of Bell storming out. What was that about?

Jeremiah glowered as Vick returned to the table. "What the heck did you say to her?"

"The truth."

Two words, and they weren't much of an answer.

Jeremiah stood. He was absolutely going after her, but he had to find out what he was up against, first. "Which is what?"

"That I don't think the two of you should be dating. She doesn't know a thing about you, and neither do I."

"You're joking, right?" Stifling a groan, Jeremiah dragged a hand down his face. This guy was serious. Part of dating was learning about each other. Trying to discover if you made a good match. Not that he had any doubt about him and Bell. Every fiber of his being told him they would be great together.

"What is wrong with you? Do you have your head so far up your—"

"Hey. Sorry, I'm ..." It was Jeremiah's sister. She paused and glanced between him and Vick. "Hmm. Clearly you two are having a thing."

Focusing on Amanda, Jeremiah inhaled and calmed down. If anyone could handle a dimwitted dick, it would be his sister. "Mandy, can you do me a favor and keep an eye on this dip-wad while I go fix his mess?"

"Excuse me?" Vick glared at Jeremiah and balled up his fists. "Where do you get off calling me a dip-wad?"

"I'm just calling it like I see it. Now, if you'll excuse me …"

As Jeremiah strode toward the doors, Vick growled and took a step forward. "Where do you think—?"

"Oh, no you don't." Amanda stepped in front of Vick, and he stopped dead in his tracks.

Alex got to her feet, prepared to grab a hold of Vick's arm if necessary. "Let him go," she said.

Vick spun around and faced Alex. "But we don't know anything about him. He could be a rapist for all we know."

Alex lifted her hand to silence Jeremiah's sister, who responded by crossing her arms.

"Come on Vick," Alex said. "Do you really believe that?"

"Well, no, but—"

"But nothing. You need to give Bella the benefit of the doubt. She's a smart girl and fairly capable of making her own decisions. Listen, you were spot on when it came to Heather. But this? I think you're overreacting."

Alex had only spoken to Jeremiah for a few minutes, but she read people well. He was one of the good ones. And for the first time, she saw a rather happy, outgoing Bella. It would be nice if this version stuck around.

Pinching the bridge of his nose, Vick sighed. "Maybe I was a little harsh."

"A little?" Amanda sputtered.

"Not now." Alex glared over Vick's shoulders at the girl.

"Um, yeah, I think now." Dropping her hands to her hips, Amanda said, "I mean, it is my brother the two of you are discussing. As if I'm not even here."

"It's, okay." Vick squeezed Alex's shoulder and turned to Amanda, straightening his spine. "Go ahead."

Alex covered her mouth to hide her smile. Vick's change in posture hadn't gone unnoticed. By either her or Amanda.

But Amanda didn't comment. She just said, "I don't want you to get the wrong idea about my brother. He's a decent guy, and he really likes her. Trust me. I have heard non-stop about Bella for the last three days. I haven't even officially met her, and I already know too much. You feel me?"

Just then Alex noticed another person heading their way. Oh, God. She didn't want to have to deal with him, too—but it seemed she was going to have to.

"Who's been talking about Bella?"

Amanda turned so she could see who had stopped behind her. "My brother."

"Oh." David shrugged and shifted his gaze. "Hey, Alex, can I talk to you really quick?" Then, as if what Amanda said caught up with him, he looked back to Amanda. "Nothing bad I hope."

"I doubt it. He likes her." Amanda snickered.

Alex hung her head. Here, she thought lunch couldn't get any more exciting. Stepping around Vick, she snagged David's hand and tugged him off to the side. "Come on. Let's talk."

David planted his feet and refused to budge. "Who's her brother, Alex?"

Great. Maybe she could ... No. She wasn't going to be bullied in discussing her best friend. "None of your business. All you need to know is Bella has made her choice, and it isn't you."

"You know as well as I do no one will treat her the way I would."

The way he would? Oh, brother. Alex rolled her eyes. "Please. I know you don't really want her. You only want the image of her you've dreamed up in your head."

"What image? I don't see her for anything more than she is, and that's what I want. She isn't like the other girls here. That's why I like her. It's why I've always liked her."

Was he yanking her leg? Had to be. No way a guy of his stature felt anything for anyone without thinking about image.

"See, I'd love to believe you, but the timing of it all just doesn't add up. First Mike, then you. Wow." Alex started to walk away.

Snagging her arm, David pulled her back. "What about Mike?"

Alex eyed his grip on her arm, then him. If he didn't let go in two seconds, she was going to kick him where the sun didn't shine. David released his hold.

"Mike Riley asked Bella to the spring formal last year. And when she got there, she found him making out with your sister. Turned out it was a big joke. Then you asked her to prom a couple weeks later. Suffice it to say, she wouldn't be played for the fool twice."

"Mike did what?"

"Ask him, yourself. Or better yet, ask your sister."

Bella looked up from her seat on the hall floor. Sure, she thought. I just got into a fight with one of my best friends. Still, she nodded at Miah. "Yeah, I'm okay."

"Good. I'm glad. I mean ..." Miah shoved his hands in his pockets and stared at the floor. "Mind if I join you?"

Bella shrugged. He seemed nervous, too. Kind of refreshing, actually. Especially after all the hand holding. Miah dropped down on the floor beside her. He was so lithe. He flowed like a waterfall. Absolutely magnificent. His light brown skin seemed soft and strong. His buzzed brown hair, upon closer inspection, waved ever so slightly. His emerald green eyes mesmerized her. With one look, he could probably see everything she tried and failed to be. She turned her gaze toward the floor. Hopefully he hadn't caught her staring.

"I'm sorry about lunch."

"You don't have to apologize. Besides, if you're okay, then I don't think lunch is quite ruined."

"Except I ran out."

"True, but if you hadn't then we would still be sitting at the lunch table with everyone else. Which would mean you and I wouldn't get to talk."

"I would laugh if it didn't seem like you know my friends so well." She peeked at Miah. She was pretty sure she and Vick had been far enough away that no one at the table had heard their conversation. Alex would've been understanding, but would Miah? Given he had been the topic at hand.

"And yet I hardly know them."

Bella giggled. "I guess they're easy to read."

"To a degree. I'm not really interested in your friends, though."

"If you were, you'd be in there, not out here with me." Finding an excuse to look away, she glanced at her watch.

"How much longer do we have?"

"Twenty minutes." Should she be upset or happy at the time remaining?

"Would you like to go back to the lunch room?"

She still had her lunch with her. And, yeah, she and Alex normally used this time to plan the weekend, but she could hit her up in last period.

"No."

"Would you like to walk the halls with me?"

Bella peered at Miah. It sounded like a great plan. Despite her brother's concerns, she trusted the male beside her. "Yeah. Let's go."

"Cool." Miah stood and offered her his hand.

Bella placed her hand in his. "I'm sorry about Vick."

"You don't need to apologize for him, either. He didn't go about it the right way, but I know he's just looking out for you. Brothers do that. Blood or not." Miah grinned, then just looked at her.

Shivers crawled up Bella's spine, along her shoulders, and all the way down to her elbows. Diverting her gaze, she said, "Yeah. I guess."

"Hey." Miah lifted her chin so her eyes focused on him. "I have five siblings, remember. I know all about playing big brother. So, you have nothing to apologize for. Okay?"

Nibbling on her bottom lip, she stared into his eyes. They sparkled like emeralds. Exquisite. Bella nodded. "Okay."

four

Bella scanned the books in her locker and picked out her precalculus book and notebook. She had study hall next period. As she walked down the hallway where the administrative office was located, she heard voices. Then, two teachers and two students hooked the corner and approached the office.

Bella paused mid-step and just stood there as the teachers walked David and Mike toward the main office. Mike had a split lip, bruised jaw, cut forehead, and torn jacket; David carried a couple of cuts and bruises, too, but Mike apparently took the brunt of it. What the hell happened to them? Weren't they friends? What in the world went down in the lunchroom after she left?

Fighting wasn't permitted. No matter how they spun it to the principal, they'd both be suspended. The story didn't matter to the principal, but to her it mattered.

Bella turned around and headed in back the way she came, swinging by her locker and dropping her book and notebook off. Then, she walked down the hall and out the main doors. She had no clue what car David drove. Good thing there was a place outside the building that gave her access to both the front and back parking lot.

Bella found the spot and slid down onto the sidewalk. Her work experience in the administrative office taught her David and Mike would be escorted out of the building within twenty minutes--separately. One would be taken to the front door and the other to the back door. Although she had to find out what happened, she refused to get the details from Mike Riley. She balled up her fists and clenched the material of her skirt. He was a juvenile pig who could rot in hell. Releasing her grip, she inhaled a deep breath and exhaled.

Then she changed her mind. What the hell was she thinking? The two of them could pummel each other, and she didn't need to know why. As she pushed up off the sidewalk, she stumbled right into someone. *Shit!*

"Whoa!" A hand snagged hold of Bella's arm and kept her from falling.

She looked up. "David."

"You okay?"

"Yeah." Bella tucked her hands into the front pockets of her skirt. "Sorry about that. I wasn't watching where I was going."

David readjusted the backpack slung over his shoulder. "What are you doing out here, anyway?"

Good question. Bella bit her bottom lip. Upon closer inspection, David looked worse than he'd first appeared. His eye had turned a nice shade of black and blue, the corner of his mouth had been busted open, and his knuckles were blistered red.

She sighed. "Waiting for you, actually."

"Why would you do that?"

Bella reached out and lifted one of his hands. Very gently she rubbed her fingers across his damaged knuckles. "This. I saw you and Mike outside the main office."

"Oh." David removed his hand from hers. "You should go back in. You've never been in trouble and it shouldn't start now. Not on my account." David stepped around her and headed toward the parking lot.

Bella was confused. Was he looking out for her? Was she looking out for him? Had they become friends? Jogging across the lot behind him, she shouted, "I'm not going inside until you tell me what happened between you and Mike."

David stopped mid-stride. "It's not important."

"The heck it isn't. You and Mike have been best friends for three years. Guys don't fight over nothing important."

"Guys fight all the time."

"Bullshit," she said, just like Alex did when she called Bella on her stuff.

David's eyes bugged out as if he had just witnessed a meteor hit the ground in front of him. Then, getting a grip, he said, "Can we not talk about this here?"

"Fine. We can walk and talk or sit in your car and talk. Either way, you're telling me what happened." Bella crossed her arms and narrowed her eyes. If she glowered harder it might burn a hole in his skin.

"Can't I just do something nice for you and have you let it go?"

"Me? What do I have to do with this?"

David rolled his neck like he was irked by the pressure she was placing on his shoulders. "Please. Let this go."

"No. If I had anything to do with you and Mike fighting, you're going to explain it to me."

"Christ, you don't give up. Okay, okay. I'll talk, but not here. You drink coffee?"

Bella raised an eyebrow and walked after him. "I'm half Brazilian. Of course, I do."

"Let's go to the coffee shop around the corner and talk there."

The five-minute drive to the coffee shop had been quiet. Small talk had never been Bella's forte. At the shop, after David ordered an ice coffee and Bella ordered a hot mocha latte with an extra shot of espresso, they sat opposite one another at a corner table and Bella asked, "Are you going to tell me what happened, now?"

"Let's just say I found out something about Mike, and he deserved a beat down."

"That's a crap explanation. Try again."

David rubbed his eyes and then groaned into his hands.

"Can't you just accept what I told you?"

"No. There's more to it and I want to know what."

"Have you always been this difficult?"

"Stop dodging the question." Although he made an excellent point, she wasn't budging. Maybe her friends were starting to rub off on her. Or maybe it was something else entirely?

David sighed as if he was giving in, but nothing came out of his mouth. Instead, he leaned back in the chair, drummed his fingers on the table, and sipped his coffee. He returned his cup to the table and glanced out the window to his right.

Finally, he spoke. "Alex told me what Mike did last year."

Bella's lips pinched together. His reluctance to share that vital piece of information made sense. Alex knew because she'd helped Bella get home after the ordeal. The question was, how much had her best friend revealed?

David stared at her. "Is that why you said no when I asked you to prom?"

Just like that, a conversation she'd avoided for a year dropped into her lap. Bella sighed. Fidgeting with her cup to buy time, she realized she had to see the conversation through. She lifted her eyes to David's face. "The truth? When you asked me to go to prom last year, for a moment, I was excited. Then I remembered Mike, and I didn't believe I could trust you actually wanted me to go with you."

"But I kept asking you. Even after you shot me down in front of everyone."

"I know. But of all the people in the whole school, why would you pick me? I couldn't get over that. Then when things got awkward in our tutoring sessions, I realized I had to keep it professional."

David leaned forward. "If you had stopped being my tutor, and I asked you out again, would you have said yes?"

"I don't know."

"What about now?"

She should've foreseen the leap, but she didn't. There was the pond and David jumped right in. Man, she hated breaking his heart again. At least they weren't in front of the whole school this time. "No."

"Why?"

"I met somebody, and I like him. A lot." Bella held up her hand. "I know I probably never gave you a fair shot. It wasn't right taking Mike's actions out on you, but I've never thought it was good idea for us to date, anyway. Don't get me wrong. You're a great guy. I just haven't ever thought of you that way. But we can still be friends."

David slumped back and looked away. "Friends, huh? All right. Can I at least ask who this guy is? Is it someone I know?"

"I don't know. He's new."

"Not the guy who's been leaving you presents?"

Wow. She had completely forgotten about those. So much had gone on the last couple of days. Bella shook her head. "No. His family only moved here a couple of weeks ago, so he's definitely not my secret admirer." Or whatever the present giver should be coined.

"Good. So. Who is the lucky guy?"

"His name is Jeremiah Detrone."

David's face tensed. "I have met him, and I can't believe you're going to go out with that douche." He inhaled deeply, then said, "As long as you're happy. That's all I care about. Now, come on. Let's get you back to school."

Friday evening and his dark-haired beauty hadn't left the confines of her home. Gervasio stared at the screen in front of him. The tree outside her window provided too much cover, so he clicked on a couple of different links to access his favorite view—her bedroom—where the camera had been installed in the corner by her closet. Gave him an excellent sightline of her bed and desk. There was no mic, so no sound, but he would hear the sweetest noises from her soon enough. Pressing a few buttons, Gervasio zoomed in on his honey bear.

His dark-haired beauty opened the drawer in her desk and removed a couple of items.

Gervasio zoomed closer. She held two boxes. One still had the ribbon he had carefully selected before leaving it on her front porch. The other, was long and elegant. No mark on the box, but he didn't need one to identify it.

Then, after eyeing them for a second, his girl dropped the boxes in the trash.

Gervasio growled. She cared nothing for the gifts he'd given to show his affection. They were meaningless trinkets to go out with the garbage. Jumping up, Gervasio threw the mouse at the wall. How dare she throw his gifts out?

Damn ungrateful whore was exactly like her mother.

Fists balled, he paced from one side of the room to the other. This was not the time to lose his shit. He had to get it together. His plan was so close to fruition. Gervasio glanced at the calendar. A few more days and she would be ripe for the taking. The way it should be. She had always belonged to him. And once he had her, they would forever be connected.

Gervasio punched the wall directly above the monitors. Then, taking a deep breath, he stared at his lovely one on the screen. She could throw away his gifts, but *he* would not be so easily tossed aside. Reaching out, he stroked her cheek through the screen. "Eres mia por siempre."

The front door to the warehouse opened. Better be someone with good news. Gervasio strode out of his office and stopped inches from the messenger. "You find info on *el tipo*?"

Swifty rubbed his eyebrow. "I'm still digging, but I have some information."

"Dime." It was important to know your enemies, even if they came in six-foot piece-of-shit packages.

Sighing, Bella set the pencil down. How many times had she read the same line in her history book? Five? She tugged her desk drawer open. Her date with Miah tomorrow wasn't the only thing on her mind. There was also David's reminder of her secret admirer.

Bella pulled out the two boxes she had stowed in her desk. The necklace had appeared on her doorstep three weeks ago. The earrings a week before that. A matching set, too. Silver hoops with white agate in the middle. White agate hung at the center of the necklace. Both were beautiful. Since neither box had a note or card, she had done some research. The pieces had been designed by a Brazilian artist and were a great representation of part of her heritage—but no one had owned up to delivering the items.

She'd been holding onto them because she had no idea what to do with them. There was no one to return them to and, since neither box had a label, there was no way to tell what store they had been purchased from. There was only one other option. She would donate them together. Snatching a small velvet bag from her desk drawer, she dropped the necklace and earrings inside, then tossed the boxes in the trash.

Setting the velvet bag aside, she turned her attention back to her history book. Maybe now she could get her homework done. If she finished tonight, she'd have the whole weekend free. But instead of getting to work, she strode across her bedroom to her closet and eyed the endless line of full-length skirts neatly hung there. Plus, multiples of the same blouse. What about dresses? Shoving some of the skirts out of the way, she dug in the back for the few dresses she had. Black and long. Boring. Next. Flowers, long-sleeved, and past the knee. Better, but not first date material. Next. Quarter-length sleeves, bright blue, and past the knee.

Ugh. No. Dammit.

"Honey? Is everything okay?"

Bella jumped back. Cripes, her father had scared the crap out of her. Not that she was doing anything wrong. Swiping her hair behind her ears, Bella said, "Yes, Bàba. I'm okay."

"Are you certain?"

Bella shook her head. No, she wasn't sure about anything. What if this date was a horrible idea? What if they got together and Miah realized he really didn't like her? What if he thought she was boring? Or didn't like what she wore? "I'm just nervous Bàba. I'm not exactly sure what I'm doing."

Taking a seat on the bed, her father gestured to the space beside him. "Come sit."

"Bàba, I really like him. What if he realizes I'm just a plain Jane?" Bella looked at her closet. Plain, old, boring Jane. With a defeated sigh, she slumped next to her father.

"First, you are not plain. You, my dear, are special. I know what you're thinking. I'm your father, I must say that, but that is not true. Most parents love their children from the day they are born, but not all parents are happy with how their children turn out. And I am quite proud of the young woman you have become."

"Really?"

"Yes, of course. I know I was not initially on board with you dating, but I prayed about it after we spoke. And God reminded me of Isaiah 41:10. He said, 'Fear thou not; for I am with thee: be not dismayed; for I *am* thy God: I will strengthen thee; yea, I will help thee; yea, I will uphold thee with the right hand of my righteousness.' I know he's there walking beside you, guiding you in this new adventure. And he's there, giving me courage as I watch my little girl grow up. I have faith in who you are and I know that if this young man truly likes you, he will see all the wonderful things about you that I do."

With this reassurance, the butterflies in Bella's stomach settled. All the confusion in her head disappeared, and the weight she had carried all afternoon left her body.

"Thank you, Bàba."

"I'm always here for you. You will always be my Cinderella. Just remember that." Her father hugged her tightly, then stood. "Now, why don't you call Alex and see if she can help you select something appropriate. A first date is a special occasion."

Bella bolted upright in bed, struggling to catch her breath. That nightmare again. She always woke at the same point: The beating had occurred and she'd been rushed to the hospital. But instead of being an eight-year-old child in the dream, as she'd been in real life, she was closer to her current age, sixteen—and her injuries were more severe, than they'd really been. Life-threatening. And even as she struggled to awaken, in the nightmare she was leaving, she flat-lined.

Bella touched her chest to make sure her heart was still beating. That she was alive. Then she tossed the covers aside and climbed out of bed. Rubbing the creep-crawly sensation from her arms, she crossed her bedroom floor and quietly eased her door open. Thankfully, she hadn't screamed. She glanced down the hallway. Her parents' door was still closed. Relieved, she tiptoed in the opposite direction. The large bay window in the den was her favorite spot—especially after an awful nightmare.

Bella climbed onto the window seat and stared out, trying to calm down. Both her parents' cars sat undisturbed in the driveway. She scanned the vehicles that lined the street. None were flashy, as most of the people who lived in her neighborhood were middle class. But one car stood out. It was black and boxy. She could swear she'd seen it parked around town, lately, near her usual hangouts. And now it looked like someone might be in the driver's seat. Were they watching her house?

She glanced at the clock over the mantel. It was three o'clock in the morning. As she looked back out the window at the black car, a door across the street opened and a person she couldn't identify walked out of Todd's house. Weren't they on vacation? The guy walked down the sidewalk and got into the black car, which roared to life and took off.

Bella hated nightmares. They made her paranoid about everything. Nobody was watching her house. Time to go back to bed and try to fall back asleep. She had a date to prepare for.

five

"What's this?" Bella wrapped her hands around the bag and peeked inside. She reached in and pulled out a white sundress with a daisy print, a pale yellow, short-sleeve shrug, and a pair of sandals. When she had called Alex last night and asked for her help, this wasn't exactly what she had in mind. Bella eyed her best friend. "This ... this is what you chose? I can't wear this."

"Yes, you can. The sundress will come down past your knees, the shrug will cover your shoulders and hide the spaghetti straps, and the sandals will be fine. Showing your toes won't kill you."

"Why didn't you run this by me first?"

"Because I know you. You'd never pick anything like this, and if I suggested it before buying it, you would've said no. This is your first date. One step out of your comfort zone. I'm inviting you to take another small step." Alex smiled and dropped into the chair by the desk.

Alex had so much confidence, Bella thought. For once it would be nice to be more like her. Bella stared at the dress and sandals. This dress, it was only the beginning. Sure, right now it was a tad outside her comfort zone. But if she accepted this dress, what next? A pierced navel? A tattoo?

Glancing at her closet and back to the clothes in her hands, she inhaled deeply. She had faith the Lord was by her side. It was a small step. Maybe it was different, but she still had her modesty. "Okay."

"Is that a yes?"

Bella nodded and slipped across the hall to the bathroom, where she undressed. She had shaved earlier, per Alex's instructions. Now, she changed into the sundress, shrug, and sandals. Taking a deep breath, she gathered up her clothes and headed back across the hall and stepped in front the full-length mirror. She flattened the skirt with her palms. It ended a couple inches past her knees. If she sat, it'd probably hike up a little. She'd have to be careful.

She stared at her reflection, then peeked over her shoulder at Alex.

"Well?"

"Almost perfect." Alex walked over and started to unbraid Bella's hair.

"What are you doing?"

"You have beautiful hair. It's the perfect time to show it."

"What if it's hot out?" Under normal circumstances it might seem to be a dumb question, but temperatures often spiked in Rescate County.

"Put a brush and a hairtie in your purse. You can swing in a bathroom and pull it up in a ponytail."

"Why can't I wear it that way to begin with?"

Alex scrutinized Bella's reflection. "What are you guys doing again?"

"I'm showing him downtown."

"Ponytail it is. Promise though if you go on a nice dinner date with him, you'll wear it down."

Promise now, break it later, Bella thought. Though she *might* be comfortable enough if that ever happened. One date at a time. Bella nodded. "I will."

"Good. Now, let me see nails and toes. I have a cotton-pink polish to put on them, and then some make-up, and you'll be good to go."

"Polish? Make-up? Why do I feel like I'm entering a whole new world?"

Alex laughed. "Because you are. You're entering the world of dating."

Jeremiah had parked a few blocks from the pizza parlor, where they were going to have lunch, and they'd been getting to know each other, while Bella had been showing him around downtown. "How many awards have you won?" Bella asked.

Miah shrugged. "I don't know. Five or so. It's not really about the winning for me. It's about bringing dancers together and the story they tell through their bodies."

"Still. That's pretty impressive." Bella smiled and linked her hands behind her back. The dress had one flaw. No pockets. She hadn't been sure what to do with her hands their entire walk. Let them hang at her side? Fold them together in front of her stomach? Ugh.

Slowing his pace, Miah tilted his head. "Didn't you tell me you sing?"

Singing? That was her second love. "Yes, but only as part of the church choir."

"You never sing outside of church?"

"Well ... I guess that depends on your definition." Every year for the last four years she'd sung at the Fall Festival. She'd even performed a song last year at the dance. "Most of the places I've sung have been connected to the church."

"What about at ... uh ... one of those karaoke places?"

"No. No way. I've gone to the K-Bar a couple of times, but I've never gotten up and sung."

Just then, the hairs on the back of her neck rose. Stopping mid-step, she looked left, then right. It was the same sensation she had last night in the den. As if someone was watching her. But while there were people on both sides of the street, no one was giving the two of them undue attention.

"You okay?"

"Yeah." Only a handful of people knew their plan for the day. There was no one out there, unless her over-protective father decided to follow them. Just a bit of paranoia. Probably from the nightmare she had last night. Bella grabbed Miah's forearm and squeezed. "I promise. I'm okay."

Miah raised an eyebrow, but all he said was, "All right. If you say so."

"I do. Now, are you ready to eat? Because I'm starving." Bella pointed to the door of Italiano's—best pizza in town.

Today was all about Oreo cookies. Gervasio drummed his fingers against the steering wheel. The cookie and his girl had strolled downtown for the last half hour. But he was no closer to learning more about this enemy. Why were his people having so much trouble finding details about Jeremiah Detrone?

Gervasio lifted the binoculars and eyed the piece of shit. The guy had stopped. Had they reached their destination? He shifted his gaze from Jeremiah to his dark-haired beauty. No. It was she who had stopped. Again. Every time, she searched her surroundings. Not well enough. She had yet to spot him in the black Lincoln, he believed. But he was keeping well back. Anyway, he would have preferred to be out there on foot. No better way to figure out one's enemies than to get up close and personal. Or as close as possible without detection. Too bad that wasn't possible. Not a problem. He'd Plan B it.

Oh good. His girl and Oreo were heading into Italiano's. Lunch would take at least an hour. Gave him enough time to get something on this guy. Figure out if his plans would have to be altered. Through the binoculars, Gervasio checked out Oreo's black Dodge Charger, parked a block over. Too many people around for him to break in, but he could walk by and get the tag number discreetly—which would provide him with some useful information on this Detrone guy.

Gervasio turned his binoculars back to the restaurant. His girl had gotten comfortable in a booth next to the Oreo. He had work to do, now, but she'd pay for that. Later.

Tossing the binoculars aside, Gervasio collected his phone and car keys. He got out of the Lincoln and strolled over to the next block. He casually angled his cell phone and snapped a few pictures of the license plate number as he walked by the Dodge. With everyone else's face in their own device, no one would even notice. Like everyone there, he was just another shopper. Gervasio crossed the street and ducked into the boutique across the way.

One final gift for his girl. A ring.

To symbolize the eternal connection, they would soon have.

Tucking his purchase inside his pocket, Gervasio returned to his car. He glanced at the restaurant. As he suspected, they hadn't left—and he still had plenty of time to do what he needed before they moved on. Gervasio reached into the backseat and dug out his laptop, accessed the license-plate search program, and punched in the tag number. Time to see if any real information populated on this guy. Something other than dancing bullshit.

"Hijo de puta." Jeremiah Detrone was the worst kind of enemy out there. Keeping him out of the way wasn't impossible, just tricky.

Gervasio texted Swifty. It was time he put the messenger's girlfriend to work.

Bella took a quick bow, then handed the microphone back to the karaoke jockey and headed down the steps toward the table where Miah sat. Singing at church had never made her this nervous, but the moment her foot had hit that first step, goose bumps covered her from head to toe. Not that it had shown. And, thankfully, the feeling faded as the song went on.

People complimented her as she passed by. She took a deep breath and exhaled as she dropped into the chair next to Miah.

"Beautiful. Absolutely beautiful."

"Thank you."

Miah leaned in close. "How did you know which songs to pick?"

"The way you reacted to me asking you to sing with me, I knew I'd need to pick something that was light on the male vocals. I thought 'Sometimes Love Just Ain't Enough' by Patty Smyth was perfect. Don Henley sings, but it's mostly her."

"Well, I appreciate you giving a frog a chance."

Where had he gotten the idea he sounded horrible? Maybe he wasn't perfect, but he was far from frog-like. Unless he croaked before the end of the date. Amused by her own thoughts, Bella quietly snickered. "You weren't that bad."

"Thanks, but the compliment isn't necessary."

"I'm only being honest." Talking openly had come so easy with him. The more time they spent together, the easier the words flowed. How was it possible to connect with him on such a deep level? They hardly knew one another, and yet it seemed as if they had known each other their whole lives.

"I appreciate it." Smiling, Miah stood and offered her his hand. "Shall we move on?"

Bella placed her hand in his, and they left the karaoke bar. "Where to next? Bookstore, dance studio—?" She paused. He was looking at her weird. Did she have something in her teeth? She ran her tongue across the top of her teeth. Just in case.

"Sorry. I guess I was just trying to figure out why you picked the other song."

"It's my favorite."

"Really? Isn't it from *A Walk to Remember*? That movie with ... um ... Mindy ... something."

At least he remembered the movie. Bella had to give him credit for that. "Mandy Moore, and yes."

"Why that song?"

"I don't know. I guess I like what it represents."

"What do you mean?"

Bella looked at her hands. "It's about unconditional love. Not just the kind we get from God, but the kind we have the chance for with the people He brings into our lives; the ones who give us hope when we trip over the obstacles in our lives."

"That's beautiful," Miah said. "I never thought about it like that. When I hear music, it isn't just about the lyrics. The lyrics, the beat, the music—it all comes together. Kind of like displaying a piece of your soul."

"I can see that. Dancing and singing, in that way, go hand in hand."

Miah nodded. "Yeah. I guess you can't really have one without the other. Even with classical music, though there generally aren't lyrics, the music explains something."

"Right. Each piece has a story to tell." It was why music reached people on an emotional level. The way she related to songs wasn't necessarily the way Miah related, but the point was they both related.

"Exactly." Mah paused in front of the bowling alley entrance. "Now, how about I show you how to roll a strike?"

Jeremiah leaned against his bedroom door and watched as Bell looked over every one of his trophies.

She glanced up from the trophy case. "You won an award for choreography."

"Um, yes. Last year."

"That's so amazing." Bell turned back to the trophies. "What about this one?"

"That was, uh, 2011. We came in third place. It was my first year choreographing our routine."

She was asking questions, anyway. That was a good sign.

She stepped over to the Linkin Park poster stapled to the wall. "Is this one of the groups you've choreographed to?"

"Yes. Actually, the last trophy I won used a mash-up of their song 'In the End' and Evanescence's 'Bring Me to Life.'"

"You listen to Evanescence?" Her head snapped toward him.

Of all the things he thought would catch her attention, his taste in music hadn't crossed his mind. Yeah, they had spoken about it a little earlier, but they hadn't found any bands in common. Until now. Jeremiah inched forward. "Yep. One of my favorites."

"They're one of mine, too."

"Good music. Great lyrics. Awesome beats. Mashes well with other bands."

The ice had been broken. A safe topic had been broached. But while he could talk about the different routines he'd created using various musicians' work all night, there were more important things to discuss.

Jeremiah sighed. He'd have to approach it first. "Bell, you know you can talk to me about anything. Right?"

Staring at the poster, Bell nodded.

"Care to tell me about what happened earlier?" The conversation had turned sour mid-way through dinner. And he had no idea why. Bell had been talking about the teen Bible study sessions, and before he realized what was going on, she had shut down. Completely missed everything his sister had asked about downtown and the karaoke club.

"You know, I've told that story a million times. People always ask. So, I got used to ... a watered-down version." She had yet to look at him again.

Jeremiah raised an eyebrow at her back. That had been watered down? One kid beating another because of an abusive father? There was nothing diluted about it. Unless— No. Please, God, don't let her say it.

Bell dropped her gaze to the floor.

Jeremiah realized she knew too much about the boy and what had become of him. And his own father, a sheriff and a natural inquisitor, had asked questions over dinner that pushed buttons none of them could've known to avoid.

Jeremiah closed the space between them. "You were the child he beat up."

Nodding, Bell lifted her eyes to him as tears rolled down her cheeks. "I don't really talk about it. The simple version, it's usually enough. Most people ..." she sniffled, "... they don't bother asking what happened to him."

"I'm so sorry, Bell. I can't imagine what you must've gone through." Pulling her close, Jeremiah wrapped his arms around her shoulders. Her arms came around his waist in response. "I wish I could carry this for you. That I could do more."

Wiping at the tears, Bell looked up to him without moving out of his hold. "This is enough. It's more than enough."

Bella and Miah left his bedroom hand in hand. A weight had been lifted. It had been a long time since she had felt this free. She slowed as they passed his sister's bedroom. Apologizing for her earlier actions was the right thing to do.

Bella paused. "Can you give me a few minutes?"

"Yeah. Sure. I'll be in the kitchen." Miah pressed a quick kiss to her forehead and disappeared down the hall.

Bella took a deep breath and knocked on the door. "Mandy, it's me. Can I come in?"

"It's open."

Exhaling, Bella opened Amanda's bedroom door and saw Miah's sister sitting cross-legged on the bed, with a book open and a notebook in her lap. "Am I interrupting?"

"Not really." Closing the notebook, Amanda asked, "What can I do for you?"

"I just … I wanted to apologize for earlier. I don't want you think it was intentional. I guess I …" Bella paused. How to explain? She wasn't interested in airing her unresolved issues. But there had to be a way to say it without exposing her wounds. "I'm not used to talking about myself."

"I get it. We all have things we'd rather not explore too deeply. It's okay. I'm not mad."

Right. Simply put, everyone has secrets.

Bella nodded. "Good. I'm glad. I mean, I'd really like for us to be friends."

"I'd like that too. I think the three of us should go to K-Bar. Since you and I both sing, I think it'd be fun."

"Three? You, me, and Miah?" Although Miah had gone with her earlier, she'd thought it was more for her than him, about hearing her sing.

Amanda snickered. "No. Not Miah. You, me, and Alex. Maybe we can get together Saturday night."

"Um, yeah. That sounds good." She was surprised. She didn't think she and Amanda had a lot in common. But who said people with differences couldn't be friends? Besides, it was too early to rush to judgment.

Bella hooked her thumb over her shoulder. "Okay. I need to go. I'll see you tomorrow."

"Right. Church."

"Yep, church." Where she was singing. Crap. She had a solo tomorrow. Early.

"Hey, B?"

Bella paused halfway out the door. "Yeah?"

"Is Vick ... is he single?"

Bella tilted her head. Not a lot of girls asked about her brother. Most didn't know much about him, and he preferred it that way. For once, she wanted to lie. The things she knew would chase plenty of girls away, but it wasn't her place to share his secrets—and lying would damage any friendship Amanda might have with Vick. Bella eyed Amanda. "Yes."

Gervasio stared at the listing on the computer in front of him. So many soldiers to choose from. Several would do, but, really, he needed someone disposable. A person who wouldn't be missed if they disappeared.

Every other part of his plan had been set in motion. All the pieces had been aligned. And a secondary plan had been put into place in case the first one fell through. Not that he expected anyone to fail in their assigned tasks, but one could never be too careful.

The timing was perfect. If he didn't succeed now, he would have to wait. And he was tired of waiting. The last seven weeks had been used for necessary reconnaissance. Certain pieces of information had to be collected before he could make his move. A move that had to be timed with the utmost accuracy.

All that remained was for him to choose his accomplice. It was common practice for him to take a newbie along. Best for breaking a bitch in. Something he had done a lot of over the last sixteen years. But Bella, his dark-haired beauty, she was different. He had no intention of breaking her in. In fact, she was his and his alone.

Which was he had to be so damn selective when it came to which soldier he brought with him. This soldier's purpose would only be one of support. Well, and marking. Hmm. The ability to mark his woman. This was a skill honed to its utmost by only one of his men.

Gervasio grinned. Absolutely perfect.

He sent off a text. The last chess piece was in play.

six

"Pastor Whitmore, I understand you're skeptical, but I promise I will make this the best Fall Harvest Festival you have seen in the last six years." The idea had only popped into her head that morning. Her principal would be super proud. She'd fought hard against taking the lead tutor position less than a week ago, and here she stood, practically begging the pastor to let her direct this year's production.

"Bella, you have never led anything. Even getting you to work solo has been a bit of a struggle. Look what happened last year."

She dropped her gaze and felt her cheeks warm. Of course, he had to bring that up. But it was just one incident. So what if she almost choked, on stage, in front of hundreds of people? Inhaling deeply, Bella lifted her eyes. "This year is different. I have a plan."

She could see it all—from Mandy singing, to Miah choreographing, to the various skits. Yes, this was completely out of her comfort zone, but with Miah by her side, she knew it would be perfect.

Pastor Whitmore pinched the bridge of his nose. "Please don't let me regret this."

"I promise, you won't!" Nearly jumping out of her skin, Bella grinned from ear to ear. Amazing! For a second, she'd thought she'd never convince him to take a chance.

"You can direct, but on one condition."

"Anything. You name it, and I'll do it."

"You have to take on a co-director. Someone who has leadership skills and can support you."

"Done. I know the perfect person." She just had to talk to him about it first. But no way Vick would turn this down. Right? Bella clapped her hands together. "Think we can make the announcement this morning?"

"If you get your co-director set, then yes."

"Thank you!" Bella hugged the pastor, then ran out the door. She had to find Vick. After their last conversation, he owed her. This was the least he could do to make up for that lunchtime fiasco. She charged down the hall, running by a couple of people without a second glance. Then, popping out the side door, Bella ran right into someone, and they both tumbled to the ground.

A set of emerald green eyes stared back at her. "That was certainly an exit."

Her cheeks flushed. Holy hell! Not only had she knocked Miah over, but she was also sprawled on top of him. Bella quickly scrambled to her feet. "I'm so sorry!"

"No worries. I'm still in one piece." A Cheshire grin spread to Miah's face as he stood and brushed down the front of his slacks. "Care to explain the fire?"

"Oh, um, I came out to find Vick." She had roughly twenty minutes to get her brother to agree to co-direct, otherwise her entire dream would be swallowed into non-existence.

Raising an eyebrow, Miah pointed. "He's over there talking to Mandy."

Lord, don't let that girl get hurt, Bella thought. Then, giving Miah a kiss on the cheek, she said, "Thank you. I hate to run, but I need to talk to him. I'll find you later."

Wait! Did she actually just kiss him? Yes, yes, she did. Too late to take it back. No time to think too much about it.

Approaching Vick and Amanda, Bella said, "Mind if I interrupt?"

"It's okay. I was just leaving." Amanda waved goodbye to Vick and walked off.

"Later." Vick crossed his arms and narrowed his eyes. "What can I do for you B?"

Got it. He wasn't going to make this easy. Not that she could blame him. She had ignored him in school after their discussion, and they hadn't spoken since. "Okay. I deserve that. I didn't handle our conversation very well, but don't act like you're entirely blameless."

Shoving his hands in his pockets, Vick sighed. "You're right. I'm not. I could've addressed my concerns better. I just … I worry about you."

All of his points *had* been valid. It was their validity that struck her nerves. So what if it she had recently begun to act like she had a backbone? She was still the one who had to stand up for her beliefs. "I know you mean well, but I promise I can look out for myself. Yeah, maybe I haven't done the best job, but you have to let me try."

"All right. But promise me something. If you ever need help, you'll come to me. No questions asked."

"I can do that." After all, he was family. Bella smiled. Great. They'd made up. Now, she had to ask for a favor.

"I know that look. What do you need?"

"I talked to Pastor Whitmore about directing this year's Fall Harvest Festival. He said I could."

"What? B, that's amazing! You're really stepping out. I'm so proud of you."

"Um, thanks. There's one, small, teensy problem."

"Which is?"

"I need a co-director. Someone who has the skill set of a leader."

"And you want me to do it?"

"Pretty, please." Bella clasped her hands together and batted her eyelashes.

"Must be important if you're actually begging me." With a brief chuckle, Vick agreed. "Fine. Just stop. I'll co-direct with you."

Gervasio scheduled a visit with his brother after the message he'd arranged to be delivered had been confirmed. Bronco reported back that Cristobal understood, but Gervasio insisted he see the results for himself. It would look suspicious if he visited his brother too soon after the incident. He signed in and walked to the visitation area.

Cristobal had selected a corner table. Smart. It gave them some privacy. Gervasio dropped into a chair with his back to the wall.

"Good to see you, too, Gervasio."

"Cristobal, what has happen to your face?" Gervasio reached across the table and grabbed his brother's chin.

"Got into a fight with the washer ... and lost."

Releasing his grip, Gervasio smirked. "You must be careful. Next time may not go so easy."

"I'm certain it won't."

It was good to know his brother had gotten the picture. Had it seemed a little cruel to a few of his subordinates that he had arranged for someone to attack Cristobal? Of course. But they'd also learned how far he would go to protect the truth. Swifty's conversation with his brother had revealed too much. It was necessary his men be taught a valuable lesson: Gervasio wasn't someone you crossed.

"Is that all you came for?"

"*Si*. Good leader check on result."

Cristobal leaned forward. "Is that what you think you are? A good leader?"

"Si ... 'hermano.'" Gervasio allowed the sarcasm to spread across his face in a smirk as he used the word Cristobal had repeated time and time again. Blood made them brothers. Loyalty made them nothing. Cristobal could have his God. Gervasio had power and control.

Only one thing could've made him happier, but that had been lost. Instead, he would organize, and his patience would pay off in the end. Because by the time his brother manned up, Gervasio would have already claimed the property that rightfully belonged to him.

"You have no understanding of what it takes to be a good leader."

"Still, they follow me."

"Por ahora." *For now.* With that, Cristobal got up and walked away.

Gervasio didn't react. He would give his brother the last word. This time. He stood and left the room. There was business to take care of.

Bella scanned the hallway. Good. It was empty. She turned toward the library, paused at the end of the hallway, and poked her head around the corner. Still no one. Shuffling past two rows of lockers, she darted across the hall and stopped in front of the library doors and peeked through the glass. Only a couple of librarians.

The whole cloak-and-dagger routine probably wasn't necessary. But she didn't want anyone to know what she was up to.

Bella slipped in and headed straight for the computers. She typed two words into the search engine: *Jeremiah Detrone.* It seemed wrong to go digging for videos of his dancing. Asking was more straightforward. And he probably would've shown her. But this let her be unbiased, right? Ugh. There was no way to justify what she was doing.

Her decision to go online and find a— Whoa. Gold. Bella blinked when she saw the number of videos that populated. How long had Miah been dancing? Sure, he had several trophies and ribbons, but none of that indicated the amount of work he'd put in. Unzipping her backpack, she dug out her headphones and plugged them in.

Examining bits of the description listed for each selection, she searched until she found the most recent. Six months ago. Set to go, she streamed the video. Oh, this was the one where he used the Linkin Park and Evanescence mash-up. Good beat. The two songs did work well together. Not to mention the routine. It was amazing! He had choreographed that? Wow. It was over way too fast. Bella returned to her initial search and clicked the next video. Then the next. And the next.

A hand landed on her shoulder.

Bella jumped back. Yanking the headphones from her ears, she closed the search page. "You scared me."

"Sorry." Alex giggled. "Probably a good thing I found you, though. She gestured to the library doors. "Jeremiah's been looking for you."

"Crap." Bella logged off. "Thank you."

She shoved her headphones in her backpack. She hadn't meant to get so caught up. But she was much more prepared for her request, now. Walking over to Miah, Bella cracked a smile. "I'm sorry. I got stuck in some research. I lost complete track of time."

"That's okay. You ready?"

"Yeah. Let's go." They left the library and headed toward the parking lot. How in the world was she going to approach the subject with him? She definitely didn't want to let him know she'd gone digging for videos of his dancing.

Miah interrupted her thoughts. "Hey, I was wondering if you know anything about the drama teacher."

"Mrs. Potter? Can't say I've had much contact with her, but I have heard good things about her directing skills." Bella tilted her head at Jeremiah. "Why do you ask?"

"I signed up to audition for the school play. Auditions are tomorrow. Guess I was curious about what kind of a chance I stood."

School play, huh? She learned something new every day. Dancing and acting. The two did go hand in hand. If memory served, the first production of the year was *Hamlet*. "I can't say I've ever heard anyone complain about her being unfair. Any thoughts on which role you're going out for?"

"I don't necessarily always go for the lead, but I am intrigued by the idea of playing Hamlet."

"Really?" Bella raised an eyebrow.

"Yeah, I know. Weird. I mean one of the major questions of the story is whether he's crazy or actually seeing his father's ghost, but honestly, I think Shakespeare was just onto something. After all, there are things in this world we can't begin to comprehend."

He had a point. With most stories, it's all about perspective. Two people could see the same thing and still view it quite differently. "I get it."

"Good." Jeremiah stopped mid-step. "Think you could come to auditions? For moral support?"

Why her? Bella wondered. Why not his sister? But maybe it was kind of the same reason she wanted him to participate in the Fall Harvest Festival. Not just to choreograph, but because his presence comforted her. "Yeah." Bella nodded. "I have a tutor meeting after school, but it shouldn't take long. I'll come by after that."

"Thanks. I appreciate it."

"Of course." Noting the street sign ahead, Bella realized they'd be at her house in two blocks. She needed to ask, now. "There was something I wanted to talk to you about, too."

"Oh? What's up?"

"You know how yesterday the pastor announced that I'll be directing the Fall Festival this year?"

"Yeah. Congratulations, by the way. I meant to tell you yesterday, but didn't get a chance after church. Are you excited?"

"A little excited. A lot nervous." Bella rubbed her palms on her skirt. Her plans depended so much on other people. Getting the pastor to agree to let her direct was only half the battle.

"Well, I'm confident you'll do your best. If you need me to do anything, just let me know. I'd be happy to help."

His offer had been no joke. It was entirely sincere. Tugging on the straps of her backpack, Bella regarded Miah. Okay, then. "That's kind of what I wanted to talk to you about. I was hoping you'd choreograph."

"What?"

"I want you to choreograph. I think you'd be perfect. We've had bad choreographers the past few years, and I want to make this the best show anyone has ever seen." It was one of the biggest events of the year for their church. None of the other churches did anything close. A lot of people showed up for both the production and the dance—and this year, after three years of flops, it had to be off the charts, or they would lose support and even funding.

"You want me to choreograph? Really?" Miah grinned. "Yes! I'd love to!"

Had he just said yes? He had. He said *yes*.

"I'm so excited!" Bella said, throwing her arms around Jeremiah's neck.

He grabbed her and spun her around a few times, then, setting her back down, asked, "When do we start?"

Vick collected the papers that had been left behind. "Is this the norm? One assignment?"

"For the first semester, yes," Bella answered. "It'll get busier, but for now, all we usually get are those who had tutors last year."

Bella glanced at her watch. "If you'll excuse me, I need to go." Taking the papers from Vick, she tucked them in her backpack and started for the door. "I promised Miah I'd head over to the theater for his audition."

Vick opened the library door and held it for Bella. "Guess everything is today."

"What makes you say that?"

"Soccer tryouts are this afternoon, too. That's where I'm heading, now."

"You still going to make it to Bible study?" Their first teen Bible study session was scheduled for that night, and Vick was one of the few people who agreed with her that some parts of the Bible were objective, while other parts were subjective—which was why there were so many interpretations of the same verses or passages.

"Yeah. I don't expect they'll run too much over an hour. I'll catch you later." Vick started to leave, then paused. "Hey, wish Jeremiah good luck for me."

"You, too." But Bella felt it was a sad afterthought. What kind of friend was she? Vick had mentioned soccer tryouts last week, and they had completely slipped her mind. She would certainly remember to ask him how he did, later.

With that, Bella strode toward the amphitheater. The school had a large auditorium for major productions like *Hamlet*, but the amphitheater was perfect for skits and auditions. A lot of students used it as a place to hang out and catch up between classes. It was also used as a make-shift classroom on occasion.

Bella slowed as she approached the edge of the stairs and surveyed the area. Halfway down, she saw Miah and Amanda sitting together. So, his sister had come.

Descending the stairs, Bella noticed a couple of familiar faces. Mostly drama geeks, who'd been in previous productions. Some of whom were trying to make a name for themselves.

"Hey! You made it." Miah stood and held his hand out.

Setting her hand in his, Bella smiled. Maybe he'd only offered it to make sure she didn't fall, but she liked feeling their hands together. "I said I would. I never go back on my word."

With a nod at Bella, Amanda rose. "Good. Now that you're here, I can go. I'll be back." With a quick wave, she headed up the stairs.

"Was it something I said?"

Jeremiah chuckled. "No. She's juggling me and a friend. Said we both need a cheerleader."

"Okay, then." No reason to read into it too much. There were a lot of clubs with tryouts, today. A lot of people she could be cheerleading for. Shrugging it off, Bella sat beside Miah.

"Has Mrs. Potter announced the order of auditions yet?"

"No. She just said she'd call us one at a time. And that each person has two minutes."

Bella's gaze swept the amphitheater. She counted at least thirty people. Two minutes per person. Auditions would take over an hour. Fine. She glanced at her watch again. Five o'clock, now. As long as Jeremiah was one of the first, she'd be okay.

"We're going to go ahead and get started." Mrs. Potter called out. "First up, David Warren."

"David Warren?" No way. Bella had to be hearing things. But sure as shit, David climbed onto the stage. Shouldn't he be at soccer tryouts? Why the hell was he here?

"Yeah," Miah said, with a grunt. "You know that douche-bag?"

Uh-oh. Based on that comment, Bella assumed the two had run into each other, already. Oh yeah, David had mentioned something about it when they spoke last week.

She grimaced. Oh, fun. "I tutor him. Dare I ask how you guys met?"

"Signing up for auditions. Didn't take long for him to reveal his true colors."

Blowing air from puffed cheeks, Bella glanced at her watch. It was almost six. Half the auditions were over, and Miah still hadn't been called. Shit. She had to go by the church before Bible study. Then, spotting Amanda at the top of the stairs, her body relaxed. Turning toward Jeremiah, she said, "I hate to do this, but I have to go."

"What are you talking about?"

"I'm supposed to get some paperwork from the pastor for the Fall Festival on my way home. Then, there's Bible study." Bella squeezed Miah's shoulder. "Listen. I know you're going to be fine. You've got this."

"Thanks." His eyes shifted. "Are you sure you can't stay longer?"

"I wish I could, but I'll just barely make it as it is."

The look on his face broke her heart. She should've planned better, but she had truly expected his audition to be done by now.

Staring into Miah's green eyes, she could see her little pep talk had done nothing. Confidence mattered in acting. She could try again to give it to him. "I have faith you are going to nail this. I believe in my heart that in a few months, I'm going to see you on stage as the craziest Hamlet ever." Resting her hand over his heart, Bella kissed him on the cheek.

"Thanks, Bell." A broad smile tugged the corners of Miah's mouth.

Giving his hand a squeeze, Bella walked up the stairs and paused beside Amanda. "Hey, do me a favor? Stay for his audition?"

"Yeah, sure."

"Thanks." Giving Jeremiah a last glance, she checked her watch again. There was still time. Her walk would take thirty minutes, tops. Five minutes at the church, then she'd cab it home. Vick would be there soon to help her mother with the set up, and she could finish whatever last-minute things had to be done.

It would work.

Bella exited through the main doors and headed toward downtown. She would trek along Main Street, hook the corner at the alleyway next to Italiano's, then cross Thirteenth Street, and take it the rest of the way to the church. Even though the sun was dropping behind the horizon, the walk would be easy. She'd navigated that same path a hundred times before.

As she walked, her mind buzzed with those last few minutes with Miah. Her hand on his chest. It had felt so nice. Despite the circumstances. The hugs, the touches, the kisses. Each was amazing on its own. She couldn't wait for more.

Turning the corner at the pizza parlor, Bella headed into the alleyway. All of a sudden, goose bumps crawled up her arms and the hairs on her neck prickled. Her gaze bounced back and forth between the brick walls. She picked up her pace, passing a dumpster halfway through the alley.

It smelled awful. The stink of spoiled meat, aged cheese, and five-day-old anchovies filled her nostrils. She coughed—just as someone nabbed her from behind, twisting her arm and slamming her against the wall. A large man, whose face she couldn't see, yanked her to him.

She yelped as pain radiated up her arm to her shoulder. He released her arm, spun her around, threw her to the ground and straddled her, then pressed her arms above her head against a mound of garbage bags.

Bella twisted and tried to fight back. "No!"

The man punched her face, slicing the bridge of her nose. "Be good girl, honey bear, and this go easy."

Good girl? Honey bear? Tears joined the blood that trickled down her cheeks. Then another guy appeared, a stocky man, and a ray of hope sliced the darkness.

Except what savior covered their face with a bandana and a hoodie? He wasn't there to save her. He'd come to aid her attacker.

The second man's hands replaced the ones that pinned her down. Trying to use the switch to her advantage, Bella shoved at the guy on top of her. But she wasn't strong enough. A crack filled her ears as one of the men slapped her.

Bandana guy grabbed her arm and slammed it through the pile of garbage bags, snapping it against the concrete.

Agony pierced her body, and Bella screamed, but her scream lasted only a second, as a gloved hand covered her mouth. There had to be someone who would step in and intervene. Some bystander who'd stop this. But there was no one. No one stopped. No one looked her way. No one helped.

She was alone.

Bandanna man backhanded her across the cheek, then ripped her skirt right down the middle. She shut her eyes and sobbed through heavy breaths. Then the first man grabbed her by the chin.

"Look at me."

That voice. So gravelly. Had she heard it before? No. No! She refused to open her eyes and instead squeezed them tighter.

He slapped her again, busting her lip open. Blood dripped from the corner of her mouth. There were remnants of a cigarette on his breath. She didn't want to look, but if she floated away, like she wanted to, she would die.

"Do not make me hit you again. Be good girl and look at me."

God, this was just like the beating she took when she was eight. Her face hurt so badly. The only way to protect herself was to follow his instructions. Survival. She had to live through this. By will alone, Bella opened her eyes—then she saw it: That scar! The man had a scar that ran jagged down the right side of his face. It was her nightmare come to life. That scar. It made him identifiable. And it was familiar beyond her dream. But how? An image flashed deep in the recesses of her mind.

His face flared into a wide, sadistic grin, narrowing the scar. He brushed his gloved hands over her hair. "Good. Honey bear, tell me, you going to be good girl?"

His face! That face. That scar. Something flashed in the depths of her mind again, but she couldn't focus on it. Too much noise had exploded in her ears. She couldn't respond. But she had to find a way.

"Say it!"

"I'll be a good girl," Bella whispered.

Scar-face nodded, and the other man cautiously released his grip and stood. Then Scar-face yanked her top apart.

Sobbing, she tried to look away again. One of the men slapped her. How could she be in this position again? She was older, stronger ... Bella twisted and tried to escape. Bandana man kicked her in the ribs. She cried out again, but her sounds were stifled when the man on top of her seized her chin and turned her face to him. The two of them together were too strong. There was no escape.

Scar-face leaned down and kissed her hard, then bit her lip, as he pulled away and released her chin. "Sweet. Very sweet. You always remember your first."

seven

"Thanks, Mandy. I appreciate you sticking around," Jeremiah said.

Amanda parked the Dodge alongside the curb in front of Bella's house. "I still can't believe your name disappeared off that list," she said.

"I don't know how it happened. At least Mrs. Potter let me audition." Jeremiah checked his cell phone. Seven thirty. They were late for the first Bible study session. What a way to make an impression.

Jeremiah marched across the driveway and up the front walk, Amanda beside him. He knocked, and the front door flew open.

Bell's dad, DeWei Kynaston, stood there, frantic eyes flicking from Amanda to Jeremiah, then past both of them. "Isn't Bella with you?"

"No, sir."

Isn't she here? Jeremiah wanted to ask, but, obviously, she wasn't. Where was she? It had been near six when she left school. How long had she told him the walk to church would take? Shit. He couldn't remember.

"Please, please, come in. When did you last see her?" DeWei asked.

Amanda nudged Jeremiah inside the house, where he saw Vick standing, looking deeply worried.

"An hour and a half ago," Jeremiah said.

"Did she tell you where she was going? Was she coming straight home?"

Jeremiah dragged his hand through his hair and gripped the back of his neck.

"Church. She was going by church. Have you—?"

"I'll call Pastor Whitmore." Bella's mother, Milena, appeared behind DeWei, and then disappeared into the kitchen.

It had been an hour and a half since he'd seen her. People couldn't be reported as missing unless twenty-four hours had passed. No way he'd wait that long, Jeremiah thought. If necessary, he'd make a call. He turned to his sister and nodded to her. She nodded back.

Milena returned. "The pastor says she never showed."

"I'm sorry, everyone. Given the situation, we need to cancel this evening's session," DeWei announced to the teens seated around the dining table.

There was a general rustle of jackets and study materials being gathered—and then a half dozen kids filed out the front door, nodding solemnly to DeWei as they passed him.

But not Jeremiah. No flipping way he was leaving. Not without knowing Bell was safe. His heart would not beat if she wasn't okay. "Sir, I understand the urgency of the matter, and while I respect your request, I'm not going anywhere."

Vick stepped up beside Jeremiah. "I'm with him, Mr. Kynaston. Bella's family. I'll stay as long as necessary to make sure she's all right."

DeWei stopped and regarded Jeremiah and Vick. "Boys, I understand you both mean well, but I think this is a matter best handled by the police."

"I agree." Jeremiah dug out his cell phone. He shot another look at his sister. This wasn't a call he'd ever wanted to make. "So, let me help make it happen. I promise it'll go faster this way."

The smell of the dumpster wafted through the alley behind Italiano's. A skunk's stench couldn't cover the scent that assaulted his nostrils. Jamar Detrone glanced over his shoulder at the crew dedicated to evidence collection, then returned his attention to the pizzeria's owner. "What time do you normally close up shop?"

"On a night like tonight, I'm taking the trash out about eight thirty. We had a last-minute customer, so it was closer to nine. That's when I found her."

"And you're sure you didn't hear anything?" With the state the girl had been in when she was found, Jamar was surprised the attack hadn't attracted attention. But sometimes people overlook what they actually see or hear. A cry for help can blend in with the everyday sounds they're accustomed to, and it's like it's not happening.

"No. I swear. If I had ..."

Theoretically, if the guy had found her, he would've acted sooner. Unfortunately, good Samaritans were few and far between these days. Too many people willing to record, but not get involved.

"How often does the trash go out?"

"A few times a day. We can easily fill five bags on a good day."

"When is it normally collected?" Had to be at least a week's worth of garbage she'd been found under. Awfully convenient.

"Wednesday mornings. Most of the time, the guys come around six in the morning."

Tomorrow. No such thing as a coincidence in his line of work. His gut told him this attack had been planned.

"What if it's not all in the dumpster? Will they still take it?"

"I get a citation, but, yeah, they'll haul it all off."

"Anybody else besides you toss bags out back here?"

"Me, Larry, and Wanda. Larry owns the shop next door, and Wanda has an antique shop at the other end of the alley. Space behind me is empty."

Good thing about small towns, owners of nearby shops usually knew one another. Bad thing about small towns, the owners usually knew one another. "You mind if we collect your prints for exclusionary purposes?"

"Not at all, Sheriff. I'll do whatever I can to help."

"Okay. Officer Lucas here is going to get your prints. If you think of anything else, you call me." Jamar handed the owner his business card. Fresh off the printer. They'd been delivered that afternoon. He had no clue he'd use them so quickly.

He walked closer to the pile of bags the girl had been discovered under. "I want all of these bags collected and taken back to the lab. And search every dumpster in a three-block radius. Let's do what we can to find her clothes."

Detective Russell approached with his gloved hand wrapped around the strap of a backpack. "Sheriff, I found something."

"Anything inside to tell us who she is?"

"Mostly school books. Looks like from the local high ... wait."

Russell handed Jamar a wallet. Jamar popped it open. Fifty bucks in cash. Not a lot of money, but certainly enough for a teenager of no more than sixteen or seventeen. Whoever beat the hell out of her hadn't intended to rob her.

Jamar paused on her picture ID. Dammit. His son's girlfriend. She was the victim. This wasn't good. Not good at all. His son had called a couple of hours ago about her missing. He dug his phone out of his pocket and dialed one of the detectives who'd been sent to the Kynaston residence. Missing cases weren't supposed to turn into rape cases.

Deegart picked up on the second ring.

"You still at the Kynaston residence?" Jamar asked.

"Yes, sir. We've just finished taking statements."

"Good. I'll be there in ten minutes." Though he'd read over the jackets for each of his officers after he'd accepted the position, he'd had no time to get to know them, personally. He had no idea how they'd deliver bad news. Especially with his son still there.

"Tell them we found their daughter, and she's alive. Nothing more. Understood?"

"Yes, sir."

Next, Jamar reached out to the two officers he'd sent to the hospital. When Thomas answered, Jamar said, "Give me some good news."

"We were only able to collect a few samples, sir."

"What about her condition?" The girl's survival mattered more than the evidence. Yeah, samples would be required to catch her attacker, but her life came first and foremost.

"The doctors have taken her back into surgery. Her shoulder's been dislocated, a broken arm, possibly a punctured lung, and a fresh burn on her neck."

Jamar closed his eyes for a minute. What hell Bella must've gone through. And to have survived? She had to be strong. "We've identified her as Bella Kynaston—"

"Christ," Thomas said. "That's Bella?"

"Do you know her?" While the county was middle-sized, Jamar had learned that each town was small enough that a lot of people knew one another.

"Not personally, but I've met her father. He's the counselor at the Rescate County Juvenile Detention Center."

Oh, boy. Their suspect list just increased substantially. Jamar presumed Bella had been raped. A kit would confirm his suspicions. And most rapes are committed by someone the victim knows. But this piece of information changed things. Now, it could've been done out of pure revenge.

"I'll be informing her parents. Keep me posted."

"Yes, sir."

Jamar returned his phone to his back pocket. "Russell, you're in charge. I'm heading to the Kynaston residence."

The sound of a detective's cell phone ringing told Jeremiah there was news. But was it good or bad? Lord, let it be good. Leaning forward, he strained to pick up any part of the conversation. There wasn't much to be heard. He straightened up as the call ended and Detective Deegart returned to the family room.

"Mr. and Mrs. Kynaston, your daughter's been found alive."

"Oh, thank God!" Milena cried out. "Where is she?"

"I'm afraid I don't have more news than that, but I promise you'll get some answers soon. Sheriff Detrone is on his way here now."

Jeremiah slumped. She was alive. That was good news. But if his father was coming, there was bad news. Tears prickled the corners of his eyes.

Feeling a hand squeeze his, he looked over to his sister. Amanda hugged him. "She's alive."

"Then why is he coming?"

Rising to his feet, Jeremiah stepped away and wiped at his eyes. Amanda meant well, but the situation was bad, and she knew it, too. Bell was alive, but for how long? Jeremiah looked to Deegart. If he asked, would the guy tell him more?

Before he had a chance to ask, there was a knock at the door. Even though it wasn't his house, Jeremiah raced to the door and yanked it open. "Dad, tell me. Is she okay? Don't give me any bullshit. You have to tell me! Right now."

His father pulled Jeremiah into a tight hug. "I know, son. I know. Now, come on. Let's go inside, and I'll explain everything."

Jeremiah's chest shook as he swallowed the unshed tears. He stepped out of his father's grip, and they walked into the family room, together.

"Sheriff Detrone, tell us what is going on with our daughter," DeWei demanded.

Tucking his hands into his pockets, Jamar said, "We found your daughter in the alley by Italiano's Pizzeria. She'd been attacked. I spoke with one of the detectives who went to the hospital with her not fifteen minutes ago. She's in surgery at the moment. If you'd like, we can all head to the hospital now."

Bella's eyes felt heavy, and her mouth was dry. She lifted her arm to wipe the crust from her eyes and winced. Had somebody played chopsticks on her ribs while she was asleep? Maybe if she moved the other arm. A sharp pain radiated from her shoulder. She winced again.

She managed to get one eye halfway open. The things shoved in her nostrils, the constant beep to her right, and the bright overhead light. Hospital. She'd ended up in the hospital.

"Good. You're awake." The doctor returned the chart to its holster.

"Where am I?"

"Nautica Valley General."

How had she gotten here? The last thing she remembered, the smell of burnt flesh and then ... Oh. No. God, please, no. "What happened?"

"You were attacked."

Attacked? Oh, God. Tears streamed down her cheeks. Bella closed her one good eye. Everything clicked into place and strong images flashed behind her eyelids. Her eye flipped open, again. "How ... how bad?"

The question wasn't necessary. She already knew the answer.

The doctor sat in the chair beside her bed. "You have three broken ribs, a punctured lung, a broken ulna, multiple bruises, your shoulder was dislocated, and there's a burn on your neck."

All the damage came to life as he listed each injury. It had gone dark after the burn. She must have passed out. But it had happened, hadn't it? And everything in her world had changed.

"Where ... where are my parents?"

"In the waiting room, along with a few of your friends."

No police. If those monsters left her for dead, what would they do if the police got involved? And what about her family? Her friends? God, Miah! What had they been told? What had he been told? Could they protect her from all the questions? Or would they ask them, too? No! No, no, no. No way she could tell them what she remembered.

"Police?"

"There are some things you and I need to discuss," the doctor told her. "But we don't have to do that right away. Whatever you want to do right now, that's what we'll do."

His reply confirmed her worst fear. Her body no longer belonged to her. It had been ripped apart by monsters. The doctor wanted it to be all about what she wanted, but her desire to simply disappear probably wasn't what he was thinking of.

More tears spilled from her eyes. "I ... I don't know."

"That's okay. Take your time. The police will eventually need to speak with you, but on your time, not theirs."

Bella looked away as best she could. They all were waiting outside because they all knew. She couldn't decide which was worse. Her parents or Miah seeing her like this, her having to talk to the police, or repeating everything those men had done to her. None seemed like good options. She licked at the corner of her mouth. Why couldn't they have killed her in that alley? Why had God allowed her to be so brutalized, yet survive?

Survive. Yeah, she'd survived, all right. Her parents would want to see her to believe it. What she wanted? Well, it no longer mattered. "Miah and my parents. I'd like to see them first. Then, I guess I'll talk to the police."

"Are you sure?"

"Yes." As sure as she could be, given the circumstances.

When Jamar got to the hospital, he'd spoken with the doctor and confirmed his suspicions. Bella Kynaston had been raped and left for dead. If the restaurant owner hadn't discovered her when he did, this very well could've turned into a murder case. He'd delivered the news to her parents upon their arrival. They'd taken it as well as any loved ones would: Shock. Disbelief. Who would do something like this to their daughter?

And that was exactly what he intended to find out—but questions had to be asked if he planned to get anywhere in this investigation.

"Do you know of any enemies your daughter might have?"

"No. She is a good person. Shy, but she is kind to everyone she has ever met." Milena Kynaston leaned on her husband for support.

Jamar studied the girl's father, alert for nuances, things to let him know the guy told the truth. "What about you Dr. Kynaston? I understand you're the counselor at the juvenile detention center. Do you have any enemies?"

"No one I can think of who would attack our daughter. Some people have become angry and threatened me with regards to the work I do, but nothing has ever come to fruition."

"Written threats? Or voicemail? Any record of these threats?" The man hadn't lied, but something about his response bothered Jamar.

"I am certain there are copies on record. You may—"

DeWei's words were interrupted by a doctor stepping into the room. "Dr. and Mrs. Kynaston, your daughter's awake and asking for you and Jeremiah."

All three jumped to their feet. Milena spoke first. "Oh, my goodness. May we see her?"

"Do you mind if I go, too?" Jeremiah asked, looking to Bella's parents.

DeWei nodded. "She asked for you. I think you should come. As long as it's okay with the doctor."

"Yes, of course. The nurse will take you back."

Jamar waited for the Kynastons and his son to be escorted from the room. None of them needed to hear what he was about to be told.

Once they were out of earshot, he eyed the doctor. "Give me it to me straight."

"Dislocated shoulder, fractured ulna, punctured lung, two broken ribs, several scrapes and bruises, plus, the burn on her neck."

"You have any idea how the burn was made?"

"Based on the pattern, I'd say she was branded ... with a cauterizing pen."

Branded? Like an animal? Jamar shook his head. Cases like these turned his stomach. "You get a rape kit started?"

"Not yet. Give her a few minutes with her parents and friend, then we'll get it processed. I know you want to get the bad guy, Sheriff, but I need to take care of my patient first."

Where was his girl?

Cops crawled all over the alley behind Italiano's. Crime scene unit investigators collecting evidence, photographing the scene, talking to witnesses. Standard procedure.

Binoculars trained on the entrance of the alley two blocks away, Gervasio decided it was too soon to reach out to his police contacts. He'd wait twenty-four hours and access the reports.

Digging out his cell, he checked the time. Two a.m. Someone had found her. When? A few of the shops in the vicinity used the same dumpster. She had to have been discovered by someone taking out trash for the night. It was the most likely scenario. Meant an ambulance had hauled her off hours ago to the nearest hospital.

Her body would be on the mend. The damage they had done had been substantial. More than even he believed possible. Unfortunate for her. Even though it had more to do with his partner than it did with him. If only his partner hadn't gotten greedy.

That's okay. On to the next part of his plan.

There was still a ring to deliver.

"Do you mind if I speak with Miah alone a moment?"

Jeremiah shifted his gaze from Bell to her parents. They had every right to decline her request. Instead, they both nodded, gave quick kisses, and left the room. Alone with his angel, he eyed the bruises on her face. The black and blue traveled down her arms, what he could see of them. One arm had been broken and her other shoulder had been dislocated.

Her injuries screamed at him. This was his fault.

He should've questioned his name not being called sooner. Or have insisted she wait for him. Not as if there had been any reason. Rubbing his eyes, Jeremiah sighed. "I'm sorry."

"For what? This isn't your fault. You couldn't have predicted what would happen any more than I could."

"Somewhere in my head, I'm sure I believe that." Jeremiah jumped up and started to pace from one side of the small hospital room to the other. "But then there's the part of my head that keeps telling me it's a man's job to keep his loved ones safe, and that I failed."

"Miah, please stop. You're making me dizzy."

Halting dead in his tracks, Jeremiah realized he was blaming himself and not considering what she was going through. It was her body that had been dealt the blows. Her body that had been invaded.

"I'm sorry Bell. I don't want to make this harder for you than it already is."

"Okay. Then tell me how the audition went."

"What?" He must have misheard.

"You want to help, right? Then talk to me about something besides where we're at. I don't ... I don't want to think about it. So, tell me about your audition."

This situation couldn't be ignored forever. But he could do his part to help her ignore it for right now. He returned to the chair he had previously occupied. His audition. "I was the last one to go. As you can imagine, I got to see some pretty interesting versions of Hamlet. Me, I gave it a little bit of a twist. I turned a soliloquy into a rap and included some dance. While I hate to admit it, I'm guessing it'll come down between me and David."

"I bet she liked yours better, though."

A normal conversation. Like nothing bad had happened.

Jeremiah grinned. "Postings go up in two days. I'll let you know who got it."

"Thank you."

"Anything for you. Now, you need some rest." He stood and pressed a feather kiss to her forehead. It was the safest place for his lips to go. One of the few places on her body that had no damage.

eight

"Are you certain?" her mother asked for the fifth time.

Her parents had spent the majority of the night at the hospital, only leaving her side for an hour to shower and change clothes. She loved her parents, but they had to go.

"Yes, Mãe. There are plenty of nurses and doctors here to hover over me. I'll be fine."

"If that is what you wish, your mother and I will leave." Her father pressed a gentle kiss to her hair and smiled.

"It is Bàba."

"Very well. Rest, my Cinderella. We shall return in a few hours."

Screw sleep. She had a conversation to finish with the doctor. Her parents had interrupted the previous discussion she'd had with the doctor—and he'd said they'd continue their talk later. But not if her parents had their way. Then it wouldn't matter what she decided.

After the door closed, Bella stifled a yawn. Way too much of her ached. Including her cheeks. Talking was easy enough. Yawning, though—or, hell, any deep breath—and her lungs burned. Like they'd been set ablaze.

Every part of her body hurt. Not only had those monsters broken bones, but they'd beaten her to within an inch of her life. She'd almost prayed for death several times throughout the night. Then she'd remembered the look of relief that had washed over her parents' and Miah's faces when they'd first seen her last night. Early this morning? She had no real sense of time.

Bella glanced at the call button. Had she waited long enough? Surely her parents had taken the elevator downstairs by now. The little box had been moved closer to her good hand. Less room for her to move. She depressed the button.

"Is everything okay, Miss Kynaston? Do you need some more pain medication?"

No. At least not until she'd spoken with the doctor and addressed the subject at hand. "I'm okay, for now. I just need to talk to the doctor. I've made a decision."

"What happened next?" Detective Russell asked. They had waited less than twenty-four hours before pressing her for information.

"Another man walked up. I thought he was someone off the street and maybe ..." Bella turned her head away from the two officers. More tears rolled down her cheeks. He should've been the person to save her. But there had been no one. Not even God had intervened.

"I thought he would help me, but he pinned me down instead."

"He was an accomplice?" Miah's father clarified. It was the first question he had asked since walking in with Detective Russell.

"Yes. He had on a bandana and hoodie." Most of her memories ran together, but she was doing what she could to recall the details. Which she preferred not to do. But the police insisted she tell them as much as possible.

"Can you recall anything further about this man? Hair color? Eye color? Scars? Tattoos? Something about his voice?" Detective Russell probed.

"No. He had on gloves and kept his face hidden by the hoodie. But he was stocky. Muscular. And he never spoke." Bella winced as she wiped at the tears rolling down her cheeks. She'd leaked like a damn sieve since the questions had begun. Better than screaming her head off or choking on a gasp from a nightmare, though.

"Okay. What happened next?"

"The one with the scar told me to be a good girl. He hit me when I turned away. He forced me to look at him. Like he wanted me to know who he was." Speaking about her main attacker tore her in two. He might as well have been in the room listening to every word she uttered, ripping her apart all over again.

She attempted to dry her face, but almost every move caused pain to shoot up her arm. Added to the crack in her soul.

"And you didn't recognize him at all?"

The question nagged at her. During the attack, she swore he looked familiar. Maybe he was someone she'd seen around town? Bella frowned. No. That wasn't it. How should she answer? She shuddered and winced, again, at the movement. "I don't think so."

"What happened next?"

That question took her to the top of a rollercoaster—and she wanted to get off before it plunged down the drop. "Can we please take a break?"

Miah's father gently squeezed her hand. "I know this is hard, but we need to get it all while it's fresh in your mind."

Right. "Fresh in her mind." As if she'd ever forget.

"He ... uh ... he tore my clothes. My skirt ... my blouse ... and ... uh ... my ..." Bella paused, inhaling and exhaling as deep a breath as her damaged lungs allowed. "... my underwear. He shoved my bra up when he put himself ... inside ... inside of me."

"When did you get the mark on your neck?"

"After he ..." she paused and wiped at her face despite the shooting pain. "... after he finished."

"Who branded you?"

"The guy who helped with everything." God, what if he'd had his way with her too? Everything about this nightmare continued to get worse. "Bandana guy."

"After the scar-faced man raped you?" Detective Russell asked.

More tears. The scorching pain against her neck was the last thing she remembered. Most of the physical damage had been done after she blacked out, the doctor had told her.

"Yes. The scar-faced man told the other guy to mark me. Said I was his. Then I passed out."

Miah's father snatched a tissue from a box on the nightstand and handed it to her. "I'm sorry you had to go through all this."

Bella winced as she dried the nonstop tear train. "What happens now?"

"Several things. Your rape kit is being analyzed. I'm working on getting the mark on your neck identified. Once we have any potential suspects, we'll have you either look at a photo array or come in to do a line up," Detective Russell said.

"Okay. I can ... I think I can do that." For her own sake, she had to.

The door opened and a guy stuck his head around the corner.

Jeremiah popped up from Bell's hospital bed, as if he and Bell were two teenagers caught in a compromising position by a parent. They hadn't been doing anything, but not everyone would view it that way. Jeremiah cocked an eyebrow. No one else had visited her in the last couple of days beside him and her parents.

Until now.

And it was some guy he'd never met before. He didn't like it.

Bell greeted the newcomer. "Petar. What're you doing here?"

"Hey, Bella." The fakest of smiles spread across the guy's face, as his grip tightened on the bouquet of flowers in his hand. "I hope you don't mind. Principal Owen told me where to find you. I had to check on you myself. See you were okay."

"No. Um, please, come in." Pressing her hand awkwardly into the mattress, she tried to lift herself.

"Wait a second." Jeremiah jumped to her aid. Too bad the other guy insisted on helping, too. But when Jeremiah eased a hand onto Bell's shoulder blade, she stopped him.

"I'm fine! I can do it myself!"

Jeremiah frowned. She'd never barked at him or stiffened under his touch before. Was it the other guy's presence? A memory of two guys having raped her? Or ... could this Petar actually be one of her attackers? This was something he would bring up with his father. In the meantime, he complied with Bell's request and backed up a bit.

As did Petar.

"Sorry, I, uh ... I don't ..."

"Hey, it's—"

"It's okay. You don't have to explain. Here, I brought these for you." Petar held out the bouquet and returned the smile Bell gave him.

Arms crossed; Jeremiah frowned. The guy hadn't even acknowledged his presence—and then he'd interrupted him. And the bouquet full of purple flowers the guy offered to Bella. Larkspurs. Her favorite. Like the bouquet he, himself, had brought yesterday. The one sitting on the nightstand under the television in plain sight.

Bella gestured from one to the other of them. "Um, sorry, I'm being rude. Jeremiah, this is Petar. Petar, Jeremiah."

Extending his hand, Petar grinned. "Nice to meet you."

"You, as well." Jeremiah placed his hand in Petar's hand, palm to palm. The handshake was firm. They both tightened their grip. Jeremiah didn't need to prove anything, but he refused to be outdone.

Yeah. It would be nice to know more about this guy.

"Thank you," she said.

Miah leaned back in his chair. "For what?" he asked, warily.

Bella smirked. He and Petar had played their testosterone competition well, but neither had fooled her. That endless handshake gave it away. "For not kicking his ass."

"One, we're in a hospital. I would never start a fight here. Two, I have more respect for you than that. Though, I would like to know more about him."

"Petar and I met my freshman year. In the tutor group. Somehow, over the last few years he's become a bit of a protector to me." Mentioning the near kiss didn't seem like the wisest idea, so she skipped it. Nothing had come of it. Not even much of a friendship.

"Has he always been a bit of a creep?"

Bella opened her mouth, then shut it. She couldn't defend Petar. He'd been rude. Almost knocked over Miah's larkspurs. And so competitive. She didn't remember him being like that before. Or ever giving her the willies before. Bella shuddered at the memory of his touch when he'd tried to help her sit up in the bed.

"No. He was ... different."

"Is it possible you just saw a new side of him?"

"I don't know. Maybe. I never spent much time with him outside of school.

If I did, it was always me, him, and Alex." Except for last week. When they went to the bookstore.

"I don't want you to think I'm looking for something that's not there, but he seemed a bit possessive when it comes to you."

Possessive? Had he? Last week, when they'd gotten a bite to eat, he had ordered for her. That seemed a bit out of character. He'd even insisted on buying the book she picked out. Did that count as "possessive"? Maybe. Maybe she had overlooked something.

Later that afternoon, there was a knock on the door. "Hey. Mind if I—?"

"David." Bella shifted toward him.

And he froze halfway through the door.

Shock. It stopped a lot of people when they first saw her. Bruises in various stages of healing covered her face. One eye was swelled partially shut. Her forehead and cheeks and lips were likewise swollen. Plus, the gauze on her neck.

"David?"

Snapping out of it, he stepped into the room and set a vase of larkspur under the television next to the other two. Then he offered her a purple teddy bear. A red bow was tied around its neck and it held a heart that read, "Get well soon."

"I, uh, I brought you something. I hope you like it."

"It's perfect. Thank you." His bear would be placed with the others. Only one stuffed animal stayed by her bed—a purple tiger with a special message. Miah had great taste when it came to gifts.

"Mind if I sit?"

Bella nodded gingerly, and he sank onto the chair beside her bed. Leaning into his knees, he folded his fingers together. Then he rubbed his hands on his jeans and sighed. "I want to ask how you're feeling, but you're probably tired of hearing it."

"Yeah. A question I never thought would get old." A small smile tugged at the corner of her lips as she looked down at the teddy bear he'd brought.

"Who brought the other vases of larkspurs?"

"Miah brought one—and Petar. They both know they're my favorite. How'd you know?"

"The same way I know purple is your favorite color. You told me." David gestured the stuffed animal on the bedside table. "Who's the tiger from?"

"Miah gave it to me. I'm sorry, I told you about my favorite flowers and color?" Bella questioned. "You know what. Not important." David was bit fidgety. Her wounds tended to make visitors nervous. Afraid they would say something stupid. It would be best if they spoke about something else. "Tell me how your audition for *Hamlet* went."

"I thought it was good, but I didn't get the part of Hamlet. Instead, I got cast as Claudius."

Miah had gotten the part of Hamlet. He'd even mentioned David's role. "Still, that's a pretty big part."

"I guess so. Just not what I expected. I mean, come on, do I look like a bad guy?"

Gervasio stared at the hospital entrance. His girl had yet to be released. How many days had she been there now? Three days? Four? What day was it? No. Friday. It was Friday. Three days. How much damage had he done? It was dark when he'd stripped her of her clothes. The amount of rage he'd felt was unprecedented. He'd never destroyed someone so badly. He had been in a frenzy that he couldn't comprehend any more now than three days ago.

Standing aside and allowing another to have her had proved impossible. All his other whores had been taken by himself and one of his soldiers. They'd all been broken in the same way. It was protocol. He'd never gone off on one like that before, though.

Why was the pastor's daughter so fucking different? What the hell made the little bitch so damn special? He'd taken a virgin before. Couldn't be that. He'd had a girl younger than her. Couldn't be that.

Maybe ... could it be the connection to his brother? No.

Had to be the connection to the girl's mother. He'd never taken a mother and daughter before. Yeah. That had to be it.

No. That wasn't it either. It was an unfulfilled promise.

At least he hadn't killed her. The mother had deserved no less.

But his girl, his girl was special. She was alive for a reason.

His phone rang. Gervasio snapped the thing up. "¿Si?"

"They completed a rape kit. There's DNA."

"No worry. I fix." He smirked. It would take weeks, maybe even months before the police would have the results. And he'd prepared for the situation. "You have more to say?"

"No, sir."

Gervasio hung up and tore out of the hospital parking lot. He couldn't control the girl ... yet. But he was far from finished with her. One call, and he'd ensure everything panned out the way he'd planned. Not from his cell phone, though. Not traceable.About two blocks from the hospital, he pulled into a gas station and parked. Keeping tight to the wall and using the shadows to his advantage, Gervasio tugged his baseball cap down and entered the phone booth. He dropped in some coins, then punched in the number to the precinct. One. Two. Three. Three fucking rings. Reminding himself to stay calm, he waited for the piece of shit on the other end to get out his full statement, then spoke. "Detective Simms, please."

It was quiet. Halls were empty, save for a few nurses and the occasional doctor making rounds. Gervasio pushed the cart forward. The only other people on this level were orderlies. Assistants performing routine duties. Easiest way to gain access to the hospital and sneak into his girl's room, dress like one and push a cart.

Gervasio glanced at the nurses' station. Then, broom and dustpan in hand, he slipped into Bella's room unnoticed. Holding onto the broom, he inched toward the bed, eyes on the chart. Just what he was after. Another quick check to ensure no one was around, and he eased the chart out of its holder—and as quietly as possible, flipped through the pages. He wanted one single piece of information. One drug. Had it been administered?

Spotting exactly what he had been in search of, he smiled. "That's my girl."

She had done exactly as he'd hoped. Cautiously, he returned the chart to its proper location and exited Bella's room. Catching a glimpse of a heavily pregnant woman waddling down the hall toward him, he turned in the opposite direction.

Time to get out of there.

The freckled little boy punched her in the face. Bella stumbled backward and landed on her rear. Her cheek throbbed. Had she said something wrong? All she'd done was say hello. His Sunday dress clothes confused her. A nice pair of slacks, button-up shirt, a vest.

She tried to get to her feet.

"Stupid lil' ..." He kicked her in the ribs.

Crying out, she wrapped her arms around her stomach and curled up in a ball. What had she done? She hadn't done anything to deserve this. Tears rolled down her cheeks. "Stop! Please!"

"Shut up!" the kid hollered, pummeling her. Then, his bright green eyes so filled with anger, he punched her in the face again.

Finally, someone grabbed him from behind and yanked him back before he had the chance to inflict more damage.

"Bella!"

She lifted her eyes to the face in front of hers. "Mommy! It hurts ..."

"Mother not save you this time."

His accent. Sounded like some of the Hispanic accents she'd heard every day of her life. Except his voice was coarse, rough, as if he smoked a pack of cigarettes a day. She hardly noticed the words. Now that she thought of it, what was her mother supposed to save her from?

Bella's eyes fluttered open. It was so dark, but whatever she lay on was soft. She patted her hand around. A bed perhaps?

No. It wasn't soft. It was hard. And it smelled. Oh, God, it stunk. The stench covered her. Like she'd bathed in a tub full of trash. The back of a hand collided with her cheek. She reached for her jaw, but a pain shot down her arm and stopped her.

Her whole body ...

Had gone lax. A pair of strong arms held her up. Her feet barely touched the ground. Of course, they were kind of difficult to move. Sleep would be nice. Bella shifted and tried to open her eyes, get a gander of her surroundings. Nope. Eyes wanted to stay shut. The floor thumped beneath her. Music blared. Dance floor. She had to be on the dance floor. But with who?

"Not worry, honey bear. I take good care of you."

That voice.

Bella gasped. No! Her good eye shot open—to her view of the city through her hospital window. What an awful nightmare. So many jumbled memories. From when she was a child and from the attack a few days ago. Was there also something from the Fourth of July party? She didn't remember that night, but it really felt like a piece of it was desperately trying to push its way through.

"About time you woke up."

If her body hadn't been so banged up, she might've jumped out of her skin. In the midst of her coming around, she'd overlooked the female sitting in the chair beside her bed. "Crikey. What the hell is the wrong with you?"

"Did I startle you, princess?"

"What're you doing here, Z?" Probably a good thing she was confined to the bed. Otherwise, she might've slapped the crap out of her former best friend. Frightened wasn't on her list of favorite emotions, given the circumstances.

"I heard what happened. Had to check it out for myself."

Great. If Sarresh knew, everyone knew. Bad news travelled fast. Studying the girl, Bella raised an eyebrow. "Why are you wearing a hospital gown?"

"Hmm, well, I'm here overnight myself and figured I'd see if the rumors were true."

"Right. Well, thanks for the company, but you can go now." As if she hadn't been enough of a freak before. Her one desire: forgetting any of this happened. Provided people would allow her to forget.

"B, come on. Don't act like that."

"Like what? Like we aren't friends? I'd say tough, but you were the one who made the choice."

Sarresh rubbed her hand over her pregnant belly. "I know. And I'm sorry about that."

"What?"

Yeah, Sarresh thought. If the words hadn't come out of her mouth, she would've never believed it either. But their argument had gone on far too long. She should've apologized a while ago, but her own problems had kind of taken over. Seeing her former best friend laid up in a hospital bed, covered from head to toe in bruises, though, certainly changed her perspective.

"You heard me. I said, 'I'm sorry.'"

"Why should I believe you?"

Sarresh understood. She'd been known to lie her way out of almost anything—but this apology came straight from the heart. Besides, B had always been the one person she'd been truthful with, even if she lied to everyone else.

Sarresh sighed. Words meant little. Actions would be convincing, if either of them were in a position to do something. "If I weren't so big and you weren't so banged up, I'd say let's go dig up some memories from Camp Lahoy, but I guess we'll just have to talk about them, instead."

"You're really pulling out the box? Don't you think that's a little much?"

"Not if it convinces you I'm honest-to-God sorry."

Sarresh and Bella had met at camp, where they'd cemented their friendship by burying what they'd then considered their treasures. Before all the of their high school drama—popularity and boys—had driven them apart.

And maybe some bad decisions on her end. Okay, a lot of bad decisions on her side. But fitting in had been like her own personal drug. And the constant high had had a strong hold on her, until another addiction staked its claim. Which was how she wound up in her current predicament.

"Do you even remember where we hid the box?" Bella demanded.

A smile tugged at the corners of Sarresh's lips. Secret handshake. Spit in their hands and dirt under their nails. Lots of laughter. For once in her life, she'd belonged. It had been a night to remember. "Right by the hackberry tree, behind cabin four."

"Fine."

"Does that mean you believe I'm sorry?"

"Maybe. But I'm not ready to up and forgive you."

Those were words she deserved, Sarresh knew. Getting her best friend back wouldn't be easy. "Okay. What will it take for us to get past this?"

"Tell me the truth. Did you dump them or did they dump you?"

Of course, B wanted to know what happened. Sarresh frowned. "They pushed me out. Deep down, I saw it coming, but I convinced myself they wouldn't turn their backs on me. Things changed after they found out I was pregnant, like someone forgetting to tell me about a party. Then they began going to lunch without me. Pretty soon, they ignored me, all together."

"I'm sorry. I never wished anything but the best for you."

"It's okay. I was an ass. Probably should've gotten worse than I did, but hey, it's over now." Not to mention that, by the point it had all ended, she'd had more than enough issues of her own to deal with. Like finding out about the father of her unborn child.

"Z ..."

Waving it off, Sarresh pressed her hands into the arms of the chair and hefted herself up. "Don't worry about it. Listen, get some rest. I'll pop back in tomorrow and we can talk then."

nine

Dr. Youlo closed Bella's medical chart. "Everything looks good. Your lung function has significantly improved, your bruises are starting to change colors, and your eye is a lot better."

"Does this mean I can go home?" Four days in the hospital was enough. If she could've signed herself out yesterday, she would have. But at sixteen, that particular decision still belonged to her parents.

"Not yet. You're out of immediate danger, but I'd like you to stay a few more days. Okay?"

Bella glanced at her parents, then gave the doctor a single chin nod. The worst of the burning on her neck was gone, but moving it still stung. "Not like I have much of a choice."

There was a gentle rap on the door, and Detective Russell poked his head in. "Is this a good time?"

"Yes. Please come in, Officer. The doctor has finished, for now." Bella's father shuffled around the bed and leaned against the wall beside her mother.

A conversation with the police in front of her parents. No better way to spend the afternoon.

Detective Russell slipped inside, another officer following behind him. The two stopped at the edge of the bed. "Just a few more questions, Bella."

Only a few? What hadn't they covered? Descriptions of her attackers, check;

sequence of events, check; what the two men had said, check; smells, sounds, every possible detail she remembered about the attack … check, check, check. All of which she'd never forget. But if she remained silent, would she lose the horrible memories? If her earlier nightmare was any indication, probably not. The memories would follow her until death.

Maybe, though, justice would help dull the pain.

"Okay," she said.

"Thank you. I'd like to get a list of your friends. I know you said you can't think of anyone who might want to do this to you, but maybe one of your friends can."

Bella felt a little twinge of guilt. She hadn't yet mentioned the only person she considered an enemy. Heather hated her, and the feeling was mutual. But no way the girl would set up something so drastic. So Bella hadn't mentioned her in previous conversation with the police. Unfortunately, her friends might. Especially Alex.

"Yeah. I guess that's okay. But one person? She's not really a friend."

"Oh? Who?"

"Heather Warren."

Both officers narrowed their eyes at her.

Bella frowned. Hadn't police been trained not to reveal their emotions?

"She and I may have gotten into a bit of an argument the week before I was attacked."

Detective Russell pulled out a palm-sized notebook. "What was the fight about?"

"I may have called her out on her bullying and her slutty ways and told her she was sludge."

"Maylin Nadalia Christabel Kynaston." The full name tumbled out of her mother's mouth for maybe only the tenth time in Bella's life. "I am appalled to hear of this. You were raised to act more appropriately."

"I'm sorry, Mãe, Bàba, but I swear I had my reasons."

"We will discuss them later, young lady." Her father shifted his attention back to the detectives. "My apologies. Please continue."

Detective Russell nodded. "I take it you've crossed paths with her before?"

Bella sighed. "Yeah, but I don't really think she's behind what happened."

"Well, we'll speak with her anyway. What about your friends? Anyone in particular we should reach out to?"

"Victor Hilliard and Alexandra Grayson. They're the ones I'm closest to."

"Very well." Detective Russell turned to her parents. "Any information either of you can add would be helpful."

"Actually ..." Bella's father reached for his coat and removed a tiny box wrapped in brown paper from the pocket. "This was on our front porch the other day. There's no return address, only Bella's name. I thought it was strange."

Bella blinked. The gifts. She hadn't connected them to her attack.

"My secret admirer," she said, reluctantly.

Detective Russell eyed the box and then Bella. "Secret admirer?"

"Yes. I ..." Bella paused. "This isn't the first gift."

"How many did you receive?"

"Five, no, six in total. None of them came together. They were all delivered separately. Once a week over the last month." And the last thing her admirer had written was "soon." Why hadn't she made the connection?

"Do you still have them?"

"No. I got rid of them."

"What were you given?"

"Chocolates, coffee beans, a necklace and matching earrings. Oh, and flowers. A bouquet at school. They were in my locker. Everything else I got at home. The last thing was a single red rose. I tossed everything except the jewelry. I donated that to a thrift shop. Patti's Secondhand."

"What did the jewelry look like?"

Bella pictured the pretty pieces. "They were a matching set. The earrings were silver loops set with white agate, and the necklace, it had a white agate in the center of the chain."

"All right. We'll check out the thrift store."

With that, Detective Russell pulled an evidence bag from his pocket and held it out to Bella's father for him to deposit the tiny, unopened box.

"Any luck?"

"Nothing yet, but keep digging. Her clothes have to be somewhere." Russell pawed through another box in the dumpster. The things people threw in the garbage was astounding. Thus far, he had found empty boxes, stuffed animals, and a couple of dog beds. But no clothes. At least not the ones he was looking for.

They found the jewelry at the thrift store where the Kynaston girl left it, but it looked like a dead end. Research showed they were Brazilian pieces, but they hadn't discovered any information about who had purchased them. One of the detectives was checking street camera footage around the high school, the downtown area, and the Kynaston residence. But so far, no luck.

DNA wasn't back yet, either. And probably wouldn't be any time soon. Unless they had a suspect for comparison. But the clothes she'd been wearing, they might bear the evidence needed to crack the case. Hopefully, the clothes had been dumped, they hadn't been taken by the garbage company yet.

The crime scene unit had searched any dumpsters within a three-block radius of the crime scene, but turned up nothing. Which made sense. If he had been either of the rapists, he wouldn't have dumped her clothing at the scene or even within a few blocks of it. And these guys seemed too smart to do so, either. Between them, he and Deegart covered another two-blocks from the initial radius. They wouldn't leave a piece of garbage unturned.

Russell ripped open another black trash bag. Nothing.

He tore into another one.

"Deegart!"

Deegart popped his head up from the trash bags outside the dumpster. "You find something?"

"You could say that." With a gloved hand, Russell held up a bloodied, torn blouse. It matched the description of what Bella had been wearing.

Jeremiah watched the elevator count up the floors. As one of the last people to see Bell before the attack, he knew he would have to talk to a detective, eventually. Going to the precinct was the best option—but his father's position and his relationship with Bell complicated things.

Fifth floor. The elevator dinged and the doors opened. Jeremiah stepped into the hallway and headed toward the bullpen. Lots of desks.

"Can I help you?"

"Um, yeah. I'm here for a Detective Russell."

The woman gestured to a desk in the far corner. "He's the man you're looking for."

"Thanks." Jeremiah nodded and walked across to the desk that had been pointed out. "Detective Russell?"

"You got him."

Really? This was the guy his father told him to talk to? He couldn't be a day over twenty. "Um, great. I'm Jeremiah Detrone. My dad told me to talk to you about Bella Kynaston."

"Right. You're the boyfriend. The sheriff said you'd be coming in." Glancing around, Russell stood. "Let's go somewhere more private to talk."

Boyfriend? Jeremiah thought, as he followed the detective to an empty office. He and Bell hadn't labeled their relationship yet. They had only gone on one date. Unless having dinner in the hospital counted. Then they'd had their second date. But for all intents and purposes, he guessed the title "boyfriend" worked.

"Go on, have a seat." Russell sat down and nodded to the chair across from him. "Why don't you tell me a little about your relationship with Miss Kynaston?"

"I'm not sure there's much to tell. We haven't been dating long."

"What about the day she was attacked? You were one of the last people to have contact with her, correct?"

"Yeah. She came to support me in an audition for the school play."

"And what time did she leave?"

"Around six. She had to go by the church on her way home. The pastor had some paperwork for her, but as far as I know she never made it."

Hadn't all this been gone over already? Like a million times? How did his father have any confidence in this guy? Jeremiah clenched his fists in frustration, then released his fingers.

"Do you know which way she normally walked to get to the church?"

Hadn't Bella answered this already, too? Jeremiah frowned. "I have no clue."

"What do you know about her friends? Or any enemies?"

"As far as I know, most people like her. She doesn't have any enemies that I know of. As for her friends ... Vick and Alex are nice people. They seem to genuinely care about Bell."

Jeremiah dragged his hand across the top of his head. He'd shaved it down to almost nothing the other day. Then, although Bell said she was sure the jerk wouldn't have raped her, he asked, "Has she mentioned Petar Jacobs?"

Russell dug into the console of his sedan and plucked out a pack of gum. Sure was a hell of a week to quit smoking. As of an hour ago, he'd been made lead detective on the biggest rape case he'd seen in the last ten years. Nothing like this had happened since that local gang leader disappeared—just after a local girl showed up beaten and sexually assaulted. Then their number one suspect up and vanished. Juan Castell. The search for the guy had been Russell's first in the precinct. He'd worked it with Simms, but they hadn't found much of anything. Only trace of the guy's existence in this city was a toothbrush. A DNA and background check led them to New York City, but that's where the trail ended.

But this? Another huge rape case? Had to be linked. The mark on the victim's neck, it had become a signature for the gang. That girl ten years ago been branded, too. He'd have to pull the file. For now, though, he had to focus on the case in hand.

Russell turned right onto Luna Street and slowed as he approached his destination. Pulling alongside the driveway, Russell parked, noting the teenager mowing the lawn. The kid didn't turn as he climbed out of the vehicle. Headphones. Dangerous way to handle the yard, but gave him an opportunity to study what he guessed was the witness. If that was Victor Hilliard. According to the victim, she was close to this guy. More than that, Hilliard had been one of the few to see her shortly before the assault. Hopefully, the kid could fill in blanks purposely left out by the victim.

One thing he hated about assault cases; victims always seemed to keep secrets.

A woman stepped out onto the front steps, drying her hands on a dish towel. She appeared to be in her late thirties, early forties. Probably the kid's mother.

"Afternoon. Something we can do for you?"

"Mrs. Hilliard? My name is Detective Russell. I'd like to speak with your son regarding Bella Kynaston." He remained on the driveway and displayed his credentials. In his periphery he saw the young man shut off the lawnmower and pluck the headphones from his ears.

The woman nodded. "Vick," she called. "This detective would like to discuss Bella with you."

The kid removed a t-shirt from his back pocket and wiped the sweat from his forehead. "Okay, Mom," he said, and stepping forward, extended his hand to Russell.

"Victor Hilliard?"

"Yes, sir."

"It's my understanding you were with Miss Kynaston the day of her attack. Can you tell me about that?"

Vick raised an eyebrow. "Yeah, I saw her. We're in tutor club together. There was a short meeting that afternoon. We went our separate ways, after. She went to support a friend at an audition, and I went to soccer tryouts."

"What time did the meeting end?"

Russell had asked this question of Bella. But every statement had to be checked and rechecked. Questions had to be asked of multiple witnesses—and of the same witnesses' multiple times. Victims, also, were asked to repeat their stories over and over. Too many versions, and the victim could be seen as unreliable to a jury. Allowed for more rapists to go free than he liked.

"About a quarter to five." As Bella had said.

"How long have you known Miss Kynaston?"

"Since we were kids. We met in a sandbox about ten years ago."

"Long time. Anyone you can think who might've wanted to hurt her?"

On paper, Bella Kynaston appeared to have no enemies. But things were never as they appeared. Which was why he'd begun to dig into the lives of her parents, too. Either of them could have enemies who would attack the most vulnerable person in their lives.

"I may not be much help. I've been away from the area for about a year. My mom and I just moved back a little over a month ago. B and I still talk on occasion, while I was gone, but I don't know a whole lot about anybody here—never mind someone who'd want to do something like this. You may want to talk to her friend Alex. Provided she hasn't killed all her brain cells, she'll probably be your best bet."

The kid shoved his hands in his pockets and dropped his gaze to the ground.

Russell dug a pad out his jacket pocket and flipped through his notes. Alex? Oh, yeah. Alexandra Grayson. One of the friends Bella suggested he speak with. Also, mentioned by the boyfriend. "Something I should know about Miss Grayson?"

"Let's just say she hasn't always chosen her friends wisely."

Code for drug addict. Certainly added a whole new list of suspects. Especially if anyone associated with Alex had previously met Bella. Might've been what Bella was hiding, too. Russell scribbled a reminder to look into Alexandra's background. "Okay. Anyone new in Miss Kynaston's life you know of."

"Only Jeremiah Detrone. I know they started dating recently. Other than that, there's David Warren. He's not new, but he's had a thing for Bella for the last few years. Oh ... and one other guy. He was in the tutor group last year with B. Um, Peter?"

Russell flipped a page in his pad. "Petar Jacobs?"

Vick snapped his fingers. "Yeah! That's the guy."

"How does this work?" Bella took a gander at the small stack of photographs in Detective Russell's hand.

"I'll show you the pictures one at a time. You just let me know if anyone looks familiar. Okay?"

Sounded easy. Too easy. She saw the scar-faced man in her nightmares. Bella inhaled deeply. "I think I can do that."

"All right. Here we go." Detective Russell held out the first photo.

Bella studied the image. The scar was all wrong. This guy's scar was down the middle of his face. Her attacker—his was further to the left. "No."

"Okay. What about this one?"

The scar was similar, but his nose was too small. And the eyes were wrong, too. "No."

"This one?"

What the hell? Was this a joke? Bella eyeballed both detectives. Neither budged. They couldn't be serious. Yeah, the scar was in the right location, but no way Petar was her attacker. "Why is there a picture of Petar in there?"

"So, you recognize him?"

"Yes. He's a friend of mine." A term she used loosely in his case. How the hell could they even think Petar attacked her? Bella scowled. One answer. Jeremiah opened his trap.

"But you didn't mention him before now."

"Because I don't believe he's involved. He would never hurt me." The accusation was ridiculous. So what if the guy had been creepier than usual, lately? And maybe a little more possessive and insistent on things. No way he was the scar-faced guy. They didn't even look the same. Scar-faced guy was darker. And his voice was gravelly. And, anyway, she would've recognized Petar immediately.

But there had been two.

The other guy. With the bandana and hoodie. He never uttered a word. His whole face had been covered. All she could see was his eyes. Bella looked at the picture of Petar again. Could the eyes have been his? Or the body? Petar was stocky and muscular.

Sudden tears rolled down her cheeks.

"Are you certain he's not involved?" Detective Russell asked.

"I ... I don't know."

"Okay. Tell me about your relationship with him."

Bella wiped at her face. "He's always been a bit overprotective. Watching out for me, keeping bullies away, making sure I was doing okay. It was a little much, but I thought he just cared. I wasn't really comfortable hanging out with him alone, so I invited Alex to join us a few times. But then last December ..."

"What happened?"

"We were in the library. I leaned across the table to get something, and he tried to kiss me. I backed up and told him I didn't see him that way. That I only wanted to be friends. He got angry with me. Called me a tease. Said I had been leading him on for months. I grabbed my backpack and ran out the door. He apologized to me a couple days later. Told me it was his fault for misreading things."

Bella brushed more tears away. Petar had owned up to his mistake. Didn't make sense to hold a grudge back then. Not that she was the type. But what if he was one of her attackers? Could she have prevented it? Done something to stop it from happening?

"What about his visit here? Tell me about that."

It hadn't been as disastrous as she expected. Jeremiah had been so collected.

Made her adore him more. Maybe she should've spoken up, though. Defended Jeremiah. But something about Petar's presence had shaken her.

Bella shuddered. "He was like a tightly wound ball of testosterone. Miah was here, and I think Petar wanted to prove he was better. We talked about what he was involved in at the university and his new dietary regimen."

"His dietary regimen?"

"Yeah. He had bulked up so much over the summer."

t e n

Jeremiah glanced down the hallway. Nurses and doctors drifted in and out of other rooms, checking on patients. He peeked through the window in Bell's door. His angel lay on the bed, her eyes shut, her body busy healing while she slept. Most importantly, neither of her parents were hanging around. Good. He could give her his presents without any gawking eyes.

The gifts weren't much. Just a little something to celebrate. The doctor had agreed if her test results were good, she could go home.

Jeremiah eased the door open, stepped inside, and gently closed the door behind him.

"No .... please ... stop ... please..."

His head swung in Bella's direction. That didn't sound like a peaceful dream. Releasing his grip on the balloon string and dropping the teddy bear, Jeremiah strode to her bed. Reaching around her sling, he gently took her jaw in his hand and brushed her cheek with his thumb. "Hey, Bell, wake up. Come on."

"Please ... stop ..." Rocking from side to side, she trembled beneath his touch.

She must be reliving her attack. A never-ending nightmare. Glancing at the machine monitoring her blood pressure and heart rate, he saw both had spiked. He grabbed her good shoulder and squeezed. "Bell, wake up!"

Her eyes snapped open and her gaze darted around the room before settling on his face.

"Miah?"

"Yeah. I'm right here."

"Miah ..." She whispered his name again, then turned her face into his hand and sobbed.

Having Jeremiah near her ... it was strange how his presence comforted her.

And now he was going to be even closer.

When Bella nodded, Miah slipped an arm under the covers beneath her waist and placed the other behind her shoulder blades. "Go ahead and put your arm around my neck. Then we'll shift on three."

She followed his instructions, hooking her arm, cast and all, around his neck. When she was in place, Miah counted, "One ... two ... three ...," and barely lifting her off the mattress, settled her closer to the edge.

Bella grunted at the twinge in her ribs, but she breathed through the pain.

Now that there was more room, Miah could lie on the bed beside her. The sling and cast prevented her from curling into him the way she wanted, but she managed to rest her head against his chest. His heart thumped loudly in her ear. It was beautiful. The rhythm perfect. So steady and strong.

"Comfortable?" His arm came around her and settled against hers in its sling.

"Comfortable." Calm washed over her and the constant darkness faded. For the first time in a week, her mind and body welcomed silence. The weight of her pain temporarily lifted, her eyes drifted shut. Bella forced them open. She couldn't sleep. Not yet.

"Can you do me a favor?"

"Whatever you need."

"My parents are going to talk to the doctor about the conditions of my release and me returning to school." Every time she'd spoken to her parents about going back to school, they'd denied her request—always citing the healing process. Screw healing. Bella knew she had to stay out of her own head. Otherwise it would eat her from the inside out. She'd lose her sanity if she had nothing to occupy her time.

"I take it they don't think you should go back yet."

Bella tilted her head toward Miah. She appreciated the concern she saw written all over his face.

"No. They want me to wait it out. I've tried explaining it to them, but they don't get it." *Stay home. Get better. Give it a couple of weeks. Blah, blah, blah.* She seldom defied her parents' wishes, but this was one thing she couldn't give them.

"I could advocate for you," Miah replied, to her unspoken request. He brushed his hand along the top of her head and pressed a feather kiss to her hair. "Sleep. I'll be here when you wake up. Whatever you need, I'm here for you."

"You did what?" Amanda hollered.

Maybe he should've asked his older sister if she minded before he committed them both. But, hey, it was Bell. He'd give the girl his left kidney if she asked.

Jeremiah bounced on the balls of his feet. "Come on Mandy, it's just for a few weeks."

"Oh, just a few weeks. Why didn't I think of that?"

Her comment dripped with sarcasm.

He sighed. He needed Amanda's support to make good on his promise to Bell's parents that she'd have help the entire time. Talk about people who stood firm on their ground. Until he'd made his suggestion, the doctor had been on their side. Three against one! But they'd finally agreed.

"I don't think I'm asking a lot. We'll help her get to school, around to her classes, and back home."

"Oh, no big deal, right? Did it ever occur to you I don't want to get involved in someone else's shit?"

"Language," their father piped in from the kitchen.

Jeremiah snorted. "Seriously, Mandy …"

She raised her hand. "Fine. But you owe me."

"Thanks, Sis."

"Whatever." Amanda stalked down the hallway and disappeared into her bedroom.

Their father stopped in the doorway. "Thought you'd have to fight harder to get her help."

Jeremiah smiled. "Deep down, she's really a nice person. I think she just likes to front."

"Yeah. Your sister has a big heart. So, you really like this girl, huh?"

Jeremiah nodded. "I really do. I know it won't be easy, but ... I don't know ... I can't explain it. There's a connection between us, and I'll do what I have to do to keep it."

Tomorrow, Bella returned to school. That was normal. That she could handle. Tonight, Bible study, surrounded by friends discussing various Bible verses, not so much. But running wasn't an option. And even if she could run, she had nowhere to go but her room. No way it was far enough away from God.

The doorbell rang.

"I got it." Answering the door was something she could do. She opened it and blinked. What the hell? "David?"

"Hi. Hope I'm not late."

"Here? Why?"

"I'm here for Bible study." David stepped inside.

"How did you find it?"

"The address is listed on the church website."

"I ..." What was she supposed to say? She couldn't exactly tell him to leave. Or could she? Bella peered over his shoulder. No one had seen him yet ...

But before she got the chance, David turned to the doorway on his right. "Is that where everyone gathers?"

"Yeah." Bella watched him walk into the den and introduce himself to the brunette Barbie twins, Ashley and Emily. They were exactly the type of girl he always dated, she thought—giggly and brain dead. Talk about the perfect distraction. She could watch him all night instead of participating.

The doorbell rang again. She turned to see Jeremiah stride through the front door. He paused inside the foyer. "Is it just me, or is David here?"

"You're not seeing things. He just showed up." Bella closed the door. "My dad would say, the more the merrier."

"Normally, I'd agree, but when it comes to this guy, all I can ask is why?"

Nodding toward the collected crowd, Bella grinned. "Feel free to ask him."

"You know what, I'm not going to worry about it. I came here for you."

Lord, why couldn't he be there for himself? Instead, he was being supportive. Like her parents. Great. She should be appreciative. Yet, their "support" only served as a reminder of how much her life had changed in the last week.

Looking through the doorway, Bella saw everyone started taking their seats. Right. She'd have to deal with the sympathy for tonight. She gestured toward the den. "We should probably head in."

Ephesians 4:17 - 32 played in her head over and over again. Like an endless soundtrack of the Bible. God, she hated those verses. Forgiveness, her ass. The hairs on the back of her neck prickled. Somebody was there. Bella looked up from the tray of leftovers. David stood in the doorway.

"Hey, B. Can I talk to you for a sec?"

"I guess so."

David joined her at the kitchen island. "This Fall Festival thing, what does it consist of?"

"A lot of stuff. Music, skits, dancing. Why?" She had forgotten all about the production. Had her father mentioned it? Dumb question. If David was asking, her father said something.

"Can anyone sign up?"

Oh, no. No, no, no, no. Directing the production she could handle. Having David and Miah rehearsing at the same time, not bloody likely. Dammit. But she needed the bodies. Stepping back from a botched clean-up, Bella offered David her undivided attention. "Yes. Why?"

"So, I could sign up?"

"What are you doing?" The question came out before she could stop it.

Hooking his thumbs in his belt loops, David leaned back against the island. "I think I'd enjoy it. I just wanted to make sure I could sign up."

All right. She could see that. The guy had auditioned for the school play. Plus, he hadn't been half bad. "Do you know what you would sign up for?" This was important. Gave her a heads up of placement. And exactly how much tension she might have to face between him and Miah. Even if Miah had beaten David out for Hamlet, the two still had issues.

David rocked back and forth a little. "Yeah. But you have to promise you won't tell anyone."

Not tell anyone? Was he shy all of sudden? "You do realize people from all over town come to this thing, right?"

"Yeah, but that doesn't mean they have to know beforehand. I have a reputation to protect. I play piano and sing."

No. Flipping. Way. Had to be a joke. Bella giggled. "You're serious?"

"Deadly."

Holy shit! But what if he was lying? She had never once heard him play or sing. He could be completely bullshitting her. "Okay. You can sign up, and yes, I promise I won't tell anyone. On one condition."

"What's the condition?"

"You'll play something for me on the first day of rehearsals. If you aren't horrible, then you can be in the show. If you are horrible, then you have to work backstage." Bella smiled. Win/win for everybody involved.

David held out his hand. "Deal."

"Good." With one shoulder still in a sling and the other arm casted to the elbow, the best Bella could do was shake his fingers. Which she did.

David turned to leave, but paused mid-step. "One more question. Are you still able to tutor me?"

"I don't know. Vick and I are sitting down with Principal Owen tomorrow afternoon. I'll tell you after." It was hard enough convincing her parents to let her return to school. Add in the production and tutoring, and her parents nearly blew a gasket.

"Sure. Just, if possible, please don't give me another tutor."

"I'll do what I can."

Left alone in the kitchen, Bella perked her head up and listened to the voices in the den. Who was still there? William. He was talking to her father ... about a girlfriend. When had that happened? Who else? Miah ... Vick ... They were talking to each other ... about her.

"Tonight's lesson couldn't have been easy for her," Jeremiah said—although he knew he and Vick shouldn't be talking about Bell like this. But she had been so quiet all evening. She hadn't participated in the discussion on forgiveness at all. She had shown nothing. Her face had been ... empty.

"That's true." Vick folded his arms across his chest. "I'm surprised her dad didn't change the lesson given the circumstances."

Made two of them. It would've been the sensible thing to do. Take Bell's feelings into consideration. Jeremiah frowned. Unless her father believed she could handle it. All these conversations about returning to school and being normal. Maybe that had something to do with it. "She's been so determined to get back to her old life. What if she told him not to?"

"Maybe. I know all her dad's ever wanted was the best for her."

"Yeah, this isn't like anything their family has ever dealt with before." How many times had he heard his father go on about rape trauma? How a lot of victims don't even come forward. How those that do are forced to re-live the nightmare, telling their story over and over again to police, lawyers. God, what Bell had to be going through. Jeremiah shook his head.

Dragging a hand down his face, Vick frowned. "This isn't going to be easy, is it?"

"No. I'll talk to her. See if I can get a feel for where she's at right now. In the meantime, we'll just keep reminding her we're there for her."

"Thanks, man." Jeremiah and Vick clapped hands.

Vick looked Jeremiah in the eye. "For what it's worth, I'm glad you're here."

"Me, too." Jeremiah watched as Vick left. He glanced at his watch. Enough time to talk to Bell before he headed out. Jeremiah poked his head in the kitchen. Empty. Maybe she was in her bedroom. Walking down the hallway, he saw her door ajar. He knocked.

"It's open."

Stepping inside, he found Bell sitting in a chair staring out her bedroom window. "Hey. I just wanted check on you before I left. Make sure you're okay."

"I'm fine."

Got it. It was going to be one of those conversations. How did he go about this? Wanting her to talk and getting her to talk to him were two different things. One of the few times he wished he had his sister's knack for getting people to open up. "Bell ... you know you can talk to me about anything, right?"

"I know."

Two-word responses, and she still hadn't even looked at him. Maybe he needed to try this another way. Jeremiah walked around the bed and sat down across from her. "Hey. I know tonight couldn't have been easy for you. I'm just worried. That's all."

"Is that what you were talking to Vick about?" Bella shifted a narrow-eyed gaze to Jeremiah. But at least she was looking at him. Even if she was a little upset. Better to be angry and speaking than angry and quiet.

"Yes. We're both worried about you. You were awfully quiet tonight."

"How the hell was I supposed to be? The last thing I can even think about right now is forgiving those bastards."

"None of us expect you to. Yes, the timing was poor, but that doesn't mean the lesson was directed at you. You may get there one day, but if you do, it'll be when you're ready, not because it was thrown in your face."

Forgiveness was the right thing to do, eventually. For her, not for her attackers. But he sure as hell wasn't going to push her to it anytime soon. Jeremiah reached for her fingers and gave them a gentle squeeze.

"What if I'm never ready?"

"Then that's your call. I will support you no matter what." Though he hoped she would. It might be the only way for her to move on with her life.

"Really?"

Leaning forward, Jeremiah tucked a strand of hair behind her ear. "Yes. If you don't want to ever forgive these guys, then you don't have to. Just promise me if this starts to eat at you, you'll ask for help."

"I think I can do that."

eleven

Bella listened as Mandy repeated the plan.

"Jeremiah and I will switch every other period. I'll walk you to your first class, and he'll take you to your second class, then me, him, and so forth." Amanda removed a couple of books and notebooks from Bella's locker.

Right. So, Bella was basically here to do nothing. Pretty, bruised window dressing, covered in varying shades of blue and purple—like larkspurs. And it wasn't exactly like she could carry anything.

As she stepped aside to let Amanda close her locker, she stumbled backwards and banged her head against the locker beside hers.

Amanda grabbed Bella's semi-good shoulder and prevented her from falling. "Whoa. Are you okay?"

"I'm fine." Awkwardly she maneuvered her fingers around to rub the back of her head. The painkillers must've kicked in. Wonderful pills which the doctor had reluctantly given her, only after forcing her to repeat how many she could take, and how often, five times.

"Okay. Do you have a free period?"

"Um, yeah. Fourth. Just after lunch."

Amanda checked the lock on Bella's locker. "Good. Fewer books to carry."

"Thanks, Mandy."

"No problem." Holding Bella's books and notebooks in her arms, Amanda bent and unzipped the backpack.

"Well, well, well. If it isn't the Virgin Mary. Wait, that isn't right. Wrong Mary. I meant Mary Magdalene." Heather stopped in front of Amanda and Bella.

"Hey. Wasn't Mary Magdalene a slut?" Missy giggled.

"Or a whore." Cassie tossed her red hair over her shoulder.

Bella blinked. This wasn't right. How could they stand there and compare her to ...? No, it made no sense. Yeah, she lit into Heather a couple of weeks ago, but surely this was something that would remain off limits. Why would they pick at her so soon? Where was their compassion?

Heather snickered. "A harlot, but that's close enough."

Amanda took a step forward and inserted herself between Bella and Heather, effectively becoming a shield for Bella. "If you're smart, you'll walk away right now."

"Nah, I don't think so. After all, somebody has to welcome Bella here into the world of open legs." Heather grinned.

"You open yours willingly. Not the same thing."

Amanda stayed where she was, but having the girls out of her line of sight mattered little to Bella. Her ears worked fine. They're just words, she told herself. Hurtful words, but just words. And lies to boot. She'd been brutalized. Left for dead. Ra— Attacked in a horrible way. No one should suffer the way she had. Bella backed into the lockers behind her. That man. The one with the scar. Tears prickled the corners of her eyes.

Cassie tilted her head and smirked. "I think she's gonna cry."

"Oh. Did big bad Heather hurt your feelings?" Missy rubbed at her face as if she were a weeping baby.

Amanda balled up her fist. "Last chance."

Heather laughed and looked over her shoulder to her friends. "Like she'd do anything."

The timing couldn't have been more perfect. Amanda pulled her arm back and buried her fist in Heather's face as she returned her attention forward. The power behind Amanda's punch knocked Heather into Missy and Cassie and all three fell to the ground like dominoes.

Mr. Sellers, one of the science teachers, rushed over. "What's going on here?"

"She hit me!" Heather pointed to Amanda, as she struggled to her feet.

"We saw it." Missy and Cassie nodded in agreement.

Mr. Sellers gestured to Amanda, Heather, Missy, and Cassie. "The four of you to the principal's office. Now."

"But Mr. Sellers —"

"I'm sorry, Miss Kynaston. Move it, Miss Detrone."

Amanda gave Bella a rueful look, shrugged, then headed off to the administrative office.

Bella peered at her backpack on the ground. How was she going to do this? Tears rolled down her cheeks. But this was no time to cry. She had to ...

The first bell rang, and all the students in the hall dispersed.

What was she going to do? With a groan, she began to crouch toward her backpack. Unfortunately, halfway down, her ribs protested, and she had to stand straight. Next, she tried bending over at the waist to lift the bag, but her ribs screamed at the weight. Maybe if she combined the two maneuvers it would work.

"Do you need some help?"

Her head turned in the direction of the most wonderful voice in the world. "I ..." The tears she'd struggled against came out in full force. Bella sobbed.

Miah wrapped his arms around her and brushed his hand down her tresses. "Shh. I got you. It's okay. Whatever happened, I'm right here."

Bella glanced over her shoulder. Several students walked by, all involved in their own conversations. Maybe it was something random. Nothing to do with her at all. She returned her attention to Miah.

"She probably just got her ass kicked and lied about the rest of it."

Another random comment. Certainly not about her. Chewing on the inside of her cheek, she turned a little and scrutinized the clusters of students grouped together. Two girls, a few lockers down from hers, chit-chatted. All smiles and laughter.

There was a couple on the other side of the hall in a pretty heated discussion. Other people were heading toward the front parking lot or the back.

"What about your precalculus book?"

Bella focused on the book in Miah's hand. "Oh, um, yeah. That, too."

Jeremiah had been sweet all day long. He carried her books to every class without complaint, hung out with her in the library during lunch, and helped her figure out what she needed to take home. No need to bother him with her worry over what other people thought or said about her. Anyway, what if it was all in her mind? Except for Heather and crew, no one paid any attention to her all day. The other students had gone on about their—

"She deserved what she got."

Her head snapped around. The two chattering girls had left. The couple on the other side were kissing. And the hallway had mostly emptied. There was no one there. No one who could've possibly said what she'd just heard.

A hand touched her shoulder. Bella jumped.

"Hey, hey. Only me. You okay?" Jeremiah held her nearly full backpack and was looking at her.

His voice pulled her back into ... she wasn't sure. Reality? The present? "Yeah. Fine. Can we just go?"

"Yeah, we're all set." He slipped her backpack onto his shoulder. His own occupied the other side. "You sure you're okay? I mean I know it was a rocky start this morning."

Rocky? Brutal was more like it. Made her understand why her parents pleaded with her to wait. But there was no way she could sit by and do nothing. Her body would slowly rebound. She'd eventually look good as new. Her mind ... her soul ... time? Bullshit. She had to come back. Think about something, anything other than what happened.

Bella nodded. "I'm as okay as I can be."

"Can I ask you something? Why'd you want to come back to school? I mean, I kind of jumped on board the plan without really knowing."

How to explain? Tell him the truth? No. He'd probably think she was crazy. Lie? No. It felt wrong. Down to her bones wrong. Offer a partial truth? Maybe. "The police, they don't want you to forget, but that's all I want to do. I don't want to think about what happened or how it's made me feel. I guess ... I thought returning to school, I could get part of my routine back. Find normal again."

"Okay. I get that. And getting into a routine probably helps with getting to normal, but have you considered that you're trying to jump into an old routine without accepting that what happened has changed you in some way?"

Jeremiah unlocked the car and shoved their packs in the trunk, then opened the back door for her.

Bella stared at him. Wow. No joke. No sympathy. Plain out truth. Something to think about. She climbed into the backseat. With her shoulder in a sling for the next few weeks, she had to superstar it—which might not be the best way to have this conversation, but there wasn't much choice. Unless she let it go at that.

Everything was different. But nothing had changed. Her skirts and blouses hung in the closet like normal. Her Bible lay on the desk beside the notepad she always kept there. The books were still carefully stacked in the bookcase. The corner chair with the afghan draped over the back, the chest at the end of the bed … all the same.

Bella stared at her reflection in the full-length mirror. She was different. Her room was normal. She was the anomaly. Maybe Miah was right. She'd have to find a new normal. Some way to accommodate the change.

No. She could fit back into her old life. Keep dressing as she always had. Reread some of her favorite books. As long as she had Miah, then her life was fine. She just had to figure out how to make it work.

But there had to be some change. Otherwise it would all be for nothing.

Directing the Fall Festival. That was a change.

Taking a break from tutoring. Another change.

Spending more time with Miah. The best kind of change. She could get through— No, that wasn't right. She didn't want to get through time with him.

She wanted to enjoy it. She had to enjoy it. It was too important. Not just for her sanity, but her survival. And their relationship. But how?

Bella eyed the pill bottle on the nightstand beside her bed. The painkillers. Maybe if she took an extra one at night, she could sleep. Sleep was good. She'd be less likely to space out. Might help numb the pain a little. Help her think about the attack a little less. Let her enjoy life a little more.

No. The doctor gave her specific instructions. Why was she even thinking like this? This wasn't her. Drugs weren't the answer.

Bella glanced at Miah's number tacked on the corkboard above her desk. Maybe she could just talk to him. He told her she could call at any time.

Except then he'd be sleep deprived. And he was the one who drove her to and from school. Not a good combination.

Plus, she really didn't want him to know. He might not look at her the same once he knew. She wouldn't be able to take that.

Maybe a counselor, like her parents suggested, would be best. Maybe.

Russell pulled off the dirt road and into the driveway. Nice house. Two stories. Fenced backyard. Had to be at least another five acres that weren't fenced. Not surprising. According to Alexandra Grayson's rap sheet, her family was well to do. She'd been charged for possession of a hallucinogenic substance a year ago. A misdemeanor. Surprising they didn't use their connections to get the charge dropped.

Hmm. Maybe it wasn't her first.

He climbed out of his vehicle and strode up the walkway. Hopefully this girl could shed some light on possible suspects. Right now, they only had Petar Jacobs. And the guy had no criminal record. Not even a parking ticket. Plus, DNA was still being processed. Forensics hadn't gotten back to him on Bella's clothes yet either.

Taking his credentials out, Russell knocked on the door.

A teenage girl with dirty blonde hair answered it. "Can I help you?"

"I'm Detective Russell with the Rescate County PD. Are you Alexandra Grayson?" Based on her mug shot, it was her. Best to get confirmation.

"I am. You must be here about B."

"You mean Bella Kynaston. Yes. Mind if I come in?" Russell peered inside the house. Was she the only one home?

Alex opened the door wider. "Yeah. Come on in. We can talk in the dining room."

"Thank you." Russell entered the foyer and the dining room was immediately to the right. Oh, good. There was an adult in the kitchen.

"Mom, this is Detective Russell. He's here about B." Alex took a seat at the dining table.

"Good evening, ma'am."

Mrs. Grayson nodded at him. "I do hope you catch the men who hurt Bella. She's such a sweet girl. Didn't deserve what happened to her at all."

"We're working on it, ma'am." He sat opposite Alex. "How long have you known Miss Kynaston?"

"We met freshman year. Had home-ec together. Bonded over burnt cake."

So. The girls had known one another a few years. "Can you think of anyone who might want to cause her harm?"

"Honestly, no. That's what's so weird about this. I mean, my mom wasn't joking when she said Bella is sweet. Most people like her, except for maybe Heather. But Heather's a bitch."

"Heather Warren?" It didn't seem likely the girl was involved in any way, but her name hadn't been crossed off his list.

"Yeah. Oh, plus Heather's brother, David, he has a thing for Bella."

David Warren. Another name on his list.

"Do you think he may have attacked her?"

"David? I don't know. The guy has some anger issues if you know what I mean."

Interesting. The Warren kids, their parents were the elite. At least Rescate County elite. "Can you be more specific?"

"Second day of school this year, he beat the crap out of his best friend. Is that specific enough?"

The attack on Bella was definitely personal. Obviously, David had the temper for it. "Do you know what the fight was about?"

"Yeah. David found out Mike played a prank on Bella last year, and he got pissed off."

"What about Petar Jacobs? What's his relationship with Miss Kynaston like?"

"Well, he's always acted the hero when it comes to her."

Russell flipped through a couple of pages. His notes indicated he protected both girls. Did he favor one over the other? "Didn't he help both of you?"

"Oh, no." Alex smirked. "He made it seem that way, but honestly Petar was all about Bella. We met him our freshman year. Heather was picking on B. Before I could say anything, Petar intervened. I never cared for him. Dude's a total creeper."

"What do you mean?"

"He constantly tried to get me out of the picture. Told B multiple times I wasn't a good friend. Kept trying to control the way she ate, the classes she took, the people she hung out with. He tried to kiss her once. She doesn't think I know about it, but I do. She stopped him, and he screamed at her, called her a tease."

That matched what the victim disclosed to him. Russell made a note to dig deeper into this guy's background. "How do you know all this?"

"I was at the library working on a paper when it happened. Saw the whole thing."

"Did Miss Kynaston tell you about the gifts she received?"

"Oh yeah, I know all about those. She originally thought they came from David, but he denied it. Seemed genuine, like he really had no idea what she was talking about."

Russell stood and held out his card. "Thank you for your time Miss Grayson. If I have any more questions, I'll be in touch. Or if you can think of anything else, give me a call."

"She told you about the roses in her locker?" The girl tucked his card in the back pocket of her jeans.

Russell nodded.

"Did she also tell you Petar was waiting for her outside the day she got them?"

Sitting in the farthest corner, his back against the wall, Gervasio drummed his fingers on the table. His brother was taking too long. That's okay. He'd wait however long it took. His brother pretended not to want to know when things happened, but, deep down, he always had to know. His brother's nosiness worked in Gervasio's favor. If the police ever caught up with him, and his brother broke, the guy would unintentionally give them bad information—fed to him by Gervasio.

Finally. Cristobal crossed the room to the table and sat. "You look well."

"Sweet love from something so pure make a man well." His eyes twitched, the way they did after he had a good piece of tail. Bella had been the best he ever had. And, oh, what he wouldn't give to have her again. But that would have to wait.

"Hermano ..." Cristobal's eyes narrowed.

His brother wasn't stupid. Though Gervasio hadn't come right out and uttered the entire truth, it was enough for Cristobal to understand. The look in his brother's brown eyes said so.

Gervasio grinned wide, like the cat that ate the canary. "You must know why

I come."

"No."

Gervasio reached into his pocket, pulled a beautiful gold signet ring out, and placed it on the table. The ring bore a symbol, a pair of crossed scythes—which represented Gervasio's gang. It was the mark he gave to all his property. Bella's brand was just one example.

"I love this design."

"Usted la marca."

"Si. Ella es mía." Oh yes, she was his. She had always been his. And his mark would show that to the world.

Cristobal rubbed his face. "¿Por qué? ¿Por qué hiciste esto a ella? Ella es inocente."

Innocent? His brother truly believed the girl was innocent. Because no one knew who she really was, except for him. But he wasn't about to tell his brother the truth, the real reason he had claimed her. No. Yet, he had to make Cristobal believe what he did say.

Gervasio leaned forward. "He take, I take."

"He took nothing. I am still here."

Ah. His brother fell for the lie perfectly. It started with the Bible. How much time had gone by since that visit? The one where Cristobal told him about his newfound faith in God. The faith Cristobal had garnered from the counselor's teachings. That little thing that made Cristobal disloyal in his eyes. It didn't matter it was utter bullshit. It made for a convincing story, one Gervasio used to make his brother think it was why he'd gone after Bella in the first place. After all, the counselor was her father.

Gervasio snarled. "No, you not. Heart in wrong place."

Cristobal slammed his fist on the table, causing the ring to jump. "¡Fue mi decisión!"

It was his decision. Well, yes. But if Gervasio admitted that, then anything his brother told the police wouldn't be false.

Gervasio stood. "Head filled with lies!"

Cristobal stood, too, and glowered at his brother. "Solucionar este."

"¿Cómo?" A solution. What solution? He had all the answers he needed. Gervasio ground his jaw. He knew exactly what Cristobal was going to say.

"Entrégate."

Turn himself in? "Adiós, hermano." Gervasio laughed and walked away from the table, leaving the ring behind.

twelve

"Down with the Sickness" by Disturbed blared through the speakers in the home gym. Interesting choice. Russell tucked his hands in his jeans pockets and watched as Heather attempted to get her brother's attention. The guy was so into his workout he didn't notice the two people standing there. He had to give him props.

Cupping her hands around her mouth, Heather Warren called out again. "David!"

Russell zeroed in on David Warren's face. As the boy's sneakers pounded the belt of the treadmill, his expression showed he was definitely pissed off about something.

"Screw this." His sister walked over to the control station and shut the music off.

Jumping to the sides of the belt, David pushed the stop button and eyed the doorway.

"Glad I finally got your attention. Detective Russell is here to speak with us."

David grabbed the towel from the handrail and wiped the sweat from his brow. "About?"

"Bella Kynaston. Just a few cursory questions. Background really." Though Russell would be asking this guy his whereabouts on the night of the rape.

"He's assured me we don't need a lawyer." Heather Warren strode past the treadmill and dropped onto one of the weight benches.

Ignoring his sister, David looked at Russell. "Anything we can do to help."

"Good. Glad to hear that. I understand you each have a relationship of sorts with Miss Kynaston." He used the word *relationship* loosely. According to his sources, the girl was a bully and the guy ... well, not sure friendship is how he'd describe it.

But right now, he was interested to hear how they described their respective relationships with the victim. Russell dug out his notepad and prepared to listen closely.

"Yeah, we're friends. Well, at least Bella and I are. I mean, she also tutors me."

Russell flipped to his notes on the tutoring. It had been mentioned by the victim. "How long has she been tutoring you?"

"Going on three years."

"So, you'd notice if there was anyone out of the ordinary in her life."

"Yeah, I guess so."

For someone he'd been told had a crush on the victim, that wasn't a very convincing answer. Then again, maybe the guy was trying to hide behind the half-assed response.

"Anyone new? Or someone who's been around that sticks out in your mind?"

David frowned. "I know she's seeing a new guy, Jeremiah Detrone. Then there's a guy she was in the tutor group with last year. He always followed her and Alex around like a lost puppy. Had a bit of an attitude when it came to Bella. Peter something."

"Petar Jacobs." Heather piped in. She draped one leg over the other and glared at her brother.

Interesting. Was there some animosity between the siblings? Russell turned in Heather's direction. "Do you know anything about this Petar Jacobs?"

"He was the lead tutor. And very much had a crush on Bella. Not that she ever gave him the time of day."

"Anything else?"

Folding her hands in her lap, Heather sighed. "You have to realize the guy was never that popular. He freaked a lot of the girls out, so none of us would ever date him."

"What makes you say that?" Was she playing him?

"I ran into him over the summer. I noticed a few changes in his physical appearance, so I commented on it. You know, told him he looked good. He said he'd been hitting the gym. Normal conversation. At least until I walked away. Then I heard him mutter something about having the last laugh."

That story was total bullshit. Russell could feel it. But he nodded as if he believed every word. Why was she throwing this guy under the bus?

"Got it. How about the fight you had with Miss Kynaston on the 20th?" Time to steer the conversation back into reality. Or so he hoped.

"She and I have always kind of been at odds. My brother has feelings for her, but I happen to think he's too good for her, so I make a point of doing my part to keep her at bay."

Russell looked at David Warren and saw that the veins in the boy's neck were throbbing and his jaw was clenched tight. If he hadn't been pissed before, he was definitely pissed now.

"And how do you accomplish that?"

Heather uncrossed her legs. "A couple friends of mine, Missy Watkins and Cassie Shows, and I, we comment about her clothes, looks, whatever's needed."

"So, you bully her."

Rolling her eyes, Heather smirked. "Call it what you will. The point is, she's continuously refused to go out with my brother."

Russell jotted down the other girls' names just as David added, "Ask about it all you like, Detective. The fact is, Bella won that argument. She called my sister out on some truths in front of the whole school."

Turning back to Heather, Russell said, "Which could be reason enough for you to want revenge."

The girl threw her head back and laughed. "Please. She didn't say anything the school doesn't already know about. They just don't say anything. They all know I can destroy anyone's reputation in a heartbeat."

That sounded like at least partial truth—but the girl did have a black eye. Make up only did so much to cover it. Someone must have fought back.

Russell refocused on David. "One final question, Mr. Warren. Where were you between the hours of six and nine the evening of the 27th?"

"I was on the soccer field until about six-thirty, then I hit the school gym until eight. I stopped at Raymond's Deli for a late bite on my way home."

"Anyone who can verify that?"

"Coach Yager."

Easy enough. "All right. Thank you for your time. I have enough to go on ... for now."

Heather nodded. "I'll show you out."

"No need. I can find my way."

"If you understand your rights, and you're waiving your right to an attorney, then please sign here." Russell slid the document toward Petar Jacobs.

Russell was frustrated. Bureaucratic red tape was preventing him from getting information he needed. There was a sealed juvenile record, but he didn't have enough probable cause to get the thing unsealed. And Bella's father, despite having been a counselor at the juvenile detention center for the last fifteen years, couldn't help. Which left Russell with practically nothing to get Jacobs to confess.

Petar signed the waiver and slid it back across to Russell. "Here you go. Like I said. I have nothing to hide."

"How do you know Bella Kynaston?" Only way he might get a confession would be to push this guy's buttons. Russell interlinked his fingers and studied Petar. The little tells most people didn't realize they had. The eye twitch. Lift of an eyebrow. Beads of sweat. Automatic bodily responses typically out of one's control.

"We met in high school, almost three years ago. I helped her out of a sticky situation with another classmate."

"How was it sticky?"

"A heated argument. Bella needed someone to intervene on her behalf. So, I did."

"Who was the classmate?" Funny. Alex Grayson had referenced this "sticky situation," but the other person involved hadn't uttered two words about it.

"Heather Warren. I think she saw Bella as an easy target. I made it so she wasn't. And Bella and I became friends after that."

Russell made a note to talk to Heather about this particular incident. There should be no reason for her lie about it. "Did you and Miss Kynaston ever become more than friends?"

"No. She wasn't interested in anything more."

"But you were?" The guy walked right into the question. But admitting to wanting more wasn't an admission of guilt.

"Yes, but I respected her wishes."

"When was the last time you saw Miss Kynaston?"

"A couple weeks ago. Principal Owen asked me to talk to her about her new position as lead tutor."

"You haven't seen her since?"

"No."

"Did you just talk, or did you go somewhere?"

"We went to the bookstore and dinner. I took her home afterwards. Would you like to know what we ate, Detective? Or are you going to stop wasting my time and ask me what you really brought me in for?"

"Where were you on the 27th of August between six and nine?"

"At the football stadium. I was there until around seven interviewing the new captain. Then I went to the newspaper room until eight to work on my article. Afterward, I headed back to my dorm for homework. Anything else?"

He'd head to the university tomorrow to verify this guy's whereabouts. For now, might as well ask for what he wanted. "DNA sample. Like you said, you have nothing to hide."

"Sure." Petar stood and hocked a loogie onto the table. "There's your sample."

The detectives were back at his girl's house. Gervasio zoomed the camera in closer. They had given her a new array of photographs to look at. Dammit, He couldn't get the camera in close enough to see the faces. As his girl shook her head, he dug out his phone and dialed the precinct. He refused to wait for an answer on this. Since his man wasn't there at the house, he should be at his desk. Direct dial this time. No operator. Damn whore took too long to transfer the call.

"Simms."

"The array presented to my love, who are they?"

If only he could see the faces in the array, then this call wouldn't have been necessary. Gervasio growled. Piece of shit computer.

"I'm sorry honey, but those are people I don't think you should be hanging out with."

Truly? He knew none of them? Had everything gone according to plan? "Then who are they?"

"What about that new friend of yours?"

"Excellent." That made perfect sense. They selected friends of their prime suspect. Those who probably fit a basic description given by his girl.

"All right. I love you too." The line dropped.

They were almost home free. Soon he would have everything he desired.

And she would be his forever.

It was only the first day of rehearsals, and already it was proving harder than Bella had thought it would. She had to listen to songs, select skits, watch dances, and critique everyone along the way. Forget the cast and sling. Never mind the broken ribs. It was her head. No, it was her soul. How was she supposed to make this the best production ever when she kept being reminded of that alleyway?

"How was the movie?" Amanda stood before her clutching a piece of paper.

Startled by the interruption of her thoughts, Bella took a moment to respond. "It was... different."

"That bad?"

"No, I'm just ... I'm not used to seeing fantasy come to life like that. It was an experience I'll never forget." But it was one Bella wished she could forget. The theatre had been crowded; it overflowed with teenagers and whiny, crying babies. To drown out the noise, the speaker system had to be cranked as high as it would go. The stale popcorn was drenched in butter. During dinner, Miah—who was the best part of the whole night—profusely apologized for the wretched experience she had. Bella admitted it wasn't anything like what he described and suggested they try again at a different time of day. Maybe after she healed a bit more.

Now, Bella stared at the music sheet Amanda held. Taking it from the girl, she skimmed over it. It was unfamiliar, but something about the lyrics resonated with her.

"You don't like it? That's okay, I can—"

"No. It's a beautiful song. Whose is it?"

Amanda grinned. "It's mine. I wrote it."

Bella scanned the sheet again. "You wrote this?"

"Yes. I thought if I was going to sing in the Festival, I'd like to do something of my own."

"This is ... it's perfect."

Amanda twined her fingers together. "You really think so?"

"Yes. Go ahead and take this to Vick so the band can learn it."

"Thank you." Amanda gently hugged Bella and bounced off.

Smiling, Bella turned her attention to the stage, where Miah worked with the dancers. Watching him too much was bound to get her in trouble. Everyone in the auditorium warranted equal attention. But seeing him put steps together made the world disappear. It was amazing how dance could transform into a story ... a story!

That was it! Amanda's song told a story that sounded like ... her life. One that Amanda started rehearsing.

Just a moment ago, she'd been "Vick!" she called out across the room and sat in one of the auditorium chairs.

Looking from Amanda to Bella, Vick rubbed an eyebrow and walked up the aisle. "You need me for something?"

"Yeah. There are some old skits in the pastor's office. I need you to find one that will match Mandy's song." Taking the keys from her pocket, Bella held them out. "Think you can do that?"

"Absolutely." Vick nodded and strode toward the hallway to the back offices.

Seeing Vick take off toward the back, Jeremiah held a hand up for the dancers to take five and hopped down from the stage. Something was up with Bell. She was sitting with her head in her hands. This was proving too much for her. He knew this wasn't a good idea, but she insisted. The bruises had faded, but her shoulder and arm were still out of whack. And her emotions. He made his way up the aisle to the row she occupied and crouched in front of her.

"Hey, you okay?"

"What? Yeah."

"You look a little ... lost." He glanced around. Everyone else was busy doing something. "Hey. Look at me. What is it?"

"Mandy's song. I guess. It hit close to home."

Was that all? His sister could choose another song to sing. Something that wouldn't be so soul-shattering. "Okay. I'm sure she wouldn't mind picking something else."

"No ... it's ... it's her own song. Her words."

"Oh." Right. Not easy to fix. Jeremiah sat beside Bella and brushed the tears from her cheeks. "Still, if you asked her to, I'm sure she would choose something different."

Bella wiped at the tears continuing down her face. "No. I won't be the problem with this production. I'm just ... I'll get Vick to take over some of the stuff."

"Okay. Sounds good." At least it wasn't square one. Bell asking for help was a move in the right direction. This had been a tough week for her. Rumors flying all over the school. People talking shit about her. Saying she deserved it. He'd never wanted to knock so many heads around. Jeremiah placed a hand between her shoulder blades and rubbed circles on her back. A technique he learned calmed her down.

She just seemed to be catching her breath when David appeared. "I'm rea— Am I interrupting something?"

Jeremiah glowered. Dumbass question. Was the guy blind? Keeping up with the circles, Jeremiah took a breath himself. "Give her a minute, and she'll be over there."

"Yep." David walked away.

Her shoulders relaxed under Miah's touch. It was strange how he calmed her. Her feelings about this nightmare she called life faded away. She was okay. She could do this. Looking to Jeremiah, Bella wiped at the tears. "Thank you."

"It's what I'm here for. Well, that and turning those monstrosities up there into heavenly dancers."

Bella giggled. "Then you're doing a terrible job."

"I would apologize, but I don't think I can do any better." He grinned.

Their own personal joke. He knew as well as she did how wonderful the dancers looked. The exchange had been a way to move on from the tears. Taking a deep breath, Bella offered a cock-eyed grin. "Go on. I have to go listen to David. I'm fine. I promise."

"All right." Miah hugged her tenderly and placed a chaste kiss on her forehead before he headed back to the stage where the dancers awaited his return.

Bella stood and ambled to the orchestra level below the stage. Most of the instruments had been set there ahead of time. Volunteers had numerous options.

Stepping around the piano, Bella sat in a chair off to the right. "Sorry about that. Go ahead and play."

"You sure?"

"Yeah. I'm okay." She settled in and leveled her eyes on his fingers. She hoped David's piece would be a lot less painful to hear than Mandy's. Of course, the emotional rollercoaster ride was part of the experience of listening to music, but today it was better to focus on the mechanics.

David's fingers stroked the ivory keys as if they were lovers. The notes of the music poured into the orchestra area and flowed over the empty chairs, while the different lilts told a story. One of a man betrayed by a woman he loved. Thinking he'd never find joy again, he turned to anger and fear. To one day find the woman he had dreamt of his whole life.

The last note held and the song ended. It was an excellent choice. And it was a good thing she'd stared at his hands the whole time. Otherwise she might be one big ball of mess. Again.

Bella grinned. "Exquisite."

"Does that mean I'm in the show?"

"Yes. You're in the show."

"Yes!" David jumped up and did a victory dance.

Shaking her head at his ridiculousness, Bella laughed. A deep, throaty, heartfelt laugh. He had no care over how idiotic he looked. It was all about his joy. The strength in her lungs hadn't yet returned to normal. They were still healing. But the laugh felt good for the thirty seconds her lungs could sustain it. Then she doubled over and, gripping her side, and tried to breathe through the coughing fit.

David stopped dancing and dropped to his knees in front of her. "Bella!"

"What the hell happened?!" Jeremiah hopped off the stage and landed beside her. His hand went directly to her back, and he rubbed those calming circles. "Come on, slow breaths."

Everyone stared as she inhaled and exhaled shallow breaths. Dammit. It was bad enough she had come in with a sling and cast on. Why was it her body had to draw more attention?

Bella looked from the gathered crowd to Miah and muttered, "I'm ... okay."

"You sure?"

Bella nodded as her breathing returned to normal. "Yeah. I'm okay." She shifted her gaze to the crowd. "I'm okay. Everyone back to work."

thirteen

Bella raised an eyebrow. Why would Vick start without her? The agreement was that he would take over the tutor group, but she would still be present at all meetings. She just wasn't going to tutor for a bit.

"No. I won't be long. I just need to let Alex know I'll be a little late."

"All right. Don't take too long or I'll come looking for you." Vick grinned and started toward the library.

"Didn't we do that already this year?" Bella called after him. No de ja vu for her, please. With a brief chuckle, she headed for the parking lot. Alex was probably out there waiting. The meeting wasn't last-minute, but she had forgotten to mention it during their last class.

Bella shoved through the door with her hip.

Petar stepped from behind a column as the door opened. His eyes narrowed and his nostrils flared. "What the hell is wrong with you?"

"Excuse me?" Bella blinked. Why would he ask her something like that? Nothing was wrong with her. At least as far as people knew. Excluding the obvious—the effects of the attack. The attack. Could his question be related?

"How could you even think I would rape you?"

Her eyes widened. She hadn't pointed at him as one of her attackers. Yeah, she had mentioned a few things about his temperament, but the police would've checked into him even if she hadn't. "Where did you get that idea?"

"Oh, I don't know. Maybe because the police showed up at my school and escorted me to the precinct. Or maybe it was because they asked for my DNA. Either way, honey bear, it looks to me like they think I raped you."

"What did you call me?" No. She couldn't have heard him right. Bella backed up and stared at him. No way he used the same term as her attacker. No way. No one called her that.

Behind her, the door flew open, and Miah skidded to a halt between her and Petar, just as Alex came running up from the parking lot.

Alex looked to Petar. "I don't know what the hell you're doing here, but you need to go."

"Sure. I'm done here, anyway." With a sneer, Petar walked off.

Glancing from Alex to her, Miah rested his hand on Bella's good shoulder. "Hey, you okay?"

Shrugging his hand off, Bella nodded. "I'm fine."

"You sure?"

"Yes. If you'll excuse me, I have a meeting." Without giving either of them the opportunity to question her mental state further, Bella opened the door and headed back inside the school.

Bella knew all her friends had been interviewed. Had the guys all been asked for DNA? She had no clue. If they had, none of them said anything. Would they have told her if they had?

She shook her head and told herself to focus on the meeting.

"All right. Next order of business. David Warren. He's going to need a new tutor. Looks like Algebra II. Anyone want to take him on?" Vick eyed the tutors around the table.

Her brain looped back to the question. Maybe her friends thought they were protecting her if they kept that information to themselves. But, no. That didn't make any sense. It wasn't like she was going around claiming her friends attacked her. These were people who cared about her. Petar was supposed to be the same way. So why was he so pissed?

Unless he was the only one whose DNA the police asked for. Maybe they were right to do so. He used a term of endearment no one except her attacker used. She pulled up the image of the guy in the hoodie in her mind. Bella shuddered. Don't think about the attack. Just the face. The eyes. They were brown. Chocolate brown. Petar had chocolate brown eyes, but so did half the population. It was too general.

"To be honest, none of us girls will take him. The guy is a walking slut. He hits on everything with legs."

Hayley's comment broke in on Bella's circular thinking. She really had to pay attention.

Vick sighed. "Okay. James, what about you?" "I don't think it's a good idea. He and I don't exactly get along."

"All right. Guess he's on me." Vick signed off on the change and picked up another piece of paper.

Bella started to thank Vick for taking David on, when suddenly she saw it: The bridge of Bandana man's nose, it was crooked. Her body locked. Just the face. Only focus on the face, she told herself. God, why did those images always have to barge in? Bella inhaled and exhaled deeply. What else? His forehead. The hood hadn't been pulled down all the way. There had been a straight, white line above the right eyebrow. A scar. Like the one Petar had. Oh. My. God.

"Meeting's adjourned!" Bella announced, and jumping to her feet she snatched her backpack and ran out the door.

Leaning against his locker, Jeremiah waited for Bella to disappear from his sight before he returned to collecting his books. What did he need? His English paper was due at—

"Jeremiah!" Vick jogged up. "Have you seen Bella?"

"Yeah. She just left. Why? Is something wrong?" She'd appeared okay. Determined actually. The best he'd seen her in the last week. Like things were coming together, and she was figuring out how to put her life back together.

Catching his breath, Vick said, "She was quiet through the whole meeting. Then out of nowhere she calls the meeting and runs out."

Jeremiah glanced to the door Bella walked out of mere seconds ago. She hadn't said a thing about this. "Man, I don't know if it had anything to do with it, but she had a run in with Petar before the meeting."

"What? Why didn't she say anything?"

"I don't know. Alex and I interrupted whatever was going on." Jeremiah crossed his arms and leaned back against the lockers. "Probably a good thing. Bell looked frantic to get away from him. Then Petar left and Bell went back inside—to the meeting."

He and Alex had made certain Bell was safely inside the library. Then they spent a few minutes discussing the situation. And how to handle it. Neither agreed on a solution.

Vick frowned. "I've never met the guy, but from what I've heard, I don't really want to."

Jeremiah felt the same. Too bad he *had* met the douche-bag. He pushed off the locker and shoved his hands in his pockets. "I hear you. But, anyway, I think he's a problem for the police, now."

Adopted? Russell rubbed his eyes. He couldn't be reading that right. He didn't have any chance to consider the idea further before Alexandra Grayson marched over and slammed a yearbook on his desk.

"When the hell are you going to arrest this piece of shit?" she demanded.

Her eyes weren't bloodshot, Russell noted. She didn't reek of Mary Jane, but she was definitely off her meds. Locking his screen, he raised an eyebrow.

"Who are we talking about Miss Grayson?"

She flipped open the yearbook and pointed to a picture. "Petar Jacobs. Who else would we be talking about?"

"Have a seat. What happened?" Something had gone down. Otherwise she wouldn't be in his face about this guy. Since the DNA hadn't come back, it was pointless to bring him in for another chat. Even though the guy's alibi had been completely blown apart.

Russell leaned back in his chair.

"I'm not fucking sitting." The girl glared at him and remained standing. "While you guys are playing tiddlywinks with manhole covers, he's showing up at our school accosting Bella."

Really. Hmm. The guy had something to cover. Innocent people didn't go back for a chat with a victim they were accused of raping.

Russell gestured to the chair again. "Sit. Talk."

The blonde girl groaned, but this time she sat as instructed. "I was waiting by my car. B and I were going to hang out after school. She comes out, and I see Petar step out from behind one of the columns."

"What happened next?" Russell dug into his desk drawer and gathered a pen and notepad.

"I don't know what they said. I was too far away. All I know is within a few minutes she's backing away from him. I saw that as my cue."

"Anyone else witness this?"

"Jeremiah. Detrone. He came out the doors the same time I came up from the parking lot. He got between them, and I told Petar to leave."

Girl made a good witness. Very specific. And the sheriff's son, too. Observant.

"Did Mr. Jacobs say anything before he left?" Russell glanced at his notes. They had pulled Petar in last Friday, and the guy was out there not long after trying to scare the victim.

"Just that he was 'done.' Whatever that means."

Russell leaned forward. "Listen, I appreciate you coming in with this, but I want you to let us handle it. Okay?"

"Fine. Just do it soon. Because next time he gets in my best friend's face, I go on the offensive." Alex stood and stormed off.

Right. Russell picked up the phone from its cradle. Time to lean on forensics for some results. Before things got out of hand, and civilians took justice into theirs.

"Dad, I'm telling you, this guy really freaked her out." Jeremiah set plates along one side of the table, while his father set the other side. The good news, Alex had the same idea he did. She just happened to beat him to the punch.

His father arranged the silverware and glasses. "I'm aware of this. And Russell is taking care of it."

"By doing what? Waiting on evidence? Look, I know you guys can't arrest this guy yet, but there has to be something you can do to protect Bell."

Man, he wished he'd heard what Petar said to Bella. But he got there too late. Jeremiah stared at the pile of forks and knives. He should've kicked the guy's ass when he had the chance. But Bell had been his focus. Making sure she wasn't hurt.

"I'll tell you what. I'll have Russell talk to her. If she feels truly threatened, then we'll see about a restraining order."

Restraining order? It wasn't much. But it was better than nothing. Jeremiah nodded. "Thanks, Dad."

"You do understand if she doesn't clearly state she's afraid he might hurt her, there isn't much of anything we can do until we have what we need. Right?"

"I know. It's something. I just, I can't sit back and do nothing." Jeremiah hated this. He couldn't take her pain. He couldn't heal her suffering. He couldn't keep her safe. There wasn't much of anything he could do. He had never felt so ... helpless.

"Jeremiah, you are there for her every day. How many times have you calmed her during a panic attack? Or been a shoulder to cry on? Or made sure she got where she was going safely? That isn't nothing."

Sounded like a lot when it was put that way. But was it enough? Lifting his gaze to his father, he dropped onto one of the chairs. "Sometimes, I feel like I could do more."

"Son, listen to me. You're doing everything you can in your power to help her. That's all you can ask of yourself."

"Your father's right," his mother said, from the kitchen. "Being there for Bella is half the battle. The other half ... it's her fight."

His mother's and father's insights didn't change the way he felt. But it helped. "Thank you." Jeremiah stood and finished setting his side of the dining room table.

Bella bolted upright in the chair, struggling to catch her breath. Another nightmare. She glanced around her bedroom. The closed closet doors. The empty bed. The clean desk. Her gaze settled on the tree outside her bedroom window.

That tree had been there for as long as she could remember. When she was little, it used to frighten her. Now, it comforted her.

Too bad it couldn't help her fall back asleep. She glanced across at the clock on the nightstand. Midnight. She'd managed to get a whole two hours of sleep sitting in her chair. At this rate, she'd be lucky to get another hour. And tomorrow wouldn't be any better. The nightmare disturbed her sleep every night.

Except it was worse than before. It wasn't just facing the attack all over again. Every night, when the nightmare put her back in that alleyway, she didn't see a hooded figure. She saw Petar, clear as day. Two scar-faced men forcing themselves on her. Taking her without any regard of whether she lived or died.

Bella sobbed. How was she supposed to get through this if she never left that damn alleyway? She was stuck. And there was no way out. Two men were holding her captive, and the harder she fought to escape, the tighter the reins got. Every day was a struggle. One she wasn't sure she'd survive.

There was no way ... out. Turning her head, she glanced at the clock again. An orange pill bottle sat beside it. The painkillers. She was always drowsy after taking one and often napped. The doctor had been specific about how many she could take and how many hours between each dosage. Could she ignore his instructions? Take one more? Just one extra pill at night? So she could sleep?

Bella wiped at the tears. Maybe just for tonight. She walked across the hall and filled a small cup with water. Returning to her room, she eyed the pill bottle. Opening the bottle, she dumped one pill into the palm of her hand.

Just for tonight.

Without a second thought, Bella popped the pill in her mouth, drank some water and swallowed.

Tomorrow?

Well, tomorrow was another day.

fourteen

"It's classified as horror, but I don't think it's scary. Is that okay?" Miah held up the DVD box for *Hansel and Gretel: Witch Hunters*.

Grabbing the box, Bella flipped it over. Hansel and Gretel as bounty hunters, huh? Sounded interesting. And definitely not scary. "Yeah. This should be okay."

"Good." Jeremiah walked across the living room to the DVD player. "Hey, I meant to ask if Vick got hold of you yesterday."

What? Ah, yes. The two spoke after her quick departure from the tutor meeting. "Yeah. He called last night. He wanted to know if I'd talked to David, yet. I'm not going to tutor him this semester. Vick's going to. I'll tell him tomorrow." Actually, she had to talk to David tomorrow. It was Thursday. The day set aside for his tutoring sessions. Bella hung her head. "I've kind of been avoiding him."

"Bell. Why would you do that?" Jeremiah flopped onto the couch beside her.

"Because last time he was assigned to someone besides me, he threw a fit. And I didn't feel like dealing with it again."

"So, you think he'll throw another tantrum?"

She opened her mouth and stopped. The circumstances were different. So, he might be okay this time around. Bella half-shrugged. "I don't know."

"Then how about we tell him together?"

"That's okay. I can handle it on my own." If Miah was around, David could go ballistic. The two of them could end up in a fight. Not to mention, she didn't need Miah with her every waking hour. He was already carrying so much weight for her. She didn't need to add more to the pile.

"All right. If you change your mind, you know how to find me."

"Yep." Bella nodded to the television. It was time for him to play the movie. Good thing it was a horror movie. No people falling in love. No kissing scenes. No intimacy of any kind. Good guys chasing monsters. Wow. Still too relatable. But at least these monsters were easy to spot. Hers were practically invisible.

Pushing play, Jeremiah set the remote aside and draped an arm over the back cushions.

Bella watched him out of the corner of her eye. Part of her wanted to curl up to him. Part of her screamed *run*. Why couldn't they have met sooner? When all she had to face were normal teenage anxieties about the "firsts." Instead, she'd had just a week, just one week to experience those firsts with a boy she liked. Also, a first.

It wasn't as if he hadn't touched her since the attack, of course. He'd rubbed circles on her back; they'd cuddled in the hospital. But this was different. All of that was about helping her relax. Not about intimacy.

What if they took it slow? One step at a time? No! No, she couldn't.

Eyes toward the movie, she caught another glimpse of him out of her periphery. He looked so comfortable. For crying out loud! She went five seconds without looking. Then, with a deep breath, she eyed Miah again.

Before her nerves got the best of her, she shifted closer and leaned her head against his chest. But when his hand came down on her shoulder, she jumped up. "No, no. Nope."

Snatching the remote, Jeremiah paused the movie. "What's wrong?"

Bella started pacing back and forth in front of the television. Her heart raced. It had been fine. For all of two seconds. But that wasn't enough time to settle. To get comfortable. More time. She needed more time.

"Come on, Bell. Talk to me."

"You moved." Why did he have to move? Why couldn't he have stayed put? No. Nope. They could watch the movie from opposite ends of the couch.

She stopped mid-step. Explain. Mouth had to open. God. The words wouldn't come out. Why couldn't she get them out? All the synapses in her brain fired blanks.

"Okay. I'll talk, and you nod if I'm right."

Yes. She could do that. Bella nodded.

"You curled up to me because you wanted to."

Yep, yep. That was right. She nodded again.

"Then I went to pull you closer." Hanging his head, Miah sighed. "It was too much, wasn't it?"

"Yes." Oh. Look. A word. Bella inhaled and exhaled one more time.

"I'm so sorry, Bell. I didn't even think. I'll sit in the chair. Okay?" Miah stood.

"No!" she protested. She wanted to try. With him. Bella bit her bottom lip. "One step at a time. Just ... sit. Let me get used it. I want to, I just ... I have to go slow."

Hands pinned her to the ground. Bella struggled against their hold. "Please," she whimpered. "Please, let me go."

Leaning in close, the man dipped his nose in her hair, pushing his hood back. When he sat up, she could see: Chocolate brown eyes. The jagged scar running up the right side of his face. It was Petar.

He pressed a kiss to her lips. "You belong to me, honey bear."

No! Gasping, Bella bolted upright in the chair, her eyes darting left, then right. Her bedroom was empty. She was alone.

She huffed and puffed, taking small breaths until her body relaxed. She couldn't keep dealing with this. She'd gone back to the dose her doctor prescribed—and woken to another nightmare. How often would she be subjected to the same brain loop? No more. Two pills at bedtime. Then she'd sleep through the night. It was what she had to do.

Bella glanced at the clock on her nightstand. Two a.m. No going back to sleep for her. She shivered. It was a bit on the cold side. Then the curtains shifted. Holding her breath, she studied the curtains from top to bottom. No feet peeked out beneath. She walked over and moved the curtains aside. The window behind them was open a crack. Had she forgotten to close it? No. She was certain it had been shut tight. She slammed the window and locked it.

She wasn't losing her mind, but it sure as shit felt like she was.

Then, as she turned toward her bed, she saw it. A single, long-stemmed, red rose had been laid on the middle of the desk.

Frantic, she scanned her room. Closet doors were wide open. Only skirts and blouses. A variety of ballet flats lined the floor. The bed remained unrumpled. No one in the corners. Heart beating hard, she knelt and looked under the bed. Nothing.

Jumping back to her feet, Bella ran down the hall to her parents' bedroom and threw open their door. "Bàba! Wake up!"

Her father stirred, then blinked and propped himself up on an elbow. "Bella, what's the matter?"

"He was here, Bàba. He was here." Tears streamed down her face. One of her attackers had been in her bedroom.

While she slept.

Five a.m. Way too early to be at a crime scene. Unfortunately, criminals care little about time unless it impacts their criminal activities. Russell angled the flashlight over the keyhole of the front door. The window had been a decoy move. Opened from the inside, not outside. He'd ruled out all other points of entry. There were a couple of scratches here, though. "Looks like he came in this way."

"That door was locked, with the chain on," DeWei Kynaston said.

Chain? What a joke. Turning the flashlight off, Russell said, "No offense, Dr. Kynaston, but these locks are outdated. And there are plenty of tutorials online showing how to get past a chain."

"I don't understand. We've lived here for almost twenty years, and our house has never been broken into before."

"Not an ordinary break-in. Nothing was stolen. This wasn't about theft, Dr. Kynaston, it was a message." This guy was letting them know he could still get to Bella.

One of the technicians stopped and leaned in close to Russell. "We have prints, detective."

First good thing he'd heard all morning. "I want them run A.S.A.P." Without waiting for affirmation, Russell headed back to Bella's bedroom. Man, he hoped the prints belonged to the perpetrator. Otherwise they would be added to the pile of useless crap already accruing with this case. He stared at the desk. The rose had been collected for evidence.

"It was him, wasn't it? Petar? He was here," Bella asked from the doorway.

Russell spun around. "We won't know that for sure until everything comes back."

"It has to be. He was one of my attackers. After the other day ... I know it's him."

"Miss Kynaston, I understand you fully believe that. And I believe that too. But I want to make sure this guy has no wiggle room. We will get him. When the evidence comes in. I promise you." In fact, he was going to head to the squad room and call forensics, again. DNA results were going to be delivered today if he had to go down there and run the damn test, himself.

Bella stood at her locker, rubbing her eyes. It had been a long day. The police had spent hours at her house collecting evidence and taking pictures. Not to mention the endless questions. How many times had she told them about Petar's unexpected visit at school the other day? Plus, the break. God, she was exhausted. All she wanted was to go home and curl up in her warm bed. Knocked out like there was no tomorrow.

Suddenly, David was shoving a piece of paper in her face. "Please tell me this is a joke."

"Christ! You scared the shit out of me. What is wrong with you?"

"Sorry. I didn't mean—" David stopped mid-sentence. Then pointed to the paper. "Look. I got this notice today about a switch in tutors. Is this true?"

Shit. She'd completely forgotten to talk to him. And his first tutoring session with Vick was today. Bella massaged her temples. With a sigh, she dropped her hands. "I'm sorry David. I meant to tell you earlier."

"I thought Vick was only taking over your leadership responsibilities, not your tutoring sessions, too."

"He's the only one qualified to tutor you." Okay. That was a bold-faced lie. No female was going to take that bite. David was too well known for being flirtatious. And the only male tutor besides Vick refused to take him on either. Again, David's reputation.

"That's bullshit, and you know it. I asked you to keep tutoring me. I know you have a lot going on, but I figured you could at least do this for me."

Bella grabbed the last book she'd need for homework and dropped it in her backpack. Of all days, why did he have to pick today to be difficult? She couldn't deal with this right now. Of course, it was her fault. She should've addressed the situation before he got the official notification.

She shut her locker and shrugged her backpack onto her good shoulder. "Look, I'm sorry you had to find out this way, but that's the way it is. Vick's taking over."

"You can't be serious."

"I am." With that, Bella walked away.

Pinching the bridge of his nose, Jamar returned the receiver to its cradle. Oh, the fun of being sheriff. When there was a problem with a detective's insensitivity to a victim or their family, he was the one who handled the call. And of all people, it had to be the detention center's counselor. Politics went with the job. No matter the town or county: his squad, his responsibility. Based on the verbal ass-whipping he'd just received, though, he needed to know exactly what was going on.

"Russell, get in here."

Russell stuck his head into Jamar's office. "You called?"

"Yeah. Come in. Give me a complete update on the Kynaston case."

"Prints came back on the break-in. They belong to Petar Jacobs. I just got off the phone with the ADA, and he's working on getting a judge to sign off on unsealing the kid's juvie record."

Great. The break-in had been solved in less than …? Jamar glanced at his watch. Ten hours. But that was not what he wanted to know about. "What about the rape case?"

"DNA still hasn't come in, but I put a call in to forensics this morning. They assured me the kit was being moved to the front."

DNA—when it was available and not too degraded—was the cornerstone of most rape cases. But the county was backlogged. Jamar sighed. He'd approved the overtime three weeks ago. "Is there anything else to go on? Anything that suggests Petar Jacobs is one of Miss Kynaston's rapists?"

"There are holes in the guy's story," Russell said.

Steepling his fingers, Jamar leaned back in his chair. The DNA might not be back, but they had the guy on breaking and entering. "What about the second rapist?"

"Nothing. Sketch hasn't turned up anything, and I've dead-ended on associates of Petar Jacobs that fit the description." Glancing around, Russell shut the door. "I've been checking to see if there could be any other connections. A family member of someone Dr. Kynaston counseled, maybe—or anything else that could give me a lead."

"You found something?"

"Yeah. A whole new suspect pool. Did you know Bella Kynaston was adopted?"

Before Jamar could react to that news, the door opened. It was Simms. He gave Jamar and Russell a thumbs-up. "Thought you'd want to know. The DNA on the Kynaston case just came in."

"And?" Jamar sat up. Finally.

"Perfect match to Petar Jacobs."

That was the best thing he'd heard all day. Jamar stood and grabbed his coat. "Let's go get the son of a bitch."

"For the last time, I didn't rape her. I was at the Hotel Adonné with a girl. Check with them." Petar shoved his hands through his hair.

This guy really wasn't going to give it up. But a confession wasn't necessary. They had the kid by the balls. Russell uncrossed his arms and leaned on the table. "Here's the thing. I did check with the hotel. And they don't remember you. Or this girl. In fact, there's nothing to show you even registered there at all."

"I told you. It was her room."

"Right. Jocelyn Smith." He'd asked the hotel to search that name, too. No results. This guy was a piece of work. All the proof laid out in front of him, and he still refused to cop to the rape and break-in.

Russell stood and hooked his thumbs in his belt loops. "No registration. No driver's license. So, you want to try another fictional name? Though you can spit out a hundred of them, and it still won't change the facts. Your DNA was found inside Bella Kynaston! Your prints were found in her room! On the inside of her window!"

"I don't know how any of that happened! I wasn't there!"

"It was your semen inside that girl! It was your semen on her skirt!" Russell slammed his hand down on the table. "Just tell us the name of your accomplice, and I'll put a good word in with the ADA."

"You know what? I'm done talking. Get me a lawyer."

Magic words. Crap. Russell gathered the files and left the interrogation room. Shutting the door, he eyed the sheriff. "You want me to take him back to the cage?"

"Yeah. I'll call for a lawyer and get the ADA down here. I want his accomplice off the streets."

"Roger that."

fifteen

Looking over the room one last time, his gaze stopped on a book on top of the bookcase. *Hopeless*, by Colleen Hoover. Gervasio picked it up and stared at the upper half of the picture tucked into the book, then, eyes narrowed, yanked out the photo.

It was his girl. With that damn monkey!

Upper lip curled, he hurled the book across the room—and with a roar, ripped the photograph in half.

She. Belonged. To. Him.

Gervasio knocked the bookcase over, then wrenched the drawers out of the dresser, tearing at whatever clothes he got in his hands. That whore! How dare she! Her father had promised her to him. Instead, she had gone and found herself a fucking Oreo. That piece of shit would keep them apart.

Grabbing the frame of the bed, he flipped it over. The little bitch was her mother all over again.

Striding over to the closet, Gervasio snatched skirts and blouses off hangers, splitting each in two and tossing them onto the growing pile of tattered clothes.

The sound of the front door opening, then closing, pulled his attention from the destroyed closet.

A thud followed.

Gervasio ran out of the bedroom to find Bella sprawled out on the floor.

Beside her, Marco was tucking a gun in the back of his pants.

"Is she dead?"

Swifty knelt down and placed two fingers against her neck. "No. Help me —"

Without even glancing at Swifty, Gervasio launched at Marco, landing the two of them on top of a table in the foyer that cracked under their weight. As Gervasio struggled to get to his knees, Marco punched him in the jaw and Gervasio's head snapped back. Gervasio blocked a second blow and returned an upper cut to the guy's chin; then, surging with power, Gervasio threw a right hook.

Blood gushed from Marco's nose. But it wasn't enough damage. Grabbing the sides of Marco's face, he slammed the guy's head into the ground.

From behind, Gervasio felt Swifty grab him by the armpits and try to pull him off Marco.

"Stop! You'll kill him!"

Jerking free of Swifty's grip, Gervasio stepped away. None of this was supposed to happen. It should've been a quick in and out. He eyeballed the mess.

Gervasio pointed to Marco. "Swifty, get him out of here. And get someone to clean that shit up."

"What about the girl?"

"I'll take care of her." Although his body hadn't fully relaxed, his head was back in the driver's seat. Gervasio scooped Bella up and carried her to the bedroom.

He paused in the doorway.

Shit. He had really lost it. Okay. Not a problem. If the rest of the house was ransacked, it would look like a break-in. Simple enough.

Stepping into the bedroom, he kicked the bedframe and box spring out of the way, then gently laid Bella on the mattress. There was one hell of a bump on the back of her head. Marco must've knocked her out with butt of his gun. A call to the emergency line would have to be placed. Make sure an ambulance was on the way before they left.

Brushing her hair aside, Gervasio kissed Bella's lips, then, straightening, he caught a glimpse of something orange. On the nightstand. One of the few things in the room he hadn't trashed.

It was a pill bottle. Painkillers. Filled two weeks ago. Sixty pills and the whole bottle was empty. He glanced to his girl. Was she taking them as prescribed? Or had she begun to take them recreationally?

"Boss, we need to go."

Gervasio tucked the bottle in his pocket. Walking around the mess, he gestured to the office down the hall. "We got work to do first."

Tapping his fingers against the steering wheel, Jeremiah bopped his head to "Numb," by Linkin Park. He turned onto Bella's street. He was early. Cool. If she was already home from her doctor's appointment, they'd have more time together.

He slowed the Dodge and pulled into the driveway. What the heck? Why was the front door open? Jeremiah climbed out of the car and strode up the walkway, checking out his surroundings. No other vehicles in the driveway. No broken windows. Nothing out of the ordinary. At least outside.

Inside, Bella's backpack was on the floor by the doorway. But no Bell. Jeremiah peeked into the kitchen. Empty. Same with the den. "Bell?"

A groan came from her bedroom.

Jeremiah darted toward the sound and skidded to a halt at her bedroom door. "Jesus Christ!" The room had been torn apart. What the hell happened?

He dug out his cell phone, punched in 9-1-1, then scrambled over the mess and dropped to his knees beside Bella. There was blood on the mattress beside her head. Oh, God.

"What's your emergency?"

"I need an ambulance at 1113 Pecado Avenue. My girl ... my friend's been hurt."

"An ambulance has already been dispatched to that address, sir."

Sure enough, sirens blared not far off in the distance. What? How was that possible? As he brushed some of Bella's hair out of her face, the sirens roared closer. Then Jeremiah heard the front door swing open and a male voice call out, "Hello?"

The paramedics had arrived.

"No, no, no, no. I'm not spending another night in this damn hospital." Figures.

The sling comes off only for her to get whacked in the head. Still, she refused to get stuck back in a hospital room again.

"It's just one—"

"I don't care. Get. Me. Out of here." Bella glowered at her parents. If she had to start pulling the lines from her body, she would.

Exasperated, her mother sighed. "All right. We'll speak with the doctor, but—."

"Thank you." There was no but. A mild concussion was no reason to stay overnight.

When her father and mother stepped out of the room, Bella let out a breath and lay back against the pillow. The throbbing had mostly subsided. It was now a dull ache. Whoever hit her could've caused a lot more damage.

Too bad they didn't. She wouldn't mind one bit if her memories were affected. Well. As long as she remembered Miah and everything before the attack. But no such luck. Every day of the last few weeks was with her. Including that night.

The door opened and her father stepped back in. "The doctor has given consent to release you on one condition. Your mother and I have discussed it and we agree with him."

"Which is?"

"You spend the night with the Detrones."

Standing in the hallway, Jamar looked from the study to the Kynaston's bedroom, where clothing covered the floor, drawers had been pulled out, and pillows thrown about. It was a mess, but nothing was broken.

He returned to the study, which served as a secondary office. Here, the computer had been flipped, papers littered the ground, and the chair had been laid on its side. But, as with the master bedroom, damage was minimal. And according to Milena and DeWei Kynaston, nothing was missing from either room. It was as if both had been tossed as an afterthought.

Jamar entered Bella's bedroom. Pulling on a pair of latex gloves, he eyeballed the piles of shredded clothes, the overturned bed, bloodied mattress, and shattered mirror. Books were scattered all over the floor. Chunks of dresser drawers had been chucked all over the place.

This room was different than the other two. It had received real damage. But again, nothing seemed to be missing, at least according to Bella's parents.

Something caught his eye. Jamar crouched down and reached under the bookcase. One half of a torn photograph—of his son. Where was the other half?

"You find something, Sheriff?"

Looking to Detective Russell, he held up the picture. Then he asked, "Have the Kynaston's returned yet?"

"Just got back."

"Good." Taking an evidence bag out of his jacket pocket, Jamar stood. He put the torn photograph inside and sealed it, then walked out into the hallway and removed the gloves.

"Russell."

"Sheriff?"

"Don't mention we know about the adoption yet." It was too early in the case for all their cards to be revealed. And he wanted to learn every detail before confronting the Kynastons.

"Just keep it between us."

"What do you remember about what happened?" Russell asked the girl.

"Not much."

That figured. That was about how much sense this all made. Nothing had been stolen from the Kynaston residence, but Bella had been hurt. She had walked in on something. Seen something. And he had to know what.

"That's okay. Tell me what you do remember."

"I checked the mail after the taxi dropped me off. I unlocked the door and set the mail on the table. I closed the door ... then I saw the paramedics."

"You're sure about the door?" It wasn't much, but it was something.

"I'm positive."

Jeremiah Detrone had found the door open. Meant the perpetrator left it that way. On purpose? "Anything else you remember between closing the door and seeing the paramedic?"

"A scar," Bella said. "I remember seeing a scar. It's ... like a flash. Like I caught a glimpse of it before everything went black." She paused, looking pale. "It was him. He was there."

"Who." Russell raised an eyebrow.

"The ... man who attacked me."

Russell was working under the assumption that Petar Jacobs was the primary. What if that wasn't accurate? What if it was the still-unidentified rapist who was in charge? If so, why would he have shown up at the Kynaston residence?

Gervasio spun the little orange bottle between his fingers and stared at the four monitors on his desk. All the cameras were in working order. All remained well hidden. That had been the entire reason for their visit. But his clean-up had been sloppy. Half-assed. It was his own fault. How could he have been so fucking stupid?

He watched as technicians walked in and out of his girl's bedroom. The entire scene had been photographed. Prints had been collected. Other evidence had been bagged. His grip tightened around the pill bottle. This girl. She was screwing everything up.

No. This was her father's fault. That son of a bitch. If he had held up his end of the bargain, then his girl would be by his side, where she belonged. Instead, he had been forced to break her the way he did his whores. It had been the only way to make her his.

There was a knock on the door. Gervasio looked away from the monitors. "Enter."

Tommy poked his head in. "You wanted to see me, boss."

Great. Perfect fucking timing. Gervasio cleared his throat. "*Si*. Have job." He typically used broken English around his soldiers. He preferred they underestimate his intelligence. Made them easier to manipulate. And made it less likely he'd be overthrown.

"Sure thing. Whadda ya need me to do?" Tommy stepped all the way into the office.

Gervasio tossed the pill bottle to the dealer. "Find drug and get friendly with girl. She need more soon."

"Yes, sir. Any particular deals? Or anything else I should know?"

"Talk to Swifty. He know her." As for the deal? He wanted her hooked. Unless she was pregnant. He'd much rather have her pregnant with his child than addicted to drugs. Though, if she found out she was pregnant, he was sure she'd stop using. Gervasio rubbed his chin. This was a good way to keep track of her. "Give twenty free."

"Understood."

"Good. Now go." He needed to figure out his next move.

Jamar flipped through the photos of the different crime scenes. He paused on the crisscrossed scythes burned into Bella's skin. The investigation had taken them completely away from this gang symbol. No matter how much he and Russell searched, they couldn't discover any connection between Petar and the Grim Reapers.

But DNA didn't lie. And neither did scars. Petar had been there. And the scythes had been branded onto Bella Kynaston's neck.

Dropping the pictures to the dining room table, Jamar leaned back in his chair.

"Are you still looking at those?" Christine draped an arm across his shoulders.

Wrapping an arm around his wife's waist, he pressed a tender kiss to her pregnant belly. "I feel like I'm missing something. Like the pieces don't fit."

"You don't think Bella is holding anything back, do you?"

"No. Her story has been consistent. If there's something more there, she hasn't pieced it together yet." Jamar stared at the scythes.

"I could talk to her."

Not a bridge he was ready to cross. Even if his wife and Bella were connected by similar events. Jamar laid his head against his wife's round belly. His family kept him sane. With all the ugliness in the world, they reminded him of how beautiful life could be. "I appreciate the offer, but not necessary. We're just going to have to go about this another way."

"Do you want to talk about it?"

"You see this mark?" Jamar tapped the image of Bella's neck. "This is a gang symbol. The Grim Reapers. But the guy we arrested isn't affiliated."

Christine nodded, encouraging him to continue.

"It has to be important. Right? Otherwise, why brand her?"

"I see the wheels turning. Care to share?" Christine squeezed his shoulder.

"I was thinking about the reason I was brought in." His title came with a purpose. It wasn't about being the leader the guys needed in their corner. It was about cleaning up. Rooting out the corrupt. Was he being played? Maybe. He had to go back through jackets and comb through all the evidence that had been collected. See who'd touched what. Figure out who was on his side.

As if his wife read his mind, she asked, "You think someone else is pulling the strings?"

"You know," Jamar said slowly, "I do." He stood and gathered the pictures together.

Christine backed up a step and rubbed her belly. "Honey, please tell me you're not going back to the office tonight."

The thought had crossed his mind. But Bella was here, in his house, and she had to be protected. He had men outside, sure, but suddenly, he had no idea who he could trust.

sixteen

Jeremiah startled awake. Had someone been there? He scanned his bedroom. Nothing seemed out of the ordinary. Stifling a yawn, he stretched and glanced at the clock. Was it really almost four in the morning? Tossing his covers back, he climbed out of bed. The night had been ... eventful.

Concentrating on homework had pretty much been out of the question, but they'd tried. Bell's focus had been divided. Every time the phone rang her head popped up. Jeremiah's tried to get some information from his father, when he returned home, but there was little to gain. The only thing his father confirmed was that it hadn't been a break-in, but that hadn't comforted Bell much.

Her parents had reached an agreement with her yesterday. Since she refused to stay at the hospital, overnight, they felt it best if she stayed with him and his family, where she would be safe. It wasn't exactly how he expected their first true night together would go, but life so often offers the weirdly unexpected.

Rubbing the top of his tightly shorn head, Jeremiah opened his bedroom door and headed down the hallway. He paused outside his sister's bedroom. Would Bell care if he poked his head in? His parents had placed a blow-up mattress on the far side of Amanda's room for her. Sighing softly, he continued down the hall and into the kitchen. Surely, she was asleep, and the last thing he should do was disturb her. Even if he wanted to make sure she was okay.

Bell was stronger than she gave herself credit for. But how could he convince her of that? Jeremiah grabbed a glass out of the cabinet, then turned around and stopped. They usually turned the lights out in the den, but they were on. He stepped through the entranceway and crossed the hall.

"Bell?" She was curled up on the den couch—not in his sister's room, after all.

Bella glanced at him. "Miah? What're you doing up?"

"I was going to ask you the same thing."

"I couldn't sleep."

"You want to talk about it?" Jeremiah stopped where he was.

Bella sat up and tucked her legs under her. "I just keep thinking about what happened."

"Oh? Have you remembered something?" Jeremiah sat next to Bella. When he opened her arms, she curled up to him. It was progress. A week ago, she was pulling away from him.

"No." Bella sighed as he wrapped his arms around her, and she snuggled into his body. "I just don't get why me. I don't understand why Petar did it. Or why this other guy keeps coming after me."

"I know, but you have the best people figuring that out. Leave the details to my dad. He's good at his job."

"What if they don't find the other guy?"

That was something he'd discussed with his father. He was certain Dr. Kynaston had spoken about it with him, too, because the two of them already had a plan. Too bad that plan didn't do much to comfort him. "Someone will check on you until they do."

"What do you mean?"

"A patrol car will do drivebys until they catch the guy who vandalized your home and hurt you." Jeremiah had asked his dad about assigning an actual detail to Bell, but his father had told him it wasn't necessary. Jeremiah wasn't so sure about that.

"I don't even know where we're going to stay."

"My dad is supposed to help your parents find a hotel while your house is cordoned off."

"Great. Another place that isn't home." Bella frowned.

"You have your family, and I'm sure they'll do whatever they can to make it warm. Just like I am."

Bella placed a chaste kiss on his cheek. "Thank you."

"For what?"

"Trying to make this as easy as possible on me." Bella curled back up to him and yawned.

Jeremiah leaned his head against hers and rubbed up and down her arm. "Always. Now try and get some sleep."

"Stop telling me what to do," Bella half mumbled, as she snuggled up to him and closed her eyes.

He smiled. Even falling asleep she was stubborn. It was cute as hell. There was only so much he would be able to do to help her deal with the rape and assault. And if a patrol car couldn't be assigned to watch her at all times, maybe there was something he could do instead. Their parents would be the only obstacle—but he'd convinced them to let them date, so he could certainly convince them of this. After all, it was for Bell's own safety.

A soft snore tickled his arm. Good. She had fallen asleep. He gently laid her on the couch and, keeping one arm under her back, readjusted her casted forearm over her belly. Then, slipping his other arm underneath her knees, he scooped her into his arms. Carefully, he carried her down the hall and into his bedroom. He would probably get in trouble for this, but at least this way she'd sleep the last couple hours of the night, and he'd know she was safe.

Slowly, Bella opened her eyes. Where was she? It wasn't her room or Amanda's. But those posters by the window, and the desk pushed up against the wall. Miah's room! How had she gotten here? It didn't matter. It could only mean yesterday wasn't a bad dream. Not ready to face the day, she tugged the midnight blue comforter closer to her chin.

"Good morning, beautiful."

"Does it have to be?"

"I'm afraid so." Jeremiah sat on the bed beside Bella and brushed the hair from her face.

"How did I end up here?"

"I woke up late last night and found you on the couch in the den. We talked and you fell asleep. I didn't want to leave you there."

"What time is it?"

"Six-thirty."

Bella bolted upright. "Oh, my gosh. Do your parents know I'm in your room? I don't want you to get in trouble."

Jeremiah lifted her hand to his lips and kissed it. "Bell, if I do, I do. Right now, I just want to make sure you're taken care of."

Bella buried her face in her hands and mumbled some not very nice things in Brazilian Portuguese. She wasn't directing the slurs at Miah, but at the situation. What had she done?

"Hey. None of that. Listen, don't worry about my parents. I'll deal with them. For now, get up and dressed for school, if you want to go. We can worry about everything else after."

"I'll never forgive myself if I get you in trouble." Bella peeked at him through her fingers.

Jeremiah wrapped his hand around her one good arm and peeled it from her face. "Aren't you forgetting something?"

"What?"

"You were passed out. *I* decided to bring you in here. You needed to sleep, and I made sure you did."

It would be pointless to argue. He was right. Dropping her casted arm in her lap, Bella tilted her head and smiled. "What did I do to deserve a guy like you?"

"You were just you." Miah leaned forward and pressed a tender kiss to her forehead.

It was a small kiss, but warm and loving. Bella nibbled on her bottom lip. Sometimes, she longed for more, for their lips to entangle with one another's. Her heart raced at the image. But she shook the thought away. As much as she dreamt of more, it might never happen. A couple of monsters made sure of that.

Jeremiah raised an eyebrow. "Um, Mom said to check with Mandy on clothes. She might have some you can borrow."

"Yeah, okay, I'll do that." With a deep inhale and exhale, Bella scooted back and threw the comforter aside.

Offering a hand, Jeremiah stood and helped her out of bed. "You okay?"

She smiled and nodded. No way she was opening that cage of butterflies.

"Yeah, I'm good."

"All right." Opening the bedroom door, he stepped to the side, and Bella headed into the hallway. She was as good as she could be, she thought. It would get better. Once both of her attackers were in jail. Taking another breath, Bella crossed the hall and, with a quick rap on the door, cracked it open. Amanda was decent. Good.

Bella walked in and shut the door behind her. "Hey."

"Where did you come from?" Amanda peered at Bella's reflection in the mirror.

"I ... um ..." Bella pressed her lips together. How much should she admit? Not as if they had done anything wrong.

Amanda crossed her arms. "You were in his room, weren't you?"

"Um ..." Ignore it. No need to state the obvious. *Just let me get through this in one piece.* "Your mom said you might have some clothes I could borrow."

"Unbelievable. I bet he doesn't get in trouble, either."

"Clothes?"

"Yeah. We're about the same size. Come look."

Bella scanned the closet. Mini-skirt after mini-skirt. No way, no how. And shorts. Aha! Jeans. Those would work.

Amanda grabbed a pair of shoes from the closet floor and shuffled to the dresser. She opened a drawer and tossed a pair of underwear on the bed. "You'll have to take the tag off, but at least I haven't worn these yet. Borrow shoes, too, if you need."

"Thanks."

"Sure." Amanda slid the ballet flats on her feet and left the bedroom.

Bella breathed a sigh of relief when the door closed behind Amanda. Finally. Some time alone. Exactly what the doctor ordered. She glanced at her purse on the floor next to the air mattress. Clothes could wait. She scanned the room for a bottle of water, something to drink. Nothing. Hell, she'd swallow it dry. She dug out the brand-new bottle of painkillers from her purse. One would be enough for now. Popping the pill in her mouth, Bella returned to the closet.

Sorting through the blouses, she found a white, ruffled, button-up tank and a pair of dark blue skinny jeans. Satisfied, she quickly got dressed and picked up a pair of white ballet flats to complete the outfit. As comfortable as she could be in the circumstances, Bella headed to the kitchen.

"Good morning. Come in and have some breakfast. I made pancakes." Jeremiah's mother smiled over her big belly.

"Good morning." Hopefully the knots in her stomach couldn't be heard in her voice. She hesitated, then walked toward the little nook where Miah's family ate breakfast and snacks. Thankfully, there was a place beside Miah, so she sat.

Jeremiah's father glanced in her direction. "Your dad called this morning."

"Is everything okay?"

"Yes. He found a hotel for you guys. He wants you to go to school, if you're up for it, and your mother will pick you up at lunchtime." Jeremiah's dad sat down with a plate of pancakes.

"A hotel?"

Jeremiah's mother placed a plate in front of Bella. "They can't begin to clean up the mess until it's been released. And even then, furniture replacement will take time."

"Yeah." Bella stared at the pancakes. They looked really good, golden and fluffy, but her stomach continued to do somersaults. Still, they had all been so nice, and she refused to be rude.

Jeremiah's mom rested a hand on Bella's shoulder. "Don't worry. It'll be okay."

"We'll do everything we can to find out who this guy is," Jeremiah's dad added, then shoved a bit of syrup-drenched pancake in his mouth.

"Were any of the neighbors helpful?"

"No. Nobody heard or saw anything."

"Was it ... was it my other attacker?" It had to be. The scar. The monster's scar was the only thing she could remember. Every time she closed her eyes, she saw the damn thing. Sheriff Detrone wasn't working her case, but he was kept apprised of everything, right? Bella eyed the pancakes. She didn't need Miah's father to confirm what she knew in her heart. Lifting her gaze back to the sheriff, she frowned. "It was him. Wasn't it?"

Jeremiah stared at Bell as he handed over her math book. It was strange to see her in Mandy's jeans—yesterday and again today—instead of the usual modest skirts she wore. Not that clothes made the—

"What?"

"I asked if we needed to go by your locker before lunch."

"Oh. Yeah. Sorry."

Reaching out, Bella gently squeezed his hand. "What's going on? I feel like you've been on another planet all day."

All day? That was a little dramatic. Then again, his brain had been churning out all kinds of images … Not that the jeans were very tight. And the blouse wasn't much different than what she normally had on. Except the sleeves were shorter. He wondered if this was going to be a new look for her. Actually, she looked … happy. The happiest he had seen her in the last few weeks.

"I'm sorry. You're right. I guess I'm just getting used to the new look."

"Oh." Bella's gaze dropped as she tugged at the hem of the floral top.

Insert foot into mouth. Jeremiah looked toward the sky. There had to be an idiot sign around somewhere. "I don't mean you look bad."

"But you don't mean I look good either."

"No, that's not what I'm saying." Shit. Could he get a redo? "Bell, you're beautiful. You could wear a potato sack, and you'd be gorgeous."

Bella tilted her head. "You think I'm beautiful?"

Jeremiah tucked a loose strand of hair behind her ear. "I think you're breathtaking. With every smile, the sun rises. When you laugh, the earth stops just so it can listen. My world is a better place with you in it."

"I can't imagine mine without you, either." Bella's smile lit up the hallway.

Jeremiah laced his fingers through hers. She didn't flinch. Her smile just brightened. Now was definitely the time. "I'm glad, because …" Man, he was nervous. It was like asking her out for the first time, only worse.

"Because what?"

Jeremiah inhaled softly. It was now or never.

"¿Você faria o regresso a casa comigo?"

"What?" Bella's eyes widened.

"Crap. Did I not say it right? Hold on, let me—"

Beaming, she rocked up onto her tiptoes and kissed him on the cheek. "You said it perfectly. And yes, I will go to homecoming with you."

Jeremiah hugged her close—but gently. He wanted to spin her around, but her ribs were still healing. "You just made this the best day ever."

"I agree. Now, what do you say we go to lunch?"

"My locker first, then lunch." Taking her hand, they started down the mostly empty hallway.

Bella cocked her head towards him. "But when did you learn Portuguese?"

Jeremiah grinned. His secret weapon. "I didn't. Your mom was nice enough to teach me a few key phrases."

"My mom? Has been teaching you?"

"Yes. She offered to help." Though he did have to endure an entire lesson on the difference between Portuguese spoken in Brazil and the Portuguese spoken in Portugal. He had no idea the dialects weren't the same. Jeremiah sighed, remembering.

Bella giggled. "She got on a soapbox, didn't she? I'm sorry. I know I shouldn't laugh. What other phrases did she teach you?"

"Eu gosto de você." Telling Bell he liked her in Portuguese probably would've been the best way to start the conversation. If only his foot hadn't gotten in the way.

"Oh." Bella paused. "I like you, too," she said, with a grin that matched his.

Bella kissed Jeremiah's cheek. "Someone will send you a picture of the dress."

"Promise?"

"Yes, but I'm late. I have to go or Alex and Mandy will leave without me."

Bella waved goodbye as she ran down the hall and out to the parking lot. She had no idea what one wore to a homecoming dance. Not to mention that wearing Amanda's clothes was inspiring a change of style in her—but she still fancied something on the modest side. These two friends were definitely the perfect combo of clothes advisors for her. Alex understood limits, and Amanda understood style.

Out of breath, Bella stumbled to a halt in front of the car.

"Glad you could finally make it." Amanda crossed her arms.

Alex shook her head and looked sternly at Bella and at Amanda. "Next time, we go dress shopping way in advance. I can't believe we're doing this the day before the dance. Everyone, get in the car."

Bella grinned and climbed into the backseat.

"Do you know what you're looking for?" Amanda glanced back at Bella.

"Not really. I liked the sundress Alex picked out for me, but I wasn't sure if homecoming required something fancier."

Amanda nodded. "Are you comfortable with strapless?"

Bella rubbed her temples and pushed away the onslaught of a headache. Strapless? She had no idea. Until a few days ago—until she'd been dressing from Amanda's closet—she'd dressed so modestly. She had believed in the virtue of modesty. But modesty hadn't stopped the attack.

Bella shrugged. "I don't know. But I don't want to wear a jacket this time."

"I'm sure we can find something. I wonder ... purple would look really good with your dark skin. A deep purple, not a lavender. And I'd like to put you in a straight cut. Accentuate your natural curves." Amanda narrowed her eyes and tapped a finger against her cheek.

"As long as I'm comfortable."

Alex glanced at Bella in the rearview mirror. "We'll pick out a few things, and she can decide from there."

Amanda nodded. "Sounds like a plan."

"What about you, Mandy? What are you looking for?"

Amanda half-shrugged, as if her choice of dress, or the dance, didn't matter. "Vick and I are just going as friends," she said, then folded her arms a bit too defensively and faced forward.

Bella raised her brow, opened her mouth, then closed it. Mandy and Vick's relationship wasn't her business. At the moment, she had a dress to fret over.

Bella and Amanda, with Alex providing support, had shopped for nearly two hours and still hadn't found dresses. Now, seated in the food court with her friends, sipping from bottles of water and munching pretzels (Alex, salted; Amanda, unsalted; and Bella, cinnamon), Bella scanned their surroundings.

"Hey. What about that store?" she said, pointing. "Drop Top."

Alex nodded, and Amanda said, "Okay. At this point, I'd check a thrift store."

Bella popped the last of her pretzel in her mouth, and the three tossed their trash and walked over to Drop Top.

Amanda almost immediately pulled a black and red dress off one of the racks and held it up to herself. "I'm gonna try this on."

"Cool." Alex turned back to the racks, and Bella tagged along behind her.

After about ten minutes, though, Bella was at the point of giving up. This, like most stores carried a size twelve, but even the twelves didn't always accommodate her full-figured body. She had curves and bigger boobs. Not like Alex, who was probably a size four. Amanda had the same figure as Bella, but she had a little more muscle—and more confidence.

A pair of fingers snapped her out of her head. "What—? Oh, wow. Do you think I can pull it off?"

"Try it on, and let's see."

Bella hesitated as Alex offered the hanger to her, then accepted it and walked toward the back. She paused when Amanda stepped out in a strapless dress with a red top and black skirting. A black curlicue design was embroidered into the red top. The black skirting was made of layers upon layers of tulle. It looked great on Amanda.

Amanda grinned. "I know. Perfect for me, right?"

"It's amazing." Bella grinned. Then her gaze drifted to the dress in her hand. Was she really going to try it on? It probably wouldn't look half as good as Amanda's.

"And I see you have one that'll be just as terrific. Go. Try it on. I want to see." Amanda shoved Bella into the inner sanctum of dressing rooms.

Bella went into one of the dressing rooms, hung the dress on a hook, and removed her own clothes, well aware, after trying on so many dresses that day, that this was her last hope. Slipping the dress off the hanger, she shimmied into it and pulled up the side zipper. Unfortunately, there wasn't a mirror in the room. She had to use the one out there. Where everyone could see. Brushing her hands down the soft silk, she took a deep breath, then poked her head out. Nobody waited. Good. Uncertainly, she stepped through the doorway to the three-way mirror.

"Wow. You look gorgeous." Sarresh grinned.

Bella twisted around to face her friend. They hadn't spoken a lot since she'd been released from the hospital. But here she was.

"B, I've never seen you in something like that, but I swear it's like the dress was made for you." Sarresh dropped a hand to her pregnant belly. She was bigger than the last time they ran into one another.

Bella turned around and studied her reflection in the mirror. The silky material clung to her curves. It was the deep purple Amanda had recommended. The dress crossed her chest and melded into a single shoulder strap, with a ruffle that went all the way down to her hips.

The dress made Bella feel beautiful. Despite the fact that it only had one strap, it covered everything that mattered—and she loved it. She bit her bottom lip, turned back to Sarresh and smiled. "You think so?"

"Yes." Sarresh nodded. "Whoever he is, he's lucky."

Then, Amanda and Alex emerged from between two racks.

Amanda gasped. "Holy shit."

Alex stepped up beside Amanda. "Wow."

With a thumbs up, Sarresh slipped between Amanda and Alex and left.

"What did she want?" Alex, asked, hooking a thumb over her shoulder.

"Nothing." Alex was Bella's best friend, but when it came to Sarresh, she was a bit judgmental—so Bella hadn't told Alex, yet, about her reconnection with Sarresh.

Ignoring the slight tension in the air, Amanda pulled out her phone. "Does this mean I can take a picture and send it to my brother?"

Bella had promised to have a picture sent. But … "No. I said a picture of the dress. Not me in the dress. Let me get out of it, and then you can take a picture."

Bella headed back into the dressing room. It took a bit more time to get out of the dress than into it. Damn cast was in the way. But she could do it. She wasn't a little girl who needed rescuing, but a young woman who could take care of herself. Or so she believed.

seventeen

"You're absolutely gorgeous tonight."

"Thank you. You clean up quite well, yourself." Bella grinned as she placed her casted arm on Vick's shoulder and set her hand in his. She'd never thought of him as handsome. Tonight, though, she could see why girls fawned over him. The black slacks and coat, with the red button-up and matching checkered tie, suited him. Funny, how the colors matched Amanda's dress.

"Nice of you to say. But you're the one everyone's been talking about all night."

"Really?"

"Yes." Vick smiled.

"What'd they say?"

"Mostly, how they can't believe the things Heather called you. You smoked all those old thoughts out of their brains."

Bella laughed quietly. "And to think I didn't dress for any of them."

"Who'd you dress for?"

"Myself, mostly, but Miah, too."

Vick nodded. "I'm glad to hear that. I hope you know I'm happy for you. He's a good guy and lucky to have you."

"I appreciate that. It means a lot to me to have you in my corner."

She and Vick hadn't agreed on a lot, lately. But it helped to have his support when it came to Miah. There was little she was certain of these days. Her feelings for Miah? She liked him. A lot. She just didn't trust how much she wanted to act on them.

"B, I'll always be in your corner. It's what brothers are for."

Jeremiah tapped Vick on the shoulder. "Mind if I cut in?"

Vick paused mid-step and released his hold on Bella. "She's all yours." With a grin, Vick bowed and excused himself.

"Hi." Miah lifted Bella's casted arm to his shoulder and took her free hand in his own. "Hope that was okay. I kind of wanted to share the last dance with you."

"Absolutely." Bella stared into his emerald green eyes. She liked it when he gazed back at her the way he was. When he looked at her like that, she could easily imagine their lips entangled in one another. She swallowed. If only her body was on the same page.

"You okay?"

Aside from the bile trying to climb up her throat, she was great. Bella nodded and rested her head against his chest, focusing on the sound of his heartbeat. It thumped nice and steady.

After a minute, Miah looked at her again. "What do you say we get out of here before the song ends and people dash for the door?"

Bella lightly brushed her fingers down his neck. "Okay."

Jeremiah laced his fingers through Bella's. They crossed the dance floor, and he held the door open for her before anyone had the opportunity to stop them. Once outside, he paused. "Thanks, Bell. I really had a great time."

"Me, too." The night had been special. One she would never forget. Bella rested her head against Jeremiah's shoulder. "Do you mind if we take the long way back? I know the dance is ending, but I'm not quite ready to go home."

"I think I can manage that. Why don't you stay here, and I'll go get the car?"

The hairs on the back of her neck prickled. Bella tightened her grip on Jeremiah's hand.

"Wait."

"What's wrong?"

"I don't know. I just ... I got this strange feeling. Like we're being watched or something."

Pulling her close, Miah scanned the parking lot. "I don't see anything. But if it'll make you feel better, we'll walk to the car together."

"Okay." Hand in hand, they started toward the Dodge—just as a black car peeled out and raced toward them.

Jeremiah grabbed Bella and they fell backwards together as the car nearly clipped them. "Are you okay?"

Bella eased up to sitting and checked herself. The dress might be a little dirty, otherwise she was unharmed. Miah had softened the fall. She stared in the direction the car disappeared.

"Yes," she said. "I'm okay."

Brushing himself off, Miah got to his feet and helped her up. "Are you sure? 'Cause you look like you've seen a ghost."

"No, yeah. I just ... I think I've seen that car before."

Gervasio swerved to keep from hitting the stop sign as he exited the parking lot. The tires screeched, and he narrowly missed the curb.

Dammit!

The two of them had stood too close together. He had gunned the car too slow. Or maybe too fast. How had his girl known he was there? She had stayed right beside the monkey, instead of letting him go off to get his car on his own, as Gervasio had counted on.

At least the piece of shit reacted at the right time. Otherwise he would've hit his girl. And that wasn't part of the plan. He wanted her in one piece.

He slammed his hands against the steering wheel. Shit! Shit! Shit!

If he hadn't gone all cave-man at her house a few days ago, he could've grabbed her then. Not only had he lost it in her bedroom, he'd attacked one of his own men.

This wasn't working. At the rate he was going, he'd lose his damn mind before he had his girl in his arms. Gervasio growled.

There was a better solution. But how long would he have to wait? When would be the best time? Didn't she have an event coming up in the next few weeks? Yes. That annual fall thing. A slow grin settled on Gervasio's face.

It would be perfect.

"No." Bella Kynaston shook her head emphatically.

Russell dug his elbows into his thighs as he leaned forward. He hadn't expected her to jump at the suggestion, but he was surprised she'd flat out turned it down. "Miss Kynaston, I need you understand. A protective detail is in your best interest."

"No. I'm not going to stop living my life."

This was just wrong. Another attempt had been made on her life two days ago, and she wasn't taking it seriously. Russell dragged a hand down his face. How could he convince her it was necessary?

"I don't expect you to stop living your life. I just think someone should accompany you wherever you go."

"I'm not going to have officers following me like lost puppies. This has been hard enough to deal with. Especially with the whole town knowing what happened. Having a protection detail would make it ten times worse."

"You wouldn't even know they're there. They would blend in with the crowd." They had officers' young enough to pass for high school students. There were a few he trusted to keep her safe.

"Yeah. Because that would go over so well with Principal Owen." Her words dripped with sarcasm. Then the young woman bolted to her feet. "I don't know how many different ways I can say this. The answer is no." She stomped out of the den, down the hall, and slammed her bedroom door.

Straightening, Russell looked at her parents. Surely, they understood his position. Not that either had said anything to back him up. But this unknown perp was not going to give up. And, unfortunately, they weren't any closer to discovering his identity. Until they could find that out and put him behind bars, her life would continue to be in jeopardy.

"Is there anything you can do to convince her?"

Dr. Kynaston glanced to his wife and sighed. "We'll talk to her, but I'm afraid she won't change her mind."

Like it or not, Russell couldn't force a protection detail on the girl. He could put a couple of officers undercover at her school to trail her, however. May not be the wisest idea, but it was better than leaving her to fend for herself.

Russell got to his feet. "Please try. Let me know if she accepts the detail."

"Of course. Thank you, Detective Russell." Dr. Kynaston extended his hand and the two shook hands.

Bella pushed open the doors and headed into the church auditorium. There was still so much work to do and only a little over two weeks to get it together. Good thing she arrived early and had some time to herself. Or so she thought.

Music exploded from the auditorium speakers. Annoyed at not being alone, Bella looked down toward the orchestra. It was David, sitting at the piano, playing as if he was one with the instrument. Maybe this was divine intervention or a coincidence. Either way, she owed him an apology for the way she handled the tutor thing, and this gave her a perfect chance.

Heading further down the aisle, she crossed her arms and paused to listen. He played beautifully. As the notes seeped into her brain, she found herself allowing her arms to drop to her sides. The music wasn't just beautiful, it was relaxing.

Then the tune changed … and goosebumps crawled up her arms, the hair on the nape of her neck stood on end, and the air around her thickened. With a swallow, she forced her body to breathe. If she didn't know better, she'd swear something was coming at her. She scanned the auditorium. No one but her and David. Nothing seemed out of the ordinary.

Suddenly, the music stopped, and whatever had taken hold of her released its grip. She sucked in air as if she was taking her first breaths of life. What just happened? How could such exquisite music freeze her body like that?

She shook off the sensation and walked toward the piano.

"Bella. What are you doing here?"

"I had things to take care of for the Festival."

"Oh, right." David stared down at the black-and-white keys.

"What was that you were playing?"

"I wasn't really playing anything, just messing around."

"Well, it was … good." Bella surveyed the theater. Still nothing.

David shrugged. "Thanks."

"Would you play something else for me?" Bella headed into the orchestra area. She stood next to the piano and held up her casted forearm. "I'd do it myself, but I'm kind of limited."

"Oh, right. Um, what would you like me to play?"

"You know "Bring Me to Life," by Evanescence?"

"I'm afraid not, but I can play something else." David splayed his fingers atop the keys and dropped his gaze again.

"I'm sorry." They both blurted simultaneously.

Bella grinned. Not what she expected. It wasn't like he had anything to apologize for.

She opened her mouth, but David rushed to speak.

"It's okay," he said. "I'm the one who should apologize. I was acting like a selfish brat. I guess ... you just seemed to be handling the rape so well. I figured you'd jump right back into tutoring like it was nothing."

Bella bit her tongue. She'd fooled a lot of people into thinking she was fine. She'd survived. What if one of her attackers turned out to be someone she knew and trusted? What if one of them was still out on the street? Breaking into her home? Leaving her presents? Destroying her bedroom? Trying to kill her? None of it mattered. Not. One. Single. Bit.

"Hey, you okay?"

"Huh? Oh, yeah. Fine." Turning away, Bella wiped at the tears in the corners of her eyes. "I have some, um, stuff to do in the, um, office. I'll—"

"Hey, B, come on. Just talk to me."

No. She was done talking. It was all anyone wanted anymore. The police. Her parents. Her friends. Miah. They all demanded she talk to them. Bella headed toward the staircase to the stage. "I said I'm fine."

"Bullshit." David chased after her and grabbed her good arm. "Tell me what's going on."

"Let me go." He didn't deserve the truth. He said it himself. This had all been about him being selfish. All he had thought about was what he wanted. What was it with the guys in her life? Did they all feel like she somehow owed them?

Bella yanked at her arm, but he tightened his grip.

"David, you're hurting me. Let me go!"

"Not until you talk to me." His grip twisted and tightened again.

"Ow! David—"

Jeremiah, seemingly from nowhere, inserted himself between David and Bella and forced David to release his hold. "She said to let go."

Bella rubbed her arm. At least it wasn't the other one.

"This doesn't involve you." David tried to reach around Jeremiah for Bella.

"Stay away from her." Jeremiah thrust David backward and glanced to ensure Bella remained safely behind him.

"Excuse me. This is between me and her. Now, get out of my way."

David pushed forward and Jeremiah pushed him back. No way in hell was he letting Bell get hurt again. She was still healing and this douche-bag was way too aggressive for his taste.

Then, David shoved him, and Jeremiah stumbled a few steps. Out of his periphery, he saw Bell jump forward. Holding his arm out, he stopped her. Keeping an eye on the asshole, he said, "Go to the pastor's office. I'll be right behind you."

"Okay," Bella said quietly, and then walked away.

"Do you have any idea what you're doing?" David pointed to Bella's back.

Jeremiah planted his feet and locked his stare on the shit-bag in front of him. What had just happened? It had been written all of her face. Fear. Disbelief. Something had happened between her and this pile of shit.

He needed to find out, but Bell needed him to keep his cool. As much as this good-for-nothing deserved a beat down, he wouldn't provide it. Not today. "I know exactly what I'm doing. And if you know what's good for you, you will leave her alone, like she asked."

"And if I don't, you'll do what exactly?"

"I'll kick your ass sideways and back. Now, do yourself a favor and go take a breather."

David ground his jaw and his nostrils flared. Then he shook his head and stepped back. "Fine. But not because you asked me to."

Bella picked up one of the fortune cookies. "I talked to Mitchell last night."

"The little kid that was being abused by his father and beat you up?" Jeremiah paused mid-reach.

Bella nodded.

"How did that go?"

"Weird. Interesting. Mostly, we talked about other things, but we did go back to that day. He apologized again, but I told him there was no need. He had done enough apologizing. I just wish it hadn't taken me so long to forgive him."

"But you did forgive him. That's what's important. Is he coming for a visit?"

"Yeah. Over Christmas break. We made tentative plans to hang out. I mean, I don't know what to expect, but I think it'll be okay." Bella broke her cookie in half and pulled out the fortune. What the hell? It was blank. She passed the paper across the table.

Miah took it and frowned. "Isn't that supposed to be bad luck?"

"I don't think so. If my memory serves, it's supposed to be, like, a wild card."

"Which means what?"

"If I pick a second cookie and the fortune is bad, this cookie overrides it, but if it's good, the new one will come true. But I prefer to see it as we make our own fortune. Kind of like fixing our own messes." Bella grinned.

Miah picked up the other cookie and opened it. He grimaced.

"What does it say?"

"Days of distress have yet to come."

Bella ate the last of her cookie. "What kind of fortune is that?"

"One I have no intention of helping along." He tossed the cookie back on the plate with a couple of bills. "All right. You ready to go?"

"Yeah."

Jeremiah stood and helped Bella out of her chair. Fingers entwined, they headed out the door of the Chinese restaurant and crossed the parking lot. But Jeremiah stopped when they were a few feet away from the Dodge.

"What is it?" Bell asked him.

"Stay here." Miah walked to the car, and Bella saw him pause at the front passenger side tire. He knelt down and felt over a spot, then stood, eyes scrunched up and forehead wrinkled. Quickly, he returned to Bella's side, wrapped an arm around her waist, tucked her close, and dug out his phone.

"Miah, what's going on?"

"The tires have been slashed and the door's been spray-painted," he said, before punching in a number.

"What?" Bella shivered. There were only a few scattered lamps along the street, and the lot was practically empty. As he spoke to his father, she burrowed deeper into Miah's arms. Why would someone damage the car and strand them there? Unless that person planned to cause them harm. It wasn't like they were in the best part of town. Desemper Ridge was known for ... accidents.

"Thanks, Dad." Jeremiah placed his phone back in his pocket and gave Bella a reassuring squeeze. "He's going to send a squad car to pick us up and one to investigate. And a tow truck. They can examine the car at the station."

Gently, Jeremiah led Bella to a nearby bench. They sat, and he draped an arm around her shoulders and drew her to him.

"But—?" Bella stopped before asking who could have done it. Miah knew as well as she did that her attacker was still out there. But this seemed so minimal compared to all the guy had already done. The destruction to her body. The near miss last week with the car. So, maybe it wasn't him. Maybe it was Heather getting back at her. Heather wasn't the type to let things go.

Bella tucked herself even closer to Miah, grasping at the bubble of protection he offered. It helped, but goosebumps still crawled all over her body and forced another shiver.

"You cold?"

"No. I'm freaked out."

Jeremiah placed a finger under Bella's chin, tilted her face up to his, and placed a soft kiss on her nose. "I'm right here, and I won't let anything happen to you."

"Promise?"

"Absolutely."

Comforted, the question she hadn't asked popped out. "Do you think Heather could've done this?"

"Maybe. Or she could've convinced David to do it. He is her brother. And he doesn't particularly like me."

True. David didn't like Miah, and Heather hated Bella. And Heather had concocted more schemes than Bella could remember over the last two years. But it could also be her unknown attacker, too. That worried her more than if it was Heather.

Before she could say anything else, Jeremiah caressed her arm and pointed. "Come on. Looks like our ride is here."

"Did she see what it said?"

"No. I kept her away from that side of the car."

Back off, She's mine. Those were the words the vandal had left. Jeremiah knew they weren't meant for Bell. They were a message. To him.

He looked to his father. "Is there any way you can get prints or something off the car?"

"They aren't going to find anything on the tires. Their texture doesn't hold prints. But if something was left on the rims or on the doors, my people will find it."

His dad leaned closer. "You have any thoughts who could've done this? I know you think it's her other rapist. But I have to look at all possibilities."

Jeremiah slouched against the back of the couch. Part of him hoped it was her rapist. Another part of him prayed it wasn't. He hoped it wouldn't cause any friction, but he had to put the name out there. "David Warren. The guy doesn't exactly like me."

"Okay." His father sat up straight. "Why do you think he would've vandalized the car?"

"He and I nearly got into a fight a few days ago. I'd just gotten to the church for rehearsal, and I see he's got ahold of Bell. Dad, she was trying to get away from him."

Bell had asked him to dismiss what he'd seen, but he couldn't forget the sight of the bruise that asshole left on her arm. Nothing Jeremiah said convinced her to report it. And he'd promised to keep his trap shut. Tonight changed that.

"Why didn't you tell me about this before?"

Jeremiah scowled. He should've never told her he wouldn't say anything. Her safety was all he cared about. If something happened—no. He couldn't even go there. "I told Bell I wouldn't. She insisted it was a misunderstanding."

"Damn it, Jeremiah." His father shook his head. "We didn't raise you to keep secrets."

"I'm sorry, Dad. I thought I was doing the right thing, respecting her wishes." He hadn't considered any of the consequences. Not that it made a difference. David had caused her physical harm.

Jeremiah sighed. "I'm trying to do whatever I can to help her."

"I know you are, son. Keeping secrets isn't the way to do it." His father reached out and squeezed his shoulder. "Now, tell me everything that happened the other day."

eighteen

Heather slapped Bella across the face so hard Bella fell back into the lockers and dropped her backpack. "You bitch! How dare you!"

Fuck! That hurt. Bella rubbed her burning cheek. And her shoulder throbbed, too. Damn. Why did it have to be the bad one?

Heather was right in her face. "I don't care that you accused me of slashing your damn tires, but you accused my brother! What the hell is wrong with you?"

"I didn't accuse you or your brother of anything," Bella protested.

Heather slapped Bella across the face again. "Liar!"

Students gathered around the two girls in silent anticipation of a fight. Bella kept her mouth shut and considered the implications of continuing the conversation. Her parents had encouraged her to speak openly with Detective Russell—so she had mentioned all the scenarios she and Miah'd considered regarding the attack on the Dodge. Including David's recent argument with Jeremiah. She hadn't wanted the discussion to become public knowledge, though. Crouching down, she lifted her backpack over her good shoulder, and turned away from the girl. This was one of those moments where the right thing was simply to leave.

But Heather wouldn't let it go. "This isn't over," she shouted, grabbing Bella's arm.

Bella tugged herself free from Heather's grip as gently as she could, but Heather balled up her fist and stepped back, preparing to lunge.

Before she could make another move, David appeared and grappled his sister from behind, lifting her off her feet. "Calm down, sis. This won't help anything."

"Put me down!" Heather struggled to get free from David's grip.

Jeremiah shoved his way through the crowd and stopped beside Bella. "You okay?"

"I'm okay." That wasn't entirely true. Her cheek burned like hell; her arm stung where Heather had grabbed it. Plus, there was a twinge in her shoulder like nobody's business—and her pride was pretty much shredded.

Jeremiah turned to David, who had his hands full restraining Heather. "Get her the hell out of here, or the next time the cops show up at your doorstep, it'll be to arrest her for assault."

Heather glared at Jeremiah. "If your little bitch —"

David whispered something in Heather's ear and waited for her to take three deep breaths. Once she had, he searched the crowd, nodded to an athletic-looking guy that Bella didn't know, and set Heather on her feet. "Jimmy, walk her to her car, please."

"Sure." Jimmy slipped his arm in Heather's and pulled her away from the scene.

After Heather disappeared, the crowd followed, leaving David, Bella, and Jeremiah to sort things out.

Bella waited, and finally, David spoke. "I'm really sorry about that. I guess she was still worked up. I tried to tell her you weren't to blame."

"You need to keep your sister away from Bell," Miah said, stepping between Bella and David.

David held up his hands. "I'll do what I can. Again, I'm really sorry. I understand if you feel you have to press charges."

Bella maneuvered around Jeremiah. He was doing his protective thing, but she had two feet, and she could stand on them. "No. It ... it isn't necessary."

"Bell, are you sure?" Jeremiah wrapped an arm around her shoulders.

Ow. Bella grimaced. That stung. Her shoulder needed ice—now. But all she said was, "Yeah. I just want to go home." She turned to Miah. "Can we just go?"

Miah kissed her forehead. "Let's get out of here." He slipped an arm around her waist. They headed for the doors toward the parking lot. Miah's parents had rented a car, which he was driving until the Dodge was repaired.

"Did the police find anything?" Bella asked.

"No. There weren't any prints."

"There weren't?" Detective Russell had told her about the message painted on the car door. The message didn't make sense if Heather was behind it, and she'd really hoped Heather or David had been behind it. Then again, it could've been David. If he was trying to get Miah out of the picture. But if it wasn't, that left only one other option—her attacker. He was still out there. Bella shivered. This wasn't over.

David flung open his twin's bedroom door. He was hot with fury, and the thud of the door slamming into the wall resounded loudly.

Heather, who'd been lying down reading a magazine, jumped. "What the —"

David stepped to the bed and backhanded her across the cheek. Then, glowering at her, he shoved his finger in her face. "What is wrong you with!?"

"I just did what you asked!" Heather flipped her blue-black hair back and caressed her cheek. "That hurt."

"Good! It should hurt. I told you to make some noise, but at no point did I say a goddamned thing about hitting Bella. What the hell were you thinking?"

"That it needed to look real."

David grasped the back of his thick neck tightly and started pacing. This was a bad idea. His sister hadn't found any dirt on Jeremiah, so she had convinced him to make some. Plotting with his sister was the dumbest thing he could've done. He obviously hadn't thought it through.

"It wasn't part of the plan."

"It made you look good, didn't it?"

"That isn't the point."

Heather rolled her eyes. "Oh, please. You being her freaking hero is the point. If we'd gone with the plan I suggested, this wouldn't be a problem."

Originally, Heather had proposed he show up at the restaurant, leave shortly after Bella and Jeremiah, and offer them a ride when he saw them sitting there stranded. One coincidence would've been acceptable. That many coincidences and he would've been in the line of fire.

"I told you it would look too suspicious. It worked out the way it should have, and nothing can prove we were involved."

But how were the tires to be slashed. He hadn't bothered to ask, then. Maybe he should, now. "By the way, how did you manage the tires?"

"Someone I know took care of it." Heather stood and walked to her dresser. As she checked out her cheek, she tugged a brush through her hair.

David folded his arms. She was hiding something. She'd been doing that a lot lately. Hiding things.

"Who?"

Heather groaned, dropped the brush on the dresser, and spun on her brother. "Christ! You don't know him. All you need to know is the ball is rolling and, before long, you'll have your tramp. Got it?"

"I don't like this."

"Yeah, well, you can't stop it. Deal with it."

David snarled. His relationship with his sister had been damaged a long time ago, but if anything happened to Bella ... well, "damaged" wouldn't cover what he would do. "Fine, but she better not get hurt. Or we'll have issues like you can't begin to imagine."

"Careful, bro. Your true colors are showing." Heather smirked and walked away, leaving David standing alone in her room.

David stared at the wall in front of him. He knew Heather could be devious, but she hadn't revealed anything to him. If he opened up to the authorities about his and Heather's involvement, Bella wouldn't look at him ever again. Any hope he had of being with her would be destroyed. For now, he would just have to keep his mouth shut.

He left Heather's room and headed down the hall to his own.

Russell dug through the pictures from the ten-year-old Caprise rape case. Just as he thought, both Gabriella Caprise and Bella Kynaston had been marked with the crisscrossed scythes. Both branded. Gabriella on her chest, Bella on her neck. And the fingerprints were an exact match.

There were only these two related cases in Rescate County. But maybe ...

Russell typed in a search and expanded it to include the entire state, but was interrupted by a quick knock at his desk.

"Finally got what you're looking for." Assistant District Attorney Perez held out a file.

Smirking, Russell reached for it. "It must be good if you're hand delivering it." He opened the manila folder and smiled. About damn time. Petar Jacobs' unsealed juvenile record. Russell scanned the content, pausing at the information about who Jacob had been arrested with. Talk about a familiar name.

"Must be your birthday, the way you're grinning."

"It feels like it!" Russell pulled out the bottom drawer and skimmed the files. Where was it? Aha. He removed the file folder and flipped through the stack of identification cards for the Grim Reapers. Bingo. Cristobal Rodriguez. A known member of the Grim Reapers. He always thought Petar Jacobs had to be connected to the gang somehow—and here was the link. He had been collared on an assault and battery charge four years ago with Cristobal Rodriguez. Maybe now Jacobs would give up his accomplice in the Kynaston case.

"It's not a smoking gun," he said to the ADA, "but it gives me a new lead."

"Well, hopefully, it will take you to the smoking gun," Perez said. "I'll leave you to it."

Returning to his computer search, Russell found five other cases with a similar MO. All open. He'd have to reach out to the other counties, see if he could get the case files.

Next, he searched Cristobal Rodriguez. Sixteen years old. The kid had been collared almost a year ago on yet another assault and battery charge. Sentenced to one year at the Rescate County Juvenile Detention Center with mandatory counseling. Less than two months remained of his sentence. One brother. Father deceased. Mother resided in Desemper Ridge.

Wait a second. The brother. Gervasio Rodriguez. He sorted through the Grim Reapers information, again.

There! Notes on one Gervasio Rodriguez. Suspected leader of the Grim Reapers. But no confirmed affiliation. No picture. Russell tried another search. Damn. No rap sheet for the guy. Which made sense. If he was the other rapist, his prints would've come up as match to those on the trash-bags. Collecting the files and locking everything up tight, Russell grabbed his jacket and his weapon and badge. "Hey, Simms," he called as he left. "I got a lead on the Kynaston case. If the Sheriff asks, I'm at the detention center."

Gervasio's eyes locked on the architectural schematics of the location of the Fall Harvest Festival. His girl had been working on it nonstop the last few weeks. And it was the perfect place to grab her. Half the town gathered for the festivities every year. It only had one flaw. It was held in a large, wide open space. There was no telling what booth would be where.

Getting up, he walked to the doorway of his office. His soldiers occupied both levels of the warehouse. Sports blared from the television downstairs. Music blasted from the speakers upstairs, where a couple of men stood at opposite ends of the pool table. His gaze settled on the messenger, who leaned over and lined up his next shot.

Gervasio whistled loud enough to be heard over the din. He waited for nothing. Both the stereo and television were turned down.

He stared at Swifty. "Ven aca."

"Si jefe." Swifty handed the cue stick off to one of the other men and descended the staircase.

Gervasio stepped back in his office. The messenger followed without question. "Shut door."

Swifty did. "What's up boss?"

"Have job for *novia*." The messenger's girlfriend had proved handy. She was close enough to his girl not to garner suspicion. And she couldn't be linked back to him, at all. Plus, the girl feared him. Gervasio pointed to the schematics on his desk. "Necesito información del Festival."

"¿Por que?"

Why? None of his men ever questioned his reasons for an assignment. Gervasio's eyelids lowered and he glowered at Swifty. Dropping the broken English, he shoved a finger in the messenger's face. "That is not important. All you need to know is that it is imperative I have these details. Are we clear?"

"Yes, sir."

"Good. Now get out."

His cell rang and Gervasio yanked the thing out of his pocket.

"What?" he barked at his inside man.

"Um, is this a bad time?"

"Speak." One of a few officers he had tucked neatly in his pocket. Best way to keep track of how an investigation progressed. Especially where he was involved.

"Cool, bro. Thought I'd call and let you know I was planning a visit today."

Really? The investigation had finally made its way to his brother. Exactly why he himself anticipated every possible move. Cristobal wouldn't divulge a damn thing about his activities. The attack Gervasio had completed by *verdugo* ensured his brother's silence. "No worry."

"Yeah. I'm glad to hear that. Oh, hey, you still have fingerprint kit I got you for Christmas last year?"

"I see." Gervasio studied his hand. The tips of his fingers were a little red. Healed rather nicely over the last month. So, the detectives found his prints. Wouldn't do them much good if there was nothing to compare them to. A wide grin spread across his face. "Anything else?"

"Yep. Sounds good. I'll talk to you later."

Disconnecting the line, he tucked the cell back in his pocket. It was all going according to plan. Soon, she would be his, and there wasn't a thing anyone could do to stop it.

Jeremiah brushed Bell's cheek with the back of his knuckles. They were cozied up in the backseat of the rental at the drive-in—a relic from the 'fifties and still drawing crowds. "You know I'd tell you if I knew anything, but my dad is keeping pretty tight-lipped about it." The Dodge was still in evidence. But nothing more had come of the investigation.

Bella sighed. "I don't understand why."

"Because he's a parent, and he doesn't want us to worry. Plus, I don't think he can talk about it."

"Yeah." Bell scooted a little closer and rested her head on his chest.

Jeremiah leaned his cheek against the top of her head. She'd dozed off on him the other day. They curled up on the couch in front of the television and within ten minutes she'd been out.

Now he asked, "Have you been sleeping okay?"

He felt her shake her head against his chest. "No. I fall asleep, but at some point, whatever dream I'm having turns into a nightmare. I wake up and can't go back to sleep."

"Have you told your parents?" Jeremiah asked.

"No. And as long as I don't wake up screaming, they don't have to know."

He was afraid of that. She'd refused counseling. Wouldn't talk to anyone about the rape, anymore, or the break-in, or the vandal incident. But maybe she would talk about this.

Jeremiah kissed Bell's forehead. "Will you tell me about the nightmares?"

"I don't really want to talk about it." Bella yawned.

"Not even to me?"

"I just want to forget."

Jeremiah tugged her closer. Comforting her seemed to be all he could do. If he could take the weight off her shoulders, he would. But he was helpless. He couldn't do more than he already— The gift! It was the perfect thing to cheer her up.

Jeremiah leaned forward and pulled a box from under the driver's seat. "Here," he said, and handed it to her. "I was going to wait, but I think you should have it now."

"What is it?"

"Open it."

Bella untied the ribbon, pulled the top off, and stared down uncertainly at the contents of the small box. Then she lifted out her gift and flipped it over to reveal the black glass screen of the cell phone.

"I don't get it. For me?"

The innocence and confusion on her face were absolutely adorable. Jeremiah chuckled. "Yup. Your own phone. I talked to your parents. It's so you can be reached at all times."

Jeremiah took the phone gently from her hands and powered it on. "I already programmed everyone's number in it. Even Alex's. I got it from Mandy."

Bella smiled as the phone chimed and came to life. "Thank you, so much."

"You're welcome, but it's actually pretty self-serving." Jeremiah grinned.

"Now, I can text you." And it would hopefully keep her safe. "I'll show you how to IM, too."

"What's that?" She tilted her head.

So much to learn. The nice part, he was the one who got to teach her. "IM. Basically, it's a way to shorten words to letters."

Bella dropped her gaze. Then, looking up at him with something like trepidation, she asked, "If I texted you at three in the morning, would you answer?"

"As long as I woke up, yes. Now, will you do something for me?"

Bella stifled a yawn. "Of course." Her droopy eyes were so cute.

"I can see you're tired. Curl up against me and sleep."

"Then I'll feel bad."

Jeremiah frowned. "I'll feel bad if you don't. Besides, how can you feel bad when I'm saying it's okay?"

"Are you sure?"

"Absolutely."

Bella yawned and did as he asked, snuggling good and deep. At least he made her feel safe enough to sleep. He might have to figure out a way to sneak out of the house. Something to talk to his sister about. Jeremiah trailed his fingers gently through Bella's hair. And she was out.

Each small table was draped with a red-white-and-green checked cloth and bore a flickering candle that added to the light from the chandelier. It was the pizza parlor where she had her first date with Miah. And there he was. With a smile, she waved and started for the table. Just as she arrived, Jeremiah stood. Believing he intended to pull her into his arms, Bella moved to hug him, but he turned and disappeared into the crowd. She followed, but after a few steps, lost sight of him in the crowd.

Why would he leave without her? The hairs on the back of her neck stiffened and goosebumps traveled up her body. Despite her sudden terror, she continued to search for Miah. Then, she spotted the back of his head at the door. She would know that cropped hair anywhere. He could protect her. She pushed through the throng of patrons, but when she reached the door, he was gone. She spun in circles looking for him. He must have gone outside.

She stepped out and glanced up and down the sidewalk. Even though she didn't know which way he'd gone, she started running, calling his name. Her voice echoed as if she was in a dark and empty cavern. Heart racing, she ran until the familiar became unfamiliar, then became familiar again.

She stopped, lungs heaving. Why did it look so familiar? Oh. She was on her own street, the street where she lived. How had she gotten so far? She glanced over her shoulder. A shadow shifted behind her. Swallowing, she walked toward her house.

No police tape across the door. No sign that read, "Do Not Enter." Nothing to mark the house as a crime scene. Had they finished? Had the house been released? It couldn't have. Her parents would've told her. She checked for anything out of the ordinary. Nothing stood out. Squeezing her hands into fists, she took a deep ragged breath, then stepped onto the pathway and headed up to the front door. She wiggled the knob, and the door opened.

Something was wrong. They never left the door unlocked. Why would the door have opened so easily? Unless ... Was she in a dream? "That has to be it. I'm dreaming. I just need to wake up."

But she didn't wake up. She remained outside her house ... alone. What should she do? Chewing on her bottom lip, she peeked inside.

"Hello?"

No response. She stepped inside. Should she close the door? Or leave it open? As if the house were answering, before she had a chance to decide, the door slammed shut on its own. Whipping around, she grabbed the knob and turned it, but nothing happened.

Bella pounded on the door. "Let me out! Somebody let me out!"

Silence greeted her.

Gasping, she spun around. The only sound she could hear was the beating of her own heart. She swallowed and walked toward the hallway. Her bedroom was just past the living room. If she could make it there, she'd be safe. With each step, Bella searched her surroundings. Nothing jumped out at her—though she kept thinking it would—and she reached her bedroom unscathed. Taking a deep breath, she opened the door and went in.

Everything was in its place. Both her notebook and Bible rested in their usual position on the desk. Her bed was made. The closet remained open, as she'd left it, and her clothes hung in their places. Letting out her held breath, she picked up the Bible and hugged it to her chest. God had protected her. He'd kept her safe.

Without fear, she walked through the rest of the house and found it all untouched, as well. With a smile, she returned to her bedroom ... and then, behind her, the front door banged open.

Her body stiffened. Hadn't the door been locked? Maybe her mom or dad had come home. She started to call for her parents, but before she could make a sound, she heard heavy steps striding toward her room. She struggled to close the door, but stumbled backwards when the door was shoved open to reveal a tan-skinned man with a jagged scar running down his face—who snarled and lunged at her.

Bella screamed and bolted upright. A firm hand on her shoulder caused her to jump. It was just Miah. She collapsed into his arms, sobbing.

"Shh. It's okay. I'm here."

The tears continued. Bella couldn't stop them.

"Did you have another nightmare?"

Bella nodded, then buried her face into Miah's chest. She couldn't keep holding this in. She had to tell him about the dream—but she could only cry. She was still covered in goosebumps and her heart was pounding.

"It's okay. Calm down first, then you can tell me."

Bella nodded again. Slowly her tears dried and her heartbeat slowed. Then, the words poured out of her. "It was a new dream. I went to meet you at the pizza parlor, and as soon as I got to the table, you left. I chased after you and ended up at home. I tried to get out, but I couldn't, and I thought if I got to my room, I'd be okay. Then I heard the door open ... and I saw him. It was him. He came for me."

Miah tightened his hold on her as more tears slipped free. "It's okay. It was just a bad dream. And I'll do whatever it takes to protect you. That's why I got you the phone."

Bella locked her eyes onto his. He fully believed he could protect her. Well, that made one of them. But she knew there was a sandstorm coming. And she wasn't sure anyone—not even Miah—could stop it.

nineteen

"You sure he doesn't— Whoa." Bella leaned toward the passenger side window as Sarresh drove the car around a statue of the Greek goddess Athena. She thought the gates had been awesome. But the house beat the gates, hands down. "Really? You live here?"

"Yeah. I know. Bit of a step up from my parents' house."

"I'll say. This is huge." Bella felt her eyes widen as the house—or was it a mansion? —came into full view. It was three stories and was fronted with several pairs of large, imposing columns. A wide staircase led up to the front doorway.

"Wait until you see the inside."

Bella stared at her friend. If the outside was any indication of the inside … how the hell was she going to find her way around this place? It would take time. Lots of time. But that was a non-issue, according to Sarresh.

"You're positive Mike isn't going to mind my being here?"

"Hey. I told you, it's part of our arrangement."

"I still don't get that. This whole arrangement thing." Bella was dubious. Sarresh hadn't disclosed a whole lot. All she knew about this so-called arrangement was that her friend had been emancipated and now lived with the father of her unborn child. Here. In this mansion.

"There's really not much to get," Sarresh said, breezing by what seemed a pretty big part of her life. "I told you the important stuff. Isn't that what matters?"

Sure, maybe. But they were supposed to be rebuilding their friendship. Shouldn't they share everything in that case? Then again, she hadn't done much on the sharing side, herself. Bella fiddled with the cast on her arm. "Yeah. It is."

"Good." Sarresh parked the car and shut off the ignition. "How about a tour before the movie?"

"Sounds like a plan."

After the nightmare debacle with Miah last night, she'd needed someplace to hide. He'd pushed her to talk to her parents. That was the last thing she wanted to do. Opening up to them about the nightmares would only lead down one road. And she was so not ready to have that conversation—and go down that road. So, she'd called Sarresh.

Bella and Sarresh climbed out of the car and ascended the stairs to the front door. The door swung open before them, and an older man with gray hair and a black suit bowed at the waist. "Welcome home, madam."

"Clark. Thank you." Sarresh walked past the guy like it was no big deal.

As for Bella, she stood there, mouth agape. Was he an honest to God butler? Holy shit. The girl had a butler.

"Madam, please come in."

"Sorry." Bella blurted and walked across the threshold. She got less than ten feet inside and stopped. Whoa. Her eyes travelled up the ornamented staircase to the second-floor landing and on up to the decorated ceiling.

"Clark, can you let Mrs. Adams know we'll be taking some afternoon snacks in the parlor in about an hour?"

"Of course, madam." He bent at the waist again and left the foyer.

Wait. Had Sarresh said parlor? Looking away from the vaulted ceiling, Bella turned toward her friend. "Really. How big is this place?"

"The house itself sits on a half-acre of land."

"Oh. My. God." Crikey. This wasn't a house. It was a frigging palace.

One hand on her pregnant belly, Sarresh gestured down the wide hallway. "Come on. We'll start in the greenhouse."

Jeremiah glanced at his watch. Three p.m. on the dot. According to her text, Bell wouldn't be back for a couple of hours. Seemed like the perfect opportunity to talk to her parents. He took a deep breath as he approached their hotel room door. Now or never. He knocked.

When Mrs. Kynaston opened the door, she smiled and said, "Oh, Jeremiah. I'm sorry, but Bella hasn't returned, yet."

"That's okay. I was hoping I could talk to you and Dr. Kynaston." Bell was going to be pissed at him, but he had to do something. He couldn't stand by while she shut everyone out. The nightmares meant something. Jeremiah rocked back on his heels.

"Of course. Please, come in."

He was off to a good start. But showing up was only half the journey. Jeremiah entered the hotel room and nodded to Dr. Kynaston, who looked up as he stepped into the living room.

"Is everything all right?" Mrs. Kynaston asked.

"I'm not sure." Jeremiah took in the hotel set-up. A small couch against one wall, a chair next to it, TV on the opposite side. Beyond the living room was a kitchen and table. To the right, two bedrooms. A nice suite for the three of them.

Man. How was he supposed to get into this? This wasn't the easiest of conversations. Right. Just jump in. "Has Bell spoken to either of you about the rape, recently?"

Lacing her fingers together, Mrs. Kynaston walked to the couch and sat down beside her husband. "No, she has not. I fear she refuses to speak of the issue with us."

"Has she talked to you about seeing a rape counselor?" Jeremiah dropped into the chair across from Bell's parents.

"Has something occurred?" Dr. Kynaston folded up his newspaper and set it aside.

"She's been having nightmares," Jeremiah replied. "I don't know much about them, except they all seem to center around the rape. Last night, at the movies, she fell asleep for a half hour. Maybe less. And she had a terrible nightmare. I know she has them regularly. But she won't tell me how long ago they started. Except for last night, any time I bring them up, she shuts me down."

His father had told him to be supportive, and eventually Bell would open up. Except she hadn't. Things had only gotten worse since her house had been vandalized. And then there was the car—and the message painted on it, which Bell had found out about from the detective.

Jeremiah dragged a hand over his hair. God, he should've addressed this sooner.

Dr. Kynaston glanced at his wife. "Why has she not spoken of this?"

Jeremiah leaned forward. "I've tried to convince her to talk to someone about the nightmares. A counselor, you guys. She just keeps telling me she doesn't want to discuss it."

"I'm afraid our conversations with her have become ... polite." Mrs. Kynaston sighed. "Perhaps it is time we force the issue."

The elevator dinged and the doors slid open. Bella stepped out and headed down the hallway to the suite she shared with her parents. It wasn't home. Not that home was home anymore, either. Even when they got it back.

Reaching into the pocket of her jeans, she pulled the keycard out and inserted it into the reader. When the door unlocked, she pushed it open and paused. Miah occupied the chair, and her parents sat together on the couch. Was she late? Bella eyed the clock on the table. No. It was just after four. Then he was early.

Letting the door shut behind her, Bella walked all the way in. "Give me a few minutes to ..." She paused. Each of their faces was scrunched up. Like somebody died. Oh, shit. Had something happened? "What—?"

"Have a seat, Bell." Miah stood and offered her his chair.

"Okay." What the hell was going on? Taking the seat, Bella watched as Miah propped himself against the wall.

Her father leaned toward her. "Jeremiah has been telling your mother and me some things. And we feel they should be addressed."

"Like what?" Her eyes flitted to Miah. Had he told her parents about last night? No. He would never betray her trust like that. Besides, she'd finally found a solution. Not that she'd told him about it. Or anyone, for that matter. None of them would understand.

"That you haven't been sleeping because of nightmares," her mother stated.

Bella's gaze snapped to her mother. Oh. This was an intervention. Even though they didn't know a thing about the pills, they were still stepping in and backing her into a corner. "Can't you trust that I'm handling it?"

"Your mother and I believed you were, but if you're not getting a full night's sleep, then it is not being handled."

"I am sleeping, Bàba. I swear to you." *Just don't ask if I've been sleeping all night for the last month or so.* Bella focused intently on her parents. They had to believe their interference wasn't necessary.

"As much as I'd like to believe that is true, you've already lied to us before. First about the gifts, then again with that girl at school. At this point, your mother and I have to think of what is in your best interest."

"Which means what, exactly?" They were going to lock her up in the hotel and force her to see a counselor. No. No. No. Crap. How could she get them on her side?

"You agree to see a therapist, and your mother and I will provide you with a vehicle for transportation."

Bella tilted her head. Had she heard her father, right? She takes a walk down therapy lane, and they give her a car? Sounded like a sweet arrangement. Unfortunately, she would have to go and actually do the talk thing. Hmm.

"Let me see if I have this straight. I agree to counseling, and you'll give me a car."

"Yes. We want you to get better." Her father reached across and gave her hand a squeeze.

Sure. She'd go see some psychologist or something. Didn't mean she had to open her mouth and utter one word.

"Okay. You have a deal. Now, do you mind if I talk to Miah in private?" Because she was going to rip him a new one.

"Of course." Her parents stood, hugged her, and left the hotel room.

That went better than expected. Until about five seconds ago. Jeremiah stared at the empty couch. Then her parents had to leave the two of them alone. Not a problem. He just had to head her off before she got started. "Now, Bell—"

"Don't you dare apologize." Bell hopped to her feet. "I pour my heart out to you, and the first thing you do is run to my parents. Why? Why would you do that?"

"Because I'm worried about you." Plain and simple. She could say whatever she liked about his actions, but he had done the right thing.

"I talked to you about it. Wasn't that enough?"

Jeremiah pushed off the wall. "I'm grateful for that, but, no, it's not enough. For you."

"Says who?"

"Come on, Bell. Be realistic. Tell me that our one conversation is going fix this." Jeremiah crossed his arms. It hadn't even been a full conversation. It was him holding her and promising to keep her safe. Well, this was him keeping that promise.

"I'm sorry I came to your parents, but you need help. And I didn't think you'd do it on your own." Jeremiah watched Bell's eyes narrow. "What I mean—"

"You didn't think I could handle it by myself? Screw you. You didn't even wait twenty-four hours to see if I would talk to my parents on my own."

Wait. It wasn't as if she'd even indicated she might go to them. Just the opposite. Jeremiah crossed his arms. "Well. Would you?"

"I don't know, but you didn't give me the chance!"

"Because I don't know how to trust you anymore!" Damn. What just came out of his mouth? Jeremiah reached for Bell.

Bella backed up. "Get out."

"I'm sorry. I didn't—"

"I said, get out."

Jeremiah reached for her again, but, again, she stepped back. "Bell, come on, I—"

"Get. Out." Bella spat the words.

Jeremiah stared. Venom consumed those hazel eyes of hers. He could see that he could offer a thousand apologies, and she wouldn't forgive him. Not tonight, anyway. Afraid he'd dig a deeper hole, he nodded and walked out.

"We'll do the skit, and then Mandy will close out the show with her song." Bella glanced over the last of the Festival schedule. It worked out perfectly.

Vick jotted down a few notes. "How come you haven't talked to Jeremiah?"

"I'm not discussing this with you. We have enough to worry about. We only have three days to pull the show together. Full dress rehearsals tomorrow and the next day. Everything has to be in order so this'll be the best show the church has ever put on."

"Okay. I get it, but you're still going to the dance Friday night, right?"

Bella dropped her head back against the couch. "I kind of have to. The director's required to go. I'm supposed to be welcoming people. I just don't know if I can be there with him."

"You're one of the strongest people I know. Look at everything you've done the last six weeks. This show, your recovery, and you've helped me out with the tutoring thing."

He made it sound so easy—like she'd really accomplished something. But it wasn't easy, and she hadn't accomplished the most important thing. All her activities did was give her a temporary reprieve from the memories. Nothing was likely to take them away, except maybe a lobotomy. But Vick was right. If she wanted to go to the party, she could—but did she stick with the costume she selected?

Which brought her back to Miah. "Did he tell you about our fight? What he said?"

"Yeah, and that gives you a right to be upset, but it doesn't mean you shouldn't hear him out. We all say things we don't mean in the heat of the moment."

"Did he put you up to this?" Bella raised an eyebrow. Her brother wasn't the interfering type by nature. That job belonged to her parents. And Miah.

Vick held his hands up. "I surrender. He did ask me to talk to you, but only because he knows you'll listen to me."

Bella shifted on the couch. Trust was key to any relationship. If that was what they had. Yeah, they hadn't labeled it, but it was a relationship. Maybe Miah was right not to trust her. Sometimes she didn't trust herself. On the other hand ...

"How am I supposed to be with someone who doesn't trust me?"

"That's not the right question. What you should be asking is if it's repairable. If it isn't, then you're right, you don't belong together. If it can be fixed, then maybe you should give Jeremiah another chance."

"Whose side are you on?" Bella didn't want to start another argument, but the question popped out of its own accord. Damn. Maybe Miah's words had just popped out, too.

Vick grabbed a chair, placed it in front of Bella, and sat. "I'm not on either side. I just know trust is a two-way street. And no matter what you decide, you guys need to sort it out."

"And if I don't want to?"

"Then that's your decision."

Vick's brow creased as he took Bella's hand in his and squeezed. Disappointment was written on his face clear as day, but so was his unconditional support.

"Okay. I'll talk to him before I have to climb into the Arwen dress. By the way, was Arwen ever upset with Aragorn?"

Vick raised an eyebrow, confused. "Didn't Jeremiah show you the movies?"

"No. We'd arranged it, but everything got pushed back when the house got trashed. I only know what Miah told me."

"Well, they did argue, but only once, really. And it was because she chose to give him her Evenstar and her immortality."

"Evenstar?"

"A necklace with a charm to represent Arwen's immortality."

That's what that silver necklace was her mother picked out to go with her costume. The infinite looking one with wings. "I'm with you."

Vick grinned. "Anyway, elves live forever, and Aragorn is a human. Basically, no matter what happened, she'd outlive him. She loved him so much that she'd rather have however many years with him, than live thousands of years with her people without him."

Bella blinked. Why hadn't she obtained more information on this couple before she agreed to the costume? She and Miah were only sixteen. How could they even begin to have a love like that? She nodded to Vick to go on.

"Okay. So, he goes off to war. And while he's gone, her father convinces her to go to a place where their people will be safe. Along the way, Arwen has a vision where she sees a child leaping into Aragorn's arms. Their son. Her father tries to tell her that the future isn't concrete, but she decides to wait for Aragorn, anyway. She has that much faith in him."

Wow. Bella hadn't ever disobeyed her father. Lied and kept secrets, maybe. But never outright disobedience. But this woman? She was independent and strong.

She knew what she wanted and stuck to her decisions. Bella was nothing like Arwen.

"How does it end?"

"Well, Aragorn is the true king of the land. He has to overcome the history of his ancestors, defeat the enemy, and reclaim his crown. Which he does. Then he's crowned king and marries Arwen."

The story seemed like a Brothers Grimm story. It was real and ... heroic. Kind of a tale of self-discovery and faith in true love.

Bella tilted her head. "Fine," she said. "I'll be Arwen."

Vick snagged his notepad off the floor. "Good. Now, let's finish these notes for dress rehearsal so I can go home."

"Got a big date or something?"

"No. I just want to get home." But he grinned as if he had something to hide.

Bella watched the saw cut into the cast wrapped around her forearm. Oh, what a blessed day. To think of the things she'd be able to do, now. She could finally get back to the piano. And bowling! The last time she'd been was with ... Miah.

Three days had gone by, and she ignored him in school. Classes were easy. They didn't have any together. Lunch on the other hand, was a different story. They had the same friends. It's why she had spent the last two days at Sarresh's table.

Probably why Vick had talked to her yesterday. Aside from Miah asking him to.

But she missed him. Being in the doctor's office for the next step in her recovery wasn't the same without him. Bella knew she'd screwed up. If they never worked things out, she'd only have herself to blame.

"Almost done," the nurse said.

Oh, thank God! The nurse pulled the hard part of the cast apart with some forceps-looking thing, then ripped the bandaging. Relief, but— Bella was shocked at the first sight of her wrist. It was wrinkly. Shriveled. Where had the muscle gone? Bella's withered forearm was like a dying petal on a rose. "Is it supposed to look like that?"

"Atrophy is common. Don't worry, you'll build the muscle back with some therapy. Didn't the doctor tell you the full recovery for a broken bone can be close to a year?"

Hell. She'd been in shock and hadn't paid much attention to most of what the doctors told her. Except, of course, for a few times, when she understood everything the doctor said.

She shifted her eyes back to the nurse. "A year?" No writing. No bowling. No piano.

No! She refused to give up her music. It was the only solace she had. No matter what was going on, she could always count on music.

The nurse produced a brace, which she wrapped around Bella's wrist, strapping her in nice and snug. "Not too tight? Good. The doctor has put in a referral for physical therapy, which you'll start next week. Keep the brace on until then."

Bella eyed the brace. Great. She got the cast off just to have a brace put on in its place. What's next? A splint? An ACE Bandage? Why couldn't she be done with this whole recovery thing, already? She was over it. All of it. If she never had to deal with another doctor after this, it would be too soon.

"Miss Kynaston? Do you have any questions?"

"What? Oh, no. I'm good." She was ready to get the hell out of there.

Bella glanced at her forearm one more time. The painkillers would help. She'd be able to pick up the piano like she'd never stopped playing. Yeah. With the right number of pills, she wouldn't feel any pain.

The appointment had taken about an hour. Bella paid, collected her referral paperwork, and walked out the door to the waiting room.

"Finally. I was beginning to think you'd be in there forever." Sarresh pushed herself up from the chair.

"Sorry. I didn't think it would take so long."

Sarresh rubbed her taut belly. "That's okay. I know all about doctor appointments."

"I'm sure you do." The girl was nine months pregnant. She probably had her fair share of doctors poking and prodding at her. Bella grinned.

"So, home, Jarvis?"

"Only if it's yours." Bible study was not where she wanted to be tonight. She'd call her parents and let them know. No more lessons about forgiveness for her. Not now and not in the near future. Some people deserved it, while others didn't. Herself included.

twenty

Bella stretched her fingers and balled up her fist, then repeated the motion as she opened the door to the church's auditorium. It had been two days since the cast had come off. The brace wasn't tight, but her hand was sore, nonetheless—even though all she'd done was play the piano, yesterday. And played at Sarresh's the day before that. Not that it went very well. She'd gotten in a few chords, and then her fingers tripped all over themselves.

God, please, just let her have one song. The piano used to be an escape. Like her books. A way to get out of her head and release her emotions. For now, if she could play all the way through one song, she'd give her wrists a rest. Work her way back slowly.

She stopped at the empty orchestra. Good. No David this time. No witnesses at all, in case she screwed up. Stretching her fingers on the palm of her other hand one last time, she descended the staircase. Taking a seat at the piano, Bella lifted the cover to those beautiful black and ivory keys. They were the levers that struck at the best sounds in her heart. Splaying her fingers, she poised one hand at each end of the keyboard.

One song. She prayed for one song.

Eyes closed, she began playing "Heavy in Your Arms," by Florence and the Machine. Bella belted out the opening line.

It perfectly described how she felt. As if she was weighing Miah down. They cared for one another, but was it worth fighting for? Or were they condemned to spiral into a never-ending abyss? Was their love like a stone doomed to drown in the river?

The attack had ruined her. Miah deserved more than she could give him. He deserved to be happy.

And she was so miserable.

No matter how many pills she took, nothing could make her whole again. There was no way to piece her shattered soul back together. She might as well have dragged Miah out to the river where they would both drown. God, the way she loved—

Her fingers fumbled the notes of the chorus. She opened her eyes and shifted her gaze from her hands to the piano. Both had failed her.

"Damn it!" Bella balled up her fists and pounded at the keys. Why couldn't she even get through one song?

Jeremiah stood off to the side. He didn't want to interrupt Bell. Wherever she was in her head, the song she belted out was powerful. Her body relaxed with each word she vocalized, like she was shedding a second skin. It was disturbing and exquisite.

Then something happened. The notes clashed, and Bell slammed her fists on the keyboard.

"What did it do to you?"

"What're you doing here?" No part of her moved. Her head didn't turn, and her fists stayed balled on the ivory keys.

Jeremiah walked around so he could see her face. "Figured I might be able to catch you before rehearsal. I thought we could talk."

"I don't want to talk."

"Okay. Then we won't." This wasn't going the way he hoped. Yeah, he messed up. Said some things he shouldn't have. How could they get past it if she refused to speak to him? There had to be a way. Jeremiah looked at the piano. The answer stared him right in front of the face.

"Will you play?"

"I can't."

"Why not?"

"Because my wrist keeps locking up, if you must know," Bell said.

He glanced at the instruments scattered around the orchestra. Amanda was the musical one, not him. If Bell asked him to choreograph or dance, that he could do with ease. Play the piano, guitar, drums or whatever? Not so much. But—

Jeremiah held up a finger. "I can help. Just give me a second."

He sat on the bench, straddling her from behind.

Bell glanced at him over her shoulder. "What're you doing?"

"I'm giving you my hand. I may not be able to play, but you can. You just need an extra hand."

As Miah's hand came to rest on the keyboard, Bella shivered. He was so close. His legs pressed up against hers. She could feel the steady beat of his heart. She'd treated him like shit, refused to talk about what happened, and yet here he was, trying to help. She didn't deserve him. But God, she wanted to deserve him.

Bella swallowed. "Now ... now what?"

"Put your hand on mine and guide it. Show me what to do."

It had been so long since their hands had been together. She hesitated. What if it didn't work? What if— There were so many *what ifs* running through her mind. Miah had constantly put himself out there. She had to stop the *what ifs*. It was her turn. Her turn to be brave.

Bella placed her hand on top of Miah's. Lining up their fingers, she stared at the keys. They weren't the enemy. She just had to start slow. Closing her eyes, Bella gently pressed against the keyboard. Using their entwined hands, she began to play the repetitive beginning notes of "Brave," by Idina Menzel.

It was unusual, but somehow it worked. Guiding Miah's fingers across the piano's keys, Bella trilled out the opening line. It was so different from the last song. "Brave" was all about standing on your own, finding a way to live and figuring out ... tomorrow. All things she was trying to do, had yet to accomplish, but felt like she could do with Miah by her side.

She was well into the first verse when she lost track of where Miah's hand began and hers ended. Somewhere in the middle of the song, they melded and became one.

As she played and sang, she recalled their first date, walking into his home for the first time. Miah's noisy house was as full of life as if the family had lived there for years, his siblings running around without a care in the world. Then she thought of Miah wrapping her in his arms at the hospital and him holding her after the nightmares began. There had been so many times he'd stood beside her and wiped away her tears. No matter how afraid she was, he always reassured her it would be okay.

With the memories of their time together flooding her soul, pieces of the darkness fell away. Tears streamed down her face. Her heart wasn't whole. But it could be, with the right person by her side. Sometimes the world was ugly. And sometimes it was beautiful. The past couple of months she had experienced both. But one would consume the other if she allowed it.

Bella belted out the last of the song. She brushed the tears from her eyes. It would take time to find her way, but she could do it.

She was strong enough.

She was brave enough.

She could move forward.

"Thank you," Bella said.

"You're welcome." Jeremiah swept away the tears in the corners of his own eyes. He had witnessed the most glorious transformation. It was like watching the ocean waves recede and smooth out the sand. He started to move, but Bell's hands gripped his thighs.

"Please don't."

"Uh, okay."

"I'm sorry. I ..." Loosening her hold, Bell twisted around. Her cheeks were damp from crying. "You were right."

Jeremiah caressed her cheek. "I'm sorry, too, Bell. It kills me to see you hurting and feeling like there's nothing I can do to make it better for you."

"You do make it better. You make the bad disappear. You make me feel safe."

Bell curled into his touch and placed her hand over his.

"Does this mean I'm forgiven? Because I've really missed you." He hated her not speaking to him. He'd received the silent treatment a few times in the past, but nothing was more painful than his angel purposely ignoring him. Using his thumb, Jeremiah brushed away the remnants of her tears.

"Yes. I know you were looking out for me." Bell snuggled against his chest and whispered, "I missed you, too."

He'd stay there forever if he could. Having Bell in his arms was the best feeling in the world. He nuzzled her forehead.

"I'll always look out for you." It was a man's job to keep his loved ones safe and protected. He'd do everything in his power to take care of her.

Jeremiah tucked a bit of Bell's hair behind her ear. Bell leaned in close and stroked his lips with her own. Her lips were soft and tasted like cherry. Inhaling her lavender scent, Jeremiah stared into her eyes. Their green flecks sparkled like stars. When he closed the space between them, and Bell didn't back away, he caressed her lips with his ... and then slowly deepened the kiss.

Russell studied the blueprints the church had outlined for the Fall Festival in two days. There were at least thirty different booths to cover, plus the stage. He turned to Sheriff Detrone. "We're going to have to break this up into sectors. It's the only way to make sure no corner is left open."

"That's what I was thinking. At least two officers per sector."

"Most will have to be in plain clothes. We'll need to blend." There was going to be a lot of manpower out there. There had to be. He knew this was something the church did every year, but it didn't make it easy to keep the Kynaston girl safe. She'd reluctantly agreed to have officers patrolling the Festival, as long as they dropped the push for a personal detail.

The sheriff pointed at the blueprint. "I'll post an officer at the main entrance, too. See if we can keep track of all incoming traffic."

For two in each sector, Russell knew, the grounds would have to be broken up into no more than fifteen sectors. That was nearly thirty officers. Plus, the one at the entrance and two more for the stage. "That's going to leave a skeleton crew to cover the rest of the county."

"It's what we have to do," said Sheriff Detrone.

"I don't like this. I wish she would've withdrawn as director." Not that the position made a difference. The Kynaston girl had been targeted, and if the guy was going to make a move, he'd do it even if she only participated. Hell, he'd act even if she only visited. Russell sighed. There was no way they could be everywhere at once.

"Actually, I think it's good she didn't. For the most part, her movements will be limited to backstage. Makes it easier for us to do our job."

"More so if we knew who we were looking for," Russell said. The conversations with the Rodriguez kid hadn't developed any new leads. And Petar Jacobs continued to say he was innocent—that he was being framed. But DNA didn't lie.

Jeremiah helped Bell to the stage, took a couple of steps back, and waited. So many people and a lot of different costumes. From Batman to The Flintstones. But no one compared to his Bell as Arwen. The silver-sequined dress made her stand out like a star.

Bell waved to the crowd. "Good evening. I want to thank everyone for coming out tonight. Our Fall Harvest Festival is going to be incredible. We have a wonderful set planned for tomorrow. I hope to see all of you there. Please don't forget to stop at each trunk and get a handful of candy. Thank you."

Once the music started playing, Jeremiah moved forward and, gently taking Bell's hand, escorted her down the stairs and over to a table.

"How was it?"

"It was perfect."

Bell blew out a sigh of relief. "Good. I tried to keep it short and sweet."

"Someone should tell you how wonderful a job you've done as director."

"Anyone could've pulled it off."

The girl certainly didn't take compliments all that well. "Probably, but not the way you have."

"I guess. If I walk around and get some candy, will you carry the bag?"

Jeremiah bowed to Bell. "I am at your disposal, my queen."

Bella giggled. "Are you sure your crown isn't on too tight?"

"Not at all." Jeremiah grinned, as he snagged an empty bag from the table and offered her his arm.

Together, they strolled around the room, Bell grabbing a handful of candy from each trunk. They ended at the table where they started, and Bella said, "I think I need to sit for a little bit."

"You sit. I'll get us some drinks." Jeremiah placed a kiss on Bell's forehead.

Bell pulled out a couple pieces of candy from the bag and popped one in her mouth. Jeremiah shook his head and headed around the dance floor for their drinks. The decorations were nice. He couldn't remember who Bell'd put in charge of them, but they'd done a great job.

At the punch bowl, Jeremiah picked up a cup. Vick, in his Batman costume, stepped up beside him. "Looks like you two talked," Vick said.

"Yeah. We made up. She's got a way to go, but I feel like we're in a good place. I can't thank you enough, man." Jeremiah clapped Vick on the shoulder. "Hey. Is that you or a shoulder pad?"

Staring past Jeremiah, Vick missed the jest. "Dude. That's … is that David?"

Jeremiah looked to the doorway. This had to be a joke. Was the guy seriously dressed as a grungier version of Aragorn? What the—? Jeremiah watched as a brunette stopped next to David. A brunette dressed as Arwen.

Clutching Vick's arm, Jeremiah said, "Please tell me I'm seeing things."

"I'd love to, but it'd be a lie."

"As long as they— Are they heading toward Bell?" Jeremiah couldn't believe his eyes.

"Quick. Go ask her to dance. I'll intercept them."

Bella ran her fingers down the skirt of her scoop-neck dress. Her mother had done a great job. There was a lot going on between the silver satin and the layers of organza, but it was so majestic. The ribbons braided through her hair, combined with the sparkling dress, made her feel like a queen. And this was her palace.

Her smile brightened as her handsome king approached. Bella's eyes travelled once again over the details of Miah's costume. The silver crown helped anchor his wig. A deep blue velvet cape trimmed in silver draped across his broad shoulders. He had on a pair of iridescent burgundy taffeta pants, a dark gray tunic, and a chest plate. The outfit was completed with a sword at his waist.

Miah set their drinks on the table and held out his hand. "May I have the honor of this dance?"

"You may." Bella placed her hand in his and hopped down from the chair. She laced her fingers through his. It was nice to be like this with him.

Stopping in the middle of the dance floor, Miah took her in his arms. "Does Vick always dress like Batman?"

"Only for the past couple of years."

"What about you? What have you dressed as?"

"Uh, let's see. Last year I was a gypsy. The year before I was a vampire. That was the first year he dressed as Batman. I tried to get him to go as a vampire, too, but he blatantly refused."

Jeremiah chuckled. "Before that?"

"I went as an angel, and he went as a fallen angel."

"I bet you made a pretty angel."

"I think my mom has pictures." Unless they'd been destroyed in the vandalism. No. There was no place for the ugly tonight. It was Miah and her tonight. And the relationship they were building. Bella reached up and straightened his crown.

"Better?"

"Much," Bella said. All in their world was perfect. As the music slowed, the crowd around them faded away, and Bella leaned up and brushed a tender kiss against his lips.

"What was that for? Not that I mind." Miah winked.

"A thank you. For being here with me. And not just tonight, but over the last couple of months. I know I haven't really said it, but ... I don't think I could bear it without you." There was so much for her to get through, but it was possible because of him. Otherwise the darkness might've consumed her. She might've drowned in it.

Miah caressed her cheek. "You can get through anything. Whether I'm around or not—but I can't imagine being anywhere else."

"Me, too." Bella pressed a kiss on the inside of his palm. Then her gaze caught on another couple. Was that David? And Emily? Wearing the same costumes, she and Miah wore. What the hell? No. She wasn't dealing with that this evening.

Looking away, Bella said, "Do you want to get some candy for yourself? Before it's all gone."

Miah snickered. "Yeah. I noticed the kids double-handing it, too. But really, you're all the sweet I need." Miah kissed her and wrapped an arm around her waist.

Gervasio eyed the text. He had already looked up the latest structure of the Rescate County Police Department. He also knew the number of sworn officers they had. And he'd just learned how they planned to cover the Festival. Tucking his phone in the back pocket of his slacks, he stepped out of the office.

The first floor of the warehouse was packed with soldiers. All ready to do his bidding. But for this mission, a smaller unit was better. With a quick once-over of the twenty or so men, Gervasio decided. "*Verdugo*, Swifty, Iker, Axel, and Diego. Come. The rest, you go."

Gervasio spun on his heel and walked back into his office, followed by the five men he called. "This girl, she mission." Gervasio dropped a small stack of pictures bearing Bella's face on top of the blueprints.

Swifty picked up the photographs and passed them around. "What's the location?"

"The Festival, Nautica Valley. Take two car. Park half mile from west side of fairgrounds." He spread out the blueprints and pointed to the area where the vehicles should be parked. The grounds weren't surrounded by anything more substantial than chain-link fence. It would be easy to get through. "Police be at entrance."

"Which means the whole place will be crawling with pigs," Diego said.

No shit. They intended to keep him away from his girl. But that wasn't going to happen. Gervasio scowled. "Why we split up. *Verdugo* and Iker, you with me. East side. Swifty, Axel, you take west. Diego, find happy spot. We clear?"

The soldiers all nodded.

"Good. Swifty, Check communicators. Make sure they work." Gervasio glowered at each man. He wanted to make certain they understand the next part as if their lives depended on it. Because it did. "The girl? Alive. Uninjured. *¿Entendido?*"

"Yes, boss," all five said, in unison.

"Be back tomorrow. Three sharp. Now go." Gervasio jerked his chin toward the door. "Not Diego." Gervasio waited for the office to empty and pulled out another picture. Rising to his full height, Gervasio handed the photograph over. "If you get shot, take out."

"Yes, boss." Diego nodded and left.

There was only one reason to bring a sniper on a snatch and grab mission.

To kill.

twenty-one

Miah and the other dancers took their bows and exited the stage. They'd been great—fantastic. Bella was so proud. The curtain drew shut, and two stagehands set up the beginning of the last skit, the skit Bella and Vick had agreed on.

"Ready, Skit Scene One," Bella called into the headset that she, like all the rest of the crew had been issued in the earlier meeting. During which she'd been introduced to the officers covering backstage. Though she'd lost sight of them a half-hour ago.

In Scene One of the skit, a girl was partying at a club. The audience would see that the girl was dancing slower than all the other people. At the end of the scene, the girl left with a guy.

Watching, Bella told herself she could handle this. It was just a skit. Not her life.

"Ready, Skit Scene Two."

In the second scene, the party girl and the guy she left with were parked under the stars, in the backseat of his car, making out. When he pushed for more, the girl told him no, got out of the car, and ran away.

Bella shuddered and retreated further backstage, until the scene was out of her line of sight. She was wrong. It was too soon to watch this. She scanned the backstage area. Seeing a stagehand, she handed him the clipboard and turned her headset off. "Finish the skit, and have someone find Mandy. She goes on next."

The stagehand nodded and spoke into his headset. "Ready, Skit Scene Three. Ready Mandy."

With the show in good hands, Bella went down the stairs toward the back of the booths. She could clear her head there and get away from the skit—but, since the songs could be heard throughout the whole park, she'd still be able to hear Amanda sing. It was so close to Mandisa's "The Truth about Me."

Though both had similar meanings. All about the truths one's reflection reveals. And that maybe, just maybe, they could see more if they could see themselves through another's eyes. Perspective changes everything.

As Bella heard Amanda belt out the first verse, she looked back toward the stage. Her world had shattered. Her soul was broken. She hadn't heard God in weeks. Not since ...

Shaking the memories away, Bella continued on. Yeah, she had ignored the words of the song during Mandy's rehearsals. And hearing them now, it didn't change anything. God had betrayed her when she needed him most. Over the past two months, her whole life had mutated. Her view of the world had transformed. Nothing would ever be the same for her again. No matter how people saw her.

Bella paused. She'd passed three of the five booths on the aisle. They weren't as well-lit on this side of the grounds, and there were very few people lingering nearby. She glanced around, suddenly nervous. The hairs on the nape of her neck stood on end, but she didn't see anything. With a shrug, she continued on, stopping again as she neared the end of the next booth.

Then, she felt somebody come up behind her.

"Did you miss me, honey bear?"

Bella swallowed. It was her other attacker. Scar-face. His gravelly voice gave him away.

Tears prickled the corners of her eyes. No way he'd attack her a second time. Even if they were a bit secluded, there were officers all over the place. Not that she'd bothered to tell anyone where she was going.

"Come on, honey bear. Turn around. It's time we got properly introduced."

Bella shook her head. She wouldn't survive another attack.

Scar-face pressed up against her. He thrust something small into her back and slipped a hand around her waist. Leaning in close, he brushed his lips against her ear. "You may call me Jorge."

Gervasio kept the barrel of the .38 tight against his girl's back. Not that he'd shoot her, but his girl didn't know that. And that worked in his favor. Though he introduced himself with the same name he'd used at the Fourth of July party, the likelihood of her remembering that was slim.

"Please don't hurt me," Bella said. "I'll do whatever you want."

"That's good, because we're taking a little trip." Her cooperation would make this go a hell of a lot smoother. And he wanted to get out of here fast, before anyone realized she was gone.

"Where ... where are we going?"

"No need to get ahead of ourselves." He sure as shit didn't trust her with that information. But oh, man, he couldn't wait to get her back to the place he'd purchased for them. It would make a great home. Gervasio stroked the back of her hair. "You smell so good."

"Why ... why are you doing this?"

Grabbing her arm, Gervasio spun Bella around to face him. "I'm collecting on your father's promise. He made it clear. You belong to me." He gripped the back of her neck and mashed his lips against hers. Releasing the kiss, he tightened his hold on her neck. "Always remember that. Now turn around and walk."

Jeremiah bopped his head as he watched Amanda perform. She was always wonderful, but tonight she really shone. He felt every word of the song she'd written.

Vick rushed up beside him. "I can't ... find Bella." Vick panted the words out in two heavy breaths.

"What?"

Jeremiah yanked his phone out of his pocket, texted his dad, and took off for the stairs. He ran down and started for the booths. Bella didn't eat earlier. She might've gone for food. Trying to hide his desperation, he stopped at the first booth and asked if anyone had seen her. When they said no, he quickly moved onto the next booth. Another no. He repeated the question at a third booth and got the same response.

Before he got to the next booth, some invisible force stopped him at the gap between the two booths. Quietly, he walked through the space to the backend. There, he stopped. It was too dark for him to see anything, but he heard people talking.

"Ow. I'm walking. Please ... you're hurting me."

It was Bell!

"You'll hurt more if you don't keep moving."

Was that her scar-faced attacker? Quietly, he texted his location to his father.

"Please," Bell begged.

"Don't think for one second I won't shoot you. Now move."

Fuck! The guy had a gun. Damn it, where the hell—? A hand tapped him on the shoulder. Jeremiah snapped around. His father lifted a finger to his mouth. Behind him, Jeremiah spotted a few officers as they slipped by the booth and moved the few people still loitering away from the area.

Would they be fast enough to keep Bell safe? What if the guy shot her before the police could make a move? Jeremiah slunk from his spot and headed to the other side of the booths. He would create a distraction to keep his angel alive.

Gervasio stopped and yanked his girl back against his body as he listened to the voice in his ear. Shit. They hadn't made it to the rendezvous point, yet. If the police had the area surrounded, he had to find an alternative route.

Then there was good news. "Target has been sighted," Diego came across in his ear.

Ask and you shall receive. Gervasio grinned. "Location."

Diego prattled off the distance between him, his girl, and the target.

"Is target locked?"

His sniper's *no* resounded in his ear. Glancing around, he took in their surroundings. Trees to the left. Booths to the right. The target might not be in sight, but he was there somewhere. Left him with one option—bluff.

Gervasio dug the .38 into Bella's back harder. "Do everything I say, and you'll survive. Now, be a good girl and tell me you understand."

"I ..." Bella whimpered.

"Police. Freeze," an officer said from behind.

"Not a step closer, or I put a hole in her. And while you may kill me, I promise I'll take her with me." Looking closer, Gervasio saw that the officer was one of his own. Useful.

Gervasio pressed in tight against his girl. She could be pregnant with his child. Killing her wasn't on his priority list. But if he couldn't have her, no one would.

Another officer stepped around the corner. "I'm Sheriff Detrone, and I know you want this to go easy."

Just the person he'd hoped would come out of hiding. "It's quite simple, Sheriff. The girl goes with me."

"You know I can't let that happen. Just let the girl go, and you and me can talk."

"Tell them you want to go with me," Gervasio whispered in Bella's ear.

"I want to go with him," Bella said.

Gervasio tightened his grip on his girl. This was where a great bluff came into play. "See? So, this is how it's going to work, Sheriff. Bella and I are going to go out the side, here. And you're going to let us. Otherwise, my man takes out your son."

"No!" Bella cried out.

"Shut up." Gervasio ground his jaw and inhaled deeply. This wouldn't work if he blew up. Tightening his hold on Bella, he looked toward the last place the sheriff had stood. A movement caught his eye. He nodded.

"You don't think I came alone, do you? Now, what's it going to be? Your son's life or hers?"

Bella scanned the breaks between the booths, the direction Scar-face had been looking. Where was he? Where was Miah? Tears rolled down her cheeks. God, if ever there was a choice, please take her, not Miah. He had to live.

The pressure of the gun barrel lightened. For a split second, Bella thought her attacker had decided to give up. Except he hadn't. It was only the beginning of the whirlwind. As if a tornado struck on the spot, a gun went off and she was knocked to the ground—by Miah, who landed on top of her just as another shot pierced the air.

In the sudden silence that followed, Miah rolled off her and asked, "Bell, you okay?"

Her ribs were screaming, but other than that, she was in one piece. "I'm okay." Bella sat up and her eyes drank him in from top to— His t-shirt! It was drenched in blood. Where was it coming from? She felt all over her body. It wasn't from her.

Miah fell back.

"Miah!" Bella pressed her hands against his chest where the blood was oozing. "Help! Somebody, help!"

Miah's father skidded to halt beside them. "Bella—"

"He's bleeding! I can't ... I can't stop it."

Jamar ripped his son's t-shirt up the middle. Shit! Gunshot wound to the right pectoral. God, please let it have missed major arteries.

Depressing the button on his radio, he called out, "This is Sheriff Detrone. I need an ambulance to sector thirteen immediately. I have a GSW victim to the chest."

EMS was on site, but he hadn't expected they'd be utilized. Bunching up Jeremiah's t-shirt as best he could, Jamar pressed into the wound to control the bleeding loss.

"Hold on, son. Help is on the way."

Jeremiah turned toward Bella and reached for her hand.

Quietly sobbing, Bella grasped Jeremiah's hand. "Please don't leave me."

It was gut-wrenching. But it gave him hope. The way his son looked at that girl, he'd fight to live just for her. She'd keep his son alive.

The radio responded. "EMS is on the way, sir."

Oh, thank God. Red lights flashed over the three of them. Jamar glanced up to see two paramedics coming at them at a dead run.

Bella strode up to the nurses' station. She had no idea if Miah had been taken back or how long ago. But she had to do something. "Excuse me. I'm trying to find information on Jeremiah Detrone. He was brought in by ambulance."

"Are you family?"

"I'm—" That was a hell of a question. She wasn't family, but she was important. So was he. Bella bit her bottom lip. "I'm his … girlfriend."

"I'm sorry, but I can only provide information to family."

"Well, can I at least donate blood? I'm a universal donor. That would help, right?"

Miah's dad walked up to the desk. "It's okay, ma'am, I've got this," he said to the nurse, then turned his attention toward Bella. "What are you doing here? Did you even get checked out by the paramedics?"

"I told you, I'm fine."

"Hey! That was a hard hit you took. You need to get looked at." Miah's father crossed his arms.

"Let me donate blood for Miah, and then the doctors can take a look at me." Bella winced as she tried to fold her arms across her chest. She hated that Miah's father had a point.

"Listen to me. You need to get checked out first. While you're doing that, I can have an officer collect your clothes for evidence. We gotta make sure we nail this guy. Afterward, you can donate blood." He bent closer to Bella, a kind expression on his face. "I need you to work with me on this, okay?"

This was one argument she wasn't going to win. Bella groaned. "Fine. I give."

Jamar watched as his son's girlfriend was escorted to a room. His son would never let him hear the end of it if he allowed her to donate first. Lord, this was going to be a long night, he thought, rubbing his eyes.

"You okay, Sheriff?" Detective Lacey asked.

"Yeah." Exactly who he was waiting on. With all that had gone down, it was probably better a female officer handle the evidence for Bella this time around. Almost being kidnapped nearly completed the trifecta with rape and battery. What else was this poor girl going to have go through? "Bella Kynaston has been taken to room three. Would you get some evidence bags and collect her clothes?"

"Yes, sir." Detective Lacey nodded and headed down the hall.

Turning back to the nurses' station, Jamar rapped his knuckles on the counter and said, "Please page me when you hear something about my son." Then he turned around and walked back to the waiting room.

"Where is he? Is he okay?" Christine asked, rushing in with the rest of their brood.

"He's in surgery. They took him back about thirty minutes ago. I—"

"Daddy, what's that?" His youngest, Natasha, pointed to the red stain on the bottom of his shirt.

"Oh, my God!" His wife gasped.

"Is that Jeremiah's blood?" Amanda asked, turning pale.

He glanced down at his t-shirt. His son's blood must've soaked through his over-shirt, which had already been collected for evidence. It hadn't occurred to him to look in the mirror before his family arrived. Jamar scooped up his youngest in his arms. "It's nothing for you to worry about."

"It's his, isn't it?" Amanda persisted.

Jamar squeezed his oldest daughter's shoulder. "Listen to me. Your brother is going to be fine. He has the best doctors working on him, and he got treated quickly by the paramedics."

"But we should know something soon. Right, Dad?" Connor asked.

"Yeah, son. We should know, soon." God, they shouldn't be here. His kids should be at home playing in the backyard or video games. Not in a hospital waiting to hear about a gunshot wound. Jamar reached for his three younger sons and hugged them to him.

"I promise he'll be okay."

Russell dodged various patients, nurses, and doctors as he made his way down the hall. The sheriff's kid was there getting treated. If the situation was different, he would've waited until the guy knew his son was out of the woods. But this wasn't a typical situation.

He pushed open the door to the area wing where he knew the sheriff and his family were waiting. He rounded the corner and stopped. The Kynastons were standing at the nurses' station.

"When can we see her?" Mrs. Kynaston was asking.

"The doctor should be finished with her shortly. You can see her before we take her downstairs."

"Downstairs? What's downstairs?" Dr. Kyanston asked.

"That's where blood donations are handled."

"What? Oh, no. Our daughter doesn't donate blood," Mrs. Kynaston said.

"Really? As a universal donor, she seemed happy to help."

"Universal? Her blood type isn't O negative, it's B positive," Dr. Kynaston said.

Russell shook his head. While their conversation with the nurse was puzzling, he was looking for the sheriff. He looked down the opposite hall. The waiting room. Nodding politely as he passed the Kynastons, he legged it over there.

"Sheriff, can I speak with you for a moment?"

Whispering something to his little girl, Sheriff Detrone rose from his haunches and crossed the room. "What's going on?"

"Sir, it's the shooter we arrested." Russell lowered his voice. "There's a problem with processing him."

"What do you mean?"

Once a suspect was arrested, the routine was simple. Take them to the precinct, where they got searched, fingerprinted, and tossed in a cell. But this guy threw simple right out the window. Russell leaned in close.

"He's got no prints."

"You mean he's not in the system?"

"No. I mean his fingers are damaged. All his prints have been burnt off. The only thing we have is the name on his driver's license. Jorge Smith."

twenty-two

Jeremiah grinned. "Mom." Boy, was he glad to see her again.

His mother bent over her pregnant belly to hug him. He reached toward her, then winced, and she stopped.

"Sorry. Most movement is kind of uncomfortable right now." The doctors had spent a better part of the ... evening? ... morning? He wasn't exactly sure what time it was. Or even which day. Either way, they kept telling him he was lucky. The bullet had lodged inside his lung and missed major organs and arteries.

"That's okay. I'm just ..." his mother choked up. "I'm just glad you're all right."

"Mom, come on. No bullet can put me down. I'm Superman, remember?" Jeremiah grasped his mother's hand and squeezed, watching as tears rolled down her face. Aw, man. It was probably the hormones, but he hated seeing her emotional like this.

Amanda, standing behind their mother, snickered. "I think this bullet did, bro."

"Not permanently," he retorted. "And that's what matters."

His mother wiped at her face and squeezed his hand in return.

"I'm okay," he told her. But ... "Where's Dad?"

"Your father had to go to the station. Some issue he had to handle. Speaking of which, I should go call him to tell him you're awake. I'll be right outside." His mom kissed his forehead and stepped out of the room.

Amanda plopped down in the chair beside the bed and kicked her feet up onto the clean bedding. "Aren't you going to ask?"

"Ask what?"

His sister shook her head, a look of disappointment in her eyes.

Jeremiah lifted his eyes to the television as a temporary distraction. Of course, he wanted to ask. But it might be best not to know. He remembered knocking Bell out of the way and was pretty certain she had been fine, but she hadn't come by his room yet. At least not since he'd been awake.

Amanda clasped her hands behind her head and whistled.

"All right. Just tell me. Is she okay?"

"She's fine. A couple of bruised ribs, but nothing serious."

Jeremiah blew out a breath. Bruised ribs. He could handle that. But if her injuries weren't anything to worry over, then where was she?

"Good, I'm glad."

"Really? All that and you don't even want to know where she is?"

"Of course, I do."

"That's what I thought."

That wasn't an answer. Jeremiah scowled. His sister was torturing him on purpose. "Fine. Where is she? Where's Bell?"

"Her parents took her back to the hotel. But don't worry. She told me she'd come by later so she could personally thank her hero."

"I'm no hero." Even though she hadn't gotten shot, he refused that title. He was a failure as a protector. If Bell hadn't been raped to begin with, none of this would've happened. And then his father wouldn't be involved. Hell, he might even be a failure as a son.

"Don't be stupid. Of course, you are. That dude would've killed her for sure this time."

Jeremiah returned his gaze to the television. "I don't want to talk about it anymore."

Jamar threw open the door and glowered at the secretary. "Is he in?"

"Um, yes. Go ahead."

"Good." Jamar stalked past her. The door to the prosecutor's office was already open. Slamming it behind him, Jamar tossed the folder on the man's desk. "When were you going to tell me about this?"

Assistant District Attorney Perez removed his glasses and rubbed his forehead. "This afternoon. I knew you would be upset by—"

"You're damn right I am. You should have told me the second this happened. You know good and well this Jorge Smith character would've killed her the moment they were alone—but you want to prosecute my son for the shooting?"

"It isn't my call. I know you've taken Miss Kynaston's statement of the events, but it isn't enough."

"What do you need for this to go away?"

Perez leaned back. "I'm sorry this is happening. But I need to speak with Jeremiah and go over the events from Saturday."

"It's only been two days. Can't he recover a bit, before you throw him under the bus?"

"If it were up to me, I wouldn't prosecute. But he did jump out, when all the officers we've talked say it was under control. And Mr. Smith claims he had no intention of killing her, that he just wanted her to leave with him."

"Really? Did he happen to mention the deal he placed on the table?"

"Yes. And he admitted it was a lie."

Jamar shook his head. This was pure bullshit. He was wedged between two solid rocks. "Do I need to get him a lawyer?"

"You may. For now, get forensics to reconstruct the shooting."

"Okay. But this Smith guy was out for blood. The trajectory indicated the bullet came from his gun. And it wasn't an accidental shooting."

Perez leaned forward on his desk. "You're certain of this?"

"Yes. The report from forensics is in that file. I picked it up on my way here."

Perez opened the folder and scanned the report. "Let's get a full analysis done. I don't want any fallout from this gun. Now, what about the rape?"

"I had the lab recheck their results. DNA sample isn't a match—in fact, nothing popped with this guy's DNA. Petar Jacobs is the only confirmed DNA match we have. I haven't been able to get Bella to look at another photo array, but I'm positive this Smith guy is the other rapist."

"You still don't have his real name?"

"No." And they had explored multiple avenues. Neighbors of the address on the driver's license. Picture searches in every database they could think of. The guy's social didn't turn up any leads either.

"What about this Cristobal Rodriguez?"

"I sent Russell to talk to him again, today. While he's doing that, I'll go back to Bella's friends, see if we can place Mr. Smith in any part of her life."

Jamar rubbed his chin. There was something personal between this Smith guy and Bella, something they were missing. He just had to figure out what.

Standing, Jamar said, "Let me know if this jackass posts bail." Then he marched out of the prosecutor's office and headed to the one place he was certain to get answers.

Jeremiah tossed the remote aside. Everything on TV was boring as hell. He sighed and glanced toward the door. The tube had been removed from his chest earlier. Thankfully, the doctor said he could leave in a couple days, provided everything went well.

It was weird, though. Since he'd been admitted, he'd only communicated with Bell by text. She hadn't come to see him. The whole thing with Bell had started off great, but recently it had spiraled into a pit they couldn't seem to climb out of.

There was a knock, and Jeremiah's dad poked his head in. "Good. You're alone." He sat in the chair by the bed. "I need to talk to you."

"Is Bell okay? Did something hap—"

"Whoa, whoa. She's fine."

Oh, thank God. Jeremiah slumped as his muscles relaxed.

"But I do want to talk to you about her. Do you know all of her friends? Who's known her the longest?" His father had gone into police mode. Jeremiah had seen that *ask questions until you get answers* expression many times.

Jeremiah narrowed his eyes. "Dad, what's going on?"

"Some things in the case have come into question, so I need to talk to Bella's friends. See what I can find out."

No details. Right. Jeremiah blew out a breath of air. "Well, there's Vick Hilliard. They've known each other since they were kids. And Alex Grayson.

I think they've been friends for the past couple of years. Oh. And a girl named Sarresh. Not sure. I think her last name is Zirlan? Anyway, she and Bell met before high school."

"What? Sarresh? Are you sure?"

"Yes." When Bell had first mentioned the girl, he'd meant to ask his mother if it could be who he thought it might be. The name was so unusual. But with all the other stuff going on, he'd forgotten. "Is she—?"

"Yes. She's your cousin."

His mom's sister's daughter. His cousin. He hadn't revealed his suspicion to Bella, because his mother never talked much about her sister, other than the occasional slip about how she missed the woman—and hated her at the same time. He never knew why.

"Has Bella hung out with Sarresh, lately?"

"Not that she's told me. As far as I know, they stopped talking a year ago. Had an argument that kind of ended their friendship. Bell told me that at Sarresh's last birthday party she announced to everyone that Bell had a crush on Sarresh's brother. And then he said he only saw Bell like a sister ... and she took off. After, Bell and Sarresh had a huge blowout and called each other names. And that was that."

His father scribbled a few things in his memo pad. "All right. I'll talk to Sarresh and to the others. See if anything comes up."

Then, leaning forward, hands on his knees, he said, "Bella isn't the only thing I have to talk to you about. I need to discuss the shooting."

"Okay." Jeremiah felt a little queasy at his father's serious tone. "What's up?"

"Son, there is a good probability that you may be charged with endangerment and obstruction of justice."

If Jeremiah could have bolted upright, he would have. "Can they do that?"

"Yes, if the evidence supports the claims. The suspect is saying he had no intention of killing Bella. None of my officers heard anything to the contrary. I can't even say I did. And you purposely defied my orders."

"I swear to you, Dad. He was going to kill her. He said it before you showed up!"

"Look, there's a chance this may disappear. The ADA has spoken with Bella, but he's going to have to talk with you, too. In the meantime, we're going to find you an attorney."

"But I didn't do anything wrong!"

His father scowled. "Jeremiah Christopher Detrone, you should've stayed put. Your actions could've gotten both you and Bella killed! Did you think before you jumped!?"

"I'm sorry, Dad. I just ... I flipped. I failed to keep her safe before, and I couldn't let it happen again."

"Instead, you get shot, and she could've been killed." His father crossed his arms and shook his head. "I had no intention of letting him leave with her. I would've protected her. Did you really have that little faith that my squad and I could do our jobs?"

Jeremiah hung his head. His father was right. He hadn't given the police the opportunity to save Bell—and Bell nearly got shot because of his impulsive actions. He might as well have pulled the gun on her himself. This couldn't happen again. She deserved better.

Bella paid the taxi driver and climbed out of the car. Her driving test was scheduled for next week. Until then, she'd taxi it everywhere. Unless her parents could drive her. At least today she had some time off lockdown. And freedom never tasted sweeter.

She was finally going to see Miah. It felt like forever—although, in truth, it had only been a few days. But the distance had given her time to think. To make a decision. One they had skirted around for weeks. Miah had been so patient with everything. And now she was ready. She couldn't wait to tell him the good news. Hopefully, he saw it that way, too.

Visitor's badge in hand, Bella marched to the hospital elevators. Hooking her thumbs in the belt loops on her jeans, she tapped her foot. Lord, the elevator took forever. Finally, the elevator dinged and the doors opened.

Bella hummed on the way up to the third floor. She dug her cell out and checked the text Amanda sent earlier. Room 305. On the third floor, she followed signs to Miah's wing. Three hallways later, she approached the doors standing between her and her guy. So close, yet so far away. Turning left through the door,

Bella strode down another hall. Her eyes took in the nurses' station where she'd stood that night … but she kept going.

Pausing in front of Miah's room, Bella peered through the window pane. He was laid up in the hospital bed watching television. A paper wrapper and empty pudding cup littered a tray off to the side. The good news: he was alone.

She slipped inside. "Care for some company?"

"Bell!" Shutting the television off, Miah sat up and opened his arms.

She ran across the room and hugged him. Texting hadn't been the same as seeing him every day. Being around him all the time. It didn't compare. "God, I've missed you."

"Me, too." Miah pressed his nose against her neck and inhaled deeply.

Had he just sniffed her? His breath on her neck tickled. With a soft giggle, Bella released him and sat back. "How're you feeling?"

"Good. Doc says I can go home today."

"That's great news. No more bad hospital food," Bella said.

"The food's not— Oh, who am I kidding. The food is awful. I don't know how you managed to eat this crap for a whole week."

She didn't have a choice. Not with the beating she'd suffered. Bella shook the memories away. Now was not the time to think about that. Both of her attackers were in jail, and she was with a guy she cared about deeply. "My mom used to sneak me snacks."

"Hey," Miah said. "Speaking of your mom, how'd you manage to get your parents to let you out? Or are they hovering nearby somewhere?"

"They're hiding in the bathroom. They came in while you were sleeping." Bella giggled. It was a bad joke, but funny, anyway. "Seriously, I told them I was going, and the only way they could stop me was if they tied me to chair."

"You're joking."

"It might not have been those exact words, but close enough."

"I'm impressed," Jeremiah said. But he didn't look impressed. He didn't even look like he was fully paying attention.

Bella frowned. "Are you sure you're okay?"

"Yeah. Why do you ask?" His forehead scrunched up.

"Because … I don't know. It's like you're not totally here. Tell me what's going on."

Jeremiah's eyes darted to the window. Then he sighed. "The district attorney wants to charge me for interfering in the shooting. They're saying it's my fault."

Bella jumped to her feet. "What? That's preposterous!"

"They're right."

"I'm sorry, what?" She absolutely heard what he said, but the words didn't make any sense. The shooting wasn't his fault.

"It's the truth. I didn't trust the police to handle the situation. I moved out even though they had—"

"Don't you dare say they had control!" Bella shook her finger at Miah. "Because it's bullshit!" Backing away, she walked to the other side of the room. She didn't trust herself not to slap some sense into him. He was talking like a crazy person.

"They've never had control. This whole thing has been in his hands. His rules. His plans. They still don't even know who the hell he is."

"What're you talking about?" Jeremiah asked.

"The name on his license is fake, and I guess his prints are messed up or something."

"Really?" His father hadn't mentioned any of that. "That still doesn't change what happened at the Festival."

"Are you kidding me? That asshole tried to barter our lives. And you're somehow responsible for that? How does that add up?" Bella's face was red.

"I get what you're saying, but that doesn't mean I'm not responsible for my actions. I shouldn't have interfered."

She took a deep breath. "But you did it to save my life. To protect me." She pushed off the wall and moved closer to the hospital bed.

Jeremiah blinked. "What did you say?"

"What? You were trying to protect me."

Yeah. He ran out to save her. Jeremiah rubbed his eyes. Shit. The signs had been there all along. He simply refused to acknowledge them. The car at homecoming. The message on the car. The exchange—his life for hers. The shooter had known his father was the sheriff. There was no way the guy could've made that assumption or figured it out on the spot. The only way he could have known— Shit. He and Bell had been watched.

Which clinched it. The shooting was his fault. He was the problem. His feelings for Bell caused all of this. And, yeah, the shooter was locked up. But the guy could get out at any time—on bail. Damn it.

Jeremiah lowered his gaze.

"It's my job to protect you." It was going to kill Bell, but he had to. It was the only way to ... protect her. "We need to talk ... about us."

"Thank you for coming in. Please, have a seat." Jamar gestured to the chairs in front of his desk and took a seat in his own chair. This meeting with Bella's parents was long overdue. He glanced to Detective Russell, who sat off to the side, ready to take notes.

"Of course. We'll do anything we can to help," Dr. Kynaston said.

He was sure they would. Since the adoption records were sealed, they'd had to go to the adoptive parents. Especially given what Bella had told him about her conversation with the guy calling himself Jorge Smith.

Steepling his fingers, Jamar leaned back and said, "During the course of our investigation, we discovered information regarding Bella that we realize is pertinent to the case. Tell us about the adoption."

"I'm sorry. What adoption?" Bella's father asked, raising his eyebrows, innocently.

"Dr. Kynaston, I consider myself a patient man, but the time to bring this to us on your own has passed. We know she's adopted. Not only did we find it in the records, but Detective Russell overheard your conversation with the nurse about Bella's mistake about her blood type."

From what Jamar now knew, all of last weekend's event—and the rape, and who knows what else—pointed back to someone understood to be Bella's father. But did that mean her adoptive father, the man sitting in front of him? Or her biological father? Someone who'd yet to be identified?

Mrs. Kynaston glanced at her husband for a moment and laced her fingers together. She opened her mouth to speak, but her husband held up his hand.

"Milena."

"We must tell him." Mrs. Kynaston paused, then looked Jamar directly in the eye. "You're right. Bella is not our biological daughter."

Great. An admission. That was step one. "Who are her biological parents?" That was the information they needed to figure out the connection to this Jorge Smith.

Mrs. Kynaston took a deep breath. "Her mother, her name was Ileana Costa. We were best friends and came to the United States together for college. After a few months, Ileana found work as a part-time model. Her studies became less important as the year continued. Four months prior to our first year here, she signed a modeling contract and left school. We maintained contact; however, our calls were fewer and fewer, especially once I met Dewei. Dewei and I graduated, then married. She attended our wedding. That was when I found out Ileana was pregnant, amongst other things."

"What other things?"

Dr. Kynaston crossed his arms and scowled. Obviously, the man hadn't much cared for Bella's biological mother. "Milena, you have gone this far. Now, you must advise Sheriff Detrone of everything."

Mrs. Kynaston sighed. "Ileana had become involved with many men, alcohol, and drugs. She told me she didn't know who Bella's father was, but refused to give her up for adoption. She believed Bella could save her. Two months after Bella was born, Ileana died from a drug overdose. I was contacted by a lawyer. Ileana indicated in her will that if something were to happen to her, I was to be given custody."

"Have you ever found out anything about the biological father?"

"No," Dr. Kynaston said. "His name was not on the birth certificate. Since we have not disclosed any of this information to Bella, we decided it was best not to try and find him."

"Please," Mrs. Kynaston pleaded. "You cannot share any of this information with our daughter. She doesn't know, and we believe it is best she never finds out."

Russell spoke up. "I don't think you have any right to ask us that."

"Excuse me?" Dr. Kynaston glowered at Russell, then looked to Jamar. "Sheriff, I believe you need to get your detective in line."

"I understand your position, Dr. Kynaston. But Bella wasn't a random victim. She was targeted because of her father. Whether that's you or her biological father, we have yet to determine. But I promise you, if it's her biological father, she's going to find out."

Russell stared at the case board. He was missing something. He had gone back to all of Bella Kynaston's friends. Only one of them recognized Jorge Smith. Alex Grayson identified him by that name.

And Sarresh Zirlan, if she knew Smith, he wouldn't be surprised. The crowd of people Sarresh's parents described were known law-breakers. They had led him to one person who shocked the hell out of him. Unfortunately, he hadn't had any luck getting in touch with the only do-gooder in Sarresh's life.

The social security search on Smith. That didn't turn up anything new. It had been in existence for thirty-some-odd years, and was connected to a couple of credit cards and a condo in Amorte Cliffstone. The guy was a consultant of some kind. One who owned his own business and paid all his bills on time. Just no pictures or prints on file.

The detective's desk phone rang. Stepping away from the board, he answered. "Russell."

"Hey, Owen. It's Abby. You told me to let you know if Jorge Smith got any visitors besides his attorney."

The man's high-priced New York attorney played hardball. But, at least, so far, bail hadn't been posted. A small win, but he'd take it. Anything else would be helpful.

"Tell me someone came to see him in lock-up."

"Oh, yeah. Just sent you the video."

"Thanks. I owe you one," Russell said.

"More than one, but who's counting."

"Will do." Russell returned the handset to its cradle, opened his e-mail, and clicked on the file Abby had sent. He studied the kid in the video, Smith's visitor. Couldn't be more than eighteen or nineteen. Scrawny, dark hair, maybe six foot. Hard tell with the kid sitting down.

He focused on the conversation, then paused the video and rewound it. Son. Of. A. Bitch. Russell yanked open the top desk drawer, pulled out his tablet, and walked across the bullpen to the sheriff's office. He rapped on the door once, before opening it.

"Sheriff, you need to see this."

"What is it?"

"I've had Jorge Smith's visitations monitored." Russell stepped into the office and handed Sheriff Detrone the tablet. "Listen to what Smith asks."

The sheriff pushed play and focused on what the two were saying. It wasn't so much as the conversation as it was one particular sentence. "Does your girlfriend have news on mine?"

"Makes me think this 'girlfriend' may be watching Bella. Or someone she knows," Russell said.

Just then, Deegart poked his head in. "Hey, Russell, this came in for you."

"Thanks." Russell took the file from Deegart and flipped it open. Ileana Costa's rap sheet from New York. About time. He scanned the information. She'd been collared for petty theft. Arrested with— "Son of a bitch."

"What is it?"

Russell lifted his eyes to the sheriff. "The Kynaston girl's biological mother was arrested seventeen years ago in New York City with Juan Castell."

"I take it the name's familiar to you."

"Yeah. He was the leader of the Grim Reapers, until ten years ago." Looked like they finally found the missing connection. He may have also found Bella Kynaston's biological father. "We have his DNA on file. I'll have the lab test it against the Kynaston girl."

"What else do we know about this Castell?"

Russell said, "The guy went missing. His case was never solved, but we think it was due to a hostile takeover."

"Who took over?"

"We believe Gervasio Rodriguez did." The corner of his lips tugged into a small grin. Gervasio Rodriguez and Jorge Smith could very well be one and the same. And he had a way to verify it.

Bella stared at the piano. The last time she played had been so ... intimate. A feeling she wasn't going to know again anytime soon. She had to escape the memory. Forget it ever happened. Her fingers settled against the keys and began to move—but her fingers didn't choose the song. Her heart did. Christina Perri's "The Lonely" was so apt. She felt alone. People constantly betrayed her. The shell of whoever she used to be was left to fight the ghosts.

Always alone.

Her days would forever be empty. As quiet as the church's auditorium. The stillness endured. The piano and her voice were all that could be heard. She was all that remained. Not that there was much there.

Whatever still existed barged in and smashed the last memory she had of this place. It crushed the perfection of that afternoon. Maybe she had just imagined it, anyway. Finding courage. Playing how she hoped. Singing as if her life mattered.

Now, it was all gone. Nothing but a dream. One she would never have again.

For the last time, she belted out the chorus.

The song having concluded, Bella stared at the piano. An instrument that once served as a lifeline. A way to express her emotions. And she wanted nothing more to do with it. She closed the case over the keyboard.

It was done.

The auditorium door opened. "Oh, hey. I'm not interrupting anything, am I?"

She looked to the voice and blinked. "David, what're you doing here?"

"I was kind of hoping to take advantage of the piano. I have one at home, but Heather complains about my playing."

"Oh, um, yeah, sure." Bella stood and dropped her gaze to the piano again. She stared at it, but didn't reach for it. She couldn't. It no longer desired to have her. Turning away, she ascended the nearby staircase. "It's all yours."

"Thanks," David said. "You okay?"

"Yeah. I'm fine." It was a lie, but she had grown accustomed to telling those. What was one more? Besides, she would be fine. With the right number of pills, she'd never feel anything again. Bella passed by him and made for the door.

"Hey, um, a bunch of us are going out to a movie later. Want to go?"

Bella stopped and glanced at him over her shoulder. Another memory she had to override. And what better person to do it with? Someone she had no romantic feelings for. A friend. "Yeah. Sounds good."

To be continued ...

What happened between Bella and Jeremiah? How far down the rabbit hole does Bella crawl? Have the police discovered Jorge Smith's true identity? Has Detective Russell really found Bella's biological father? Will Bella find out she's adopted?

Get all the answers in

d a m a g e d

Released November 20, 2017

Keep reading for a preview of

d a m a g e d

one

Swifty stared at the letter in his hands. He hadn't read it in quite some time. For his sixteenth birthday, he had been given the knowledge of his birth parents. The woman he had spent his life calling Madre was his caretaker, not his birth mother. The letter he'd received on his birthday that year indicated his mother had died when he was just a child. As for his father, that was a story unto itself. For his safety, he had been tendered unto the woman he knew as his mother to be cared for. Although that first and second letter held a lot of vital information, the third letter, the one he had received nearly two and a half years ago, was the one that mattered the most. It was so important that he held it in his hands now, and read through it again.

My Dearest Luis,

I understand you wish to meet. Though I would normally take this into consideration, I cannot agree. The risk is too great. You must understand. If certain individuals knew of our relationship, you would not be safe. I promised your mother long ago I would ensure your protection. It is my hope that one day I may return, and we can be a true family, as we once were. But today is not that day.

However, I believe there is a task of great importance I may ask of you. A girl, Maylin Kynaston, will be fourteen in a couple of months and starting Jackson Heights in the fall. I need you to keep an eye on her.

There are rules you will need to follow. I cannot explain why, but it is imperative for your safety and hers that you do as I say. I have listed the rules below and included a few photographs of her and of those with whom she spends time

1. *Purchase a burner phone with cash.*
2. *Learn the difference between her friends and enemies.*
3. *Get close to each, discreetly.*
4. *Discover her habits, from a distance.*
5. *Do not approach her at any point.*
6. *Do not interfere with her normal life.*
7. *Do what you can to protect her from harm.*
8. *Memorize these rules and her image from the photographs.*
9. *And then destroy them all.*

That had been nearly two and half years ago. Swifty had followed every rule except one. A fire had been started in a large garbage can in his backyard. He'd stood before it with the letter and pictures in hand, but for a reason he had yet to fathom, he couldn't bear the thought of burning it all to ashes. Instead, he'd extinguished the fire and hidden the photos and letter.

Something familiar about the girl tugged at his heart. Those hazel eyes of hers haunted him every time he looked at the photographs. Her gaze invaded his dreams nightly. It was like she held a piece of him that was missing. In the past two years, he had learned all he could about her—but discovered nothing that explained why she meant so much to him.

Maylin used the nickname Bella. Victor, she had befriended as a child. Her friend Alex was a regular *cosa* fanatic and a weekly partier. Bella had been friends with Sarresh since camp, but that appeared to have ended. She had been hospitalized only once in her life—until recent events unfolded. And she had been adopted, but the records were sealed.

Could the adoption be the connection he felt they shared?

After Swifty started dating Heather, he'd asked her to learn what more she could find out about Bella. But, although he had hoped Heather's ability to obtain information would prove useful, she'd found out nothing he hadn't already known. Heather also happened to be one of Bella's enemies—although her enmity was nothing compared to that of the obsessed Gervasio Rodriguez. If only Gervasio hadn't met Bella at the Fourth of July party. A lot of heartache could've been prevented.

Swifty had thwarted many of Gervasio's plans, but he'd ultimately failed to keep Bella safe from that asshole. A couple of weeks after the party, he learned what Gervasio had done to Bella. He'd hoped when he shared his knowledge with Cristobal, the guy would do something to intervene and stop any attack on Bella. Except nothing happened. It was then that Swifty realized he was out of his league—and he'd done the only thing he could think of, contact his father.

Unfortunately, although he'd called the phone number his father provided in his letter multiple times and sent several text messages, no response from his father had been received.

At least Gervasio was in jail, Swifty thought, now. But for how long? The man had the money to post bail, but it seemed he was biding his time. He must have some kind of scheme. If only Swifty could discover what that scheme entailed, then maybe a plan could be devised to keep Bella safe. He would be damned if she had to face Gervasio alone, again.

If his father hadn't contacted him within the next twenty-four hours, well, he'd have to break another rule. Just as Swifty tucked the letter away, the burner phone he'd purchased two and half years ago vibrated. He flipped the phone open. "Finally."

Bella half-glanced at Alex. "You look fine."

"That's what you said about the last pair of jeans."

"They were fine, too."

"You're no help!" Alex exclaimed loudly and stomped back into the changing room.

It was cruel, but Alex's reaction when Bella failed to compliment her amused the hell out of Bella. She'd only agreed to the trip to the mall to escape her parents. They were back in the house, and although her parents had been eager to return, she was the one who had to go back to the room where it all started. But between the pills and her capacity to stay out of the house, she managed to hide her pain well. Even better than she had as a child.

"What about this?" Alex stepped out in a tight, black miniskirt. The black should've washed out her white legs; instead, her skin glowed with an ethereal beauty.

"Fine."

"Fine? Again?"

Bella snorted a tiny giggle and whipped a hand to her mouth to stifle a laugh.

Alex crossed her arms. "You're screwing with me."

"Maybe. Who're you trying to impress, anyway?"

"Raul's going to be at the party." Alex blushed.

"You must really like him."

"I do. He's, you know, different."

"I'll take your word for it." Bella grinned. "Try something else. You might give the poor boy a heart attack in that skirt."

Alex brushed the skirt down and glanced at her legs. Self-loathing flitted across her face. She nodded and disappeared back into the changing room.

Bella sighed. She hadn't meant the comment to come off as negative. It was supposed to be a compliment, but it appeared her friend didn't take it that way. "Alex."

"No, no. It's okay. You're right. I'll just change into something else."

How could she forget her friends had their own demons? Alex had never accepted she was beautiful. The girl was tall and thin, and her skin was flawless, but she could pinpoint everything that was wrong with her body. Now that Bella thought about it, she had never seen Alex in a skirt. Alex had often complained about her legs. They were too long, they were too pale, people could see her freckles.

Lord, she felt so stupid. Bella had enjoyed teasing her friend about all the jeans the girl had tried on, but hadn't thought twice when she commented on the skirt.

Someone brushed against Bella's back. She flinched and her whole body stiffened. She spun around and swung, and the palm of her hand smacked the face of the guy behind her.

"What the hell!?"

Oh. It was just some stranger. *Shit!* Bella shoved a hand through her hair and inched backwards. Surely, he hadn't done it on purpose, but that never mattered.

She panicked, now, at even the slightest hint of anybody's hands near her body.

"I ... I ... I'm sorry."

"Get a grip, would ya? Sheesh." The guy shook his head and walked away.

Bella eased her back against the wall, gripped her head, and slowly slid to the floor. This wasn't the first time she'd hit some random person. Her body was a time bomb triggered by the slightest touch. She'd talked to the freaking doctor her parents asked her to see. But nothing improved. It all just got worse with every day that passed.

That monster had invaded her life and stolen all she'd had, leaving a horrible world in its place. It seemed like everything would be better if she hadn't survived. The pain she carried in her chest wouldn't exist. The fear she faced every time she left her house would be gone. There would only be peace.

Peace. Not heaven. Just peace. Bella hiccupped, and her tears subsided.

She just wanted her old life back. The time she had had with Jeremiah— *Oh God!* No. She couldn't think about him. The hole he left in her heart magnified the pain she felt from the attack. Why? Why had this happened to her? She was a good person. Nothing about her life made sense anymore. Everything had spun out of control. Someone had to take the reins. She wasn't sure how much longer she could hold on.

"Shh. Hey it's okay. You're okay." Alex's strong and steady voice broke through the haze.

A relaxing voice. That was what she needed when the panic attacks occurred. Someone to comfort and calm her ... without trying to reassure her with touch. Just a voice to pull her out of her head.

Bella blinked unshed tears from her eyes. "Alex?"

"Yeah, B. Everything's okay. Come on. Take a deep breath with me."

Bella did as her friend directed, and the darkness reluctantly disappeared. "It happened again."

"I know, but it's okay. Can you stand? Good. Come on, stand up."

As instructed, Bella stood. She wiped at her face and sniffled. "I should go."

"Okay. Just let me change back into my clothes, and we'll leave."

"No. Stay and shop. You need something for the party tonight."

"Are you sure?"

"Yeah. But get the skirt. Raul won't be able to resist you."

Jamar glared at the thin case file on his desk. The intelligence from Juan Castell's missing person's report was minimal. According to the documentation, a neighbor had reported him missing. The house had been searched, and all that had been found was a hairbrush. That was how the man's DNA had been obtained.

A half-assed search had been conducted, but no other information had been gathered. It appeared that either people didn't care that the man was missing or they assumed he'd disappeared on purpose. As for the neighbor, she died of a heart attack two years ago. If they were going to find this guy, his detectives would have to start from the beginning.

Detective Russell's knock interrupted his train of thought.

"Sheriff, they're here."

"Send them in."

Dewei and Milena Kynaston stepped into his office, followed by Russell.

After taking a seat, Dr. Kynaston got down to business. "What have you discovered?"

Jamar removed a photograph from the file and laid it on his desk. "Have you ever seen this man before?"

Bella's parents studied the picture, and Mrs. Kynaston nodded. "Yes. Once. About two years before our wedding, I spent a weekend with Ileana. She introduced this man to me as a friend."

"But?"

Mrs. Kynaston sighed. "They both had a ring tattooed on their ring finger. Ileana never confirmed nor denied they were married, but I suspected they had done so in secret."

"Did this strike you as strange?"

"Yes. Ileana and I discussed everything when we were younger. I could not comprehend why she would hide such news from me."

He could. The woman had to have known what she'd gotten herself into.

"When she introduced him to you, Mrs. Kynaston, did she tell you his name?"

"Yes. Juan ... Juan Moreno, I believe."

"What does this have to do with our daughter?" Dr. Kynaston asked.

"This man's name is Juan Castell," Jamar said, stabbing the photo with his index finger. "He was the leader of the Grim Reapers. The man who took his place is the one we believe responsible for all the attacks on Bella. Mr. Castell, though, he's her biological father."

"What?" Mrs. Kynaston gasped.

"He was arrested with Ileana for drug possession in New York nineteen years ago. Just after she died, he left New York and reappeared here. Then, in 2003, he went missing."

Mrs. Kynaston fidgeted with the strap of her purse, then glanced at her husband. "I have to tell him."

"We agreed we would follow the documents."

"To hell with the documents! This is our daughter, and I will do whatever it takes to protect her."

Dr. Kynaston leaned back in his chair. "Very well."

"Tell me." Jamar glowered at the two of them. The last time he had spoken with them, he felt they had purposely left something out. He would have guaranteed it linked back to Juan Castell. They had withheld too much information for far too long.

"You must understand, we were instructed to keep all information regarding her parents, the adoption, everything to ourselves. We signed nondisclosure agreements before the adoption paperwork proceeded."

Interesting. Jamar suspected the secrecy served the purpose of protecting Bella's true identity, as well as that of her father. Children of powerful men in the drug trade were at great risk, simply by fact of their existence. "Go on."

"First, we had to change her name. Birth records were altered to make it seem that I was her biological mother and Dewei, her biological father. Second, a bank account was established in her new name. We were given shared control. After the rape, we decided to give Bella access. We provided her a debit card to use and told her it was money we had saved for her since she was born. All of her transactions are monitored."

"By you?"

"No."

No? Jamar frowned. He didn't like where this was going. "Then by who?"

"I don't know for certain. Possibly the lawyer. I just know we got a phone call a couple of weeks ago when she withdrew two hundred dollars each day for five days."

"Do you know what she spent it all on?"

"Clothes. She has been on a shopping spree these last few weeks."

Lord, let that be the God's honest truth, Jamar thought. With access to cash like that Bella could do a lot of things.

"Okay. I need to speak with her again. But, first, the two of you are going to sit down with her and tell her she's adopted. Don't tell her who her parents are. I'll be showing her photos, and I need her reaction to be unbiased."

Three days had passed since her parents revealed the awful truth. Milena told her that Ileana was her biological mother, but had refused to provide Bella with information about her biological father. The news that they'd kept the adoption from her infuriated Bella—and her "mother's" continued refusal to share all the important details angered her more. Her rage was the reason she sat in this stupid waiting room, once again prepared to spill her guts.

Bella glanced at her watch. How much longer would she have to wait? She despised the positive phrases carefully hung on the walls. Why couldn't her shrink's outer room be sterile, like any other doctor's office?

"Bella."

Finally! She stood and exchanged greetings with the short, stout, dark-haired woman who appeared in the doorway, then walked past her doctor and crossed to the window. She normally like the view, but she was so on edge the familiar scene appeared rundown and grungy to her eyes.

"They lied to me."

"Why don't you sit on the couch? You seem quite anxious."

"I don't want to sit." Bella paced the length of the room. "How am I supposed to trust them? How am I supposed to accept that everything they did was in my best interest?"

"Is that what they've told you?"

"Yes. But I couldn't listen to them anymore, not once they told me I was adopted. They've tried explaining ... but I can only hear so much at a time."

During her last few sessions, the doctor had simply let Bella to rant—which she'd appreciated. Most of the time, Bella could find a slight hint of relief in talking, even if she shared nothing that seemed to be of real importance. But, truthfully, everything she talked about mattered to her—and her doctor said she was making progress. Now, though, they had a topic it was difficult to avoid.

"Trust is difficult to earn back once it has been damaged. It doesn't mean it is impossible."

"That's the thing. I don't care that I was adopted. I care that they didn't share that information willingly." Bella slumped onto the couch.

The doctor grabbed her notepad. "Do you think they purposely hid the truth?"

"Well, they obviously kept it from me." Not that Dewei or Milena ever explained why they'd hidden the truth—even though Bella asked. And there was so much more she needed to know. What was her mother like? Why wouldn't they talk about her father? How did her mother die? Did she have any siblings? But the people who called themselves her parents refused to answer any more questions.

"Many adoptive parents don't mention the adoption to the child because they think of the child as their own."

"That's the thing. They didn't give me any reason for having hidden the truth. Just that now they *had* to tell me because the sheriff thinks my biological parents are related to my attack."

"And you haven't seen the sheriff, yet?"

Of course, she hadn't visited him, yet. He'd called the house several times over the last two days, but Bella refused to talk to him. She would go to his office—but only when she was ready.

"What are you, inside my head, doc?"

"No. It makes sense. You're exasperated and confused by the situation. Sheriff Detrone implied that your biological parents have something to do with the rape, and you think it might be true. And that scares you. Why?"

As usual, the doctor nailed her feelings. Except it wasn't just the possibility of the horrible truth about her parents. It was more than that. Facing the man who attacked her freaked her out. What if he got released from jail? Would he come after her again? Try to kidnap her again? Her world had been shaken. This new information, it shattered what little of her old world she had left. She had nothing, now. She was emptiness personified. "Maybe I don't deserve the happiness I've had."

Swifty swallowed, grateful for the window between him and Gervasio. The man looked downright pissed. The news he'd delivered hadn't been positive.

A few days ago, he accessed the court records and learned that Bella planned to testify. In his mind, this was good. He'd given the information to his father, who hadn't responded since the conversation they'd had last week.

Unfortunately, Gervasio didn't share the joy. The only thing that seemed to please him was the intel regarding the DNA. How had the man managed to plant somebody else's DNA? Of course, Gervasio had not explained. Even if they'd been talking in code, their conversations were still monitored.

"Should I check on her?" Swifty asked into the phone that allowed them to communicate.

Into the handset on his side of the glass, Gervasio replied, "Yes. She have great problem with health. Worry too much."

Swifty winced. The only problem Bella had with her health was sitting right in front of him. But he needed to keep up appearances—otherwise, he wouldn't have bothered with this visit. "I understand, sir. And expenses?"

"Whatever it take. Is that clear?"

"Yes, sir. I'll report back."

"Good." Gervasio scowled. "And Swifty?"

He hated that nickname. The Grim Reapers had given it to him after they appointed him messenger and learned about his ability to access certain information quickly, while remaining practically invisible. "Yes, sir?"

Gervasio's gaze homed in on Swifty, and a sinister smile spread across his lips, emphasizing the jagged scar on his face. Then his gaze bounced over to the guy who stood behind Swifty—a man Swifty knew looked like just another guard watching the room. "You should get small gift for your ... girlfriend."

"Yes, sir. I understand. Is there anything else?"

"No. That all. You may go."

Swifty returned the phone to its cradle. This would be one of those moments where serving as the underrated courier benefited him. He exchanged a handshake with the waiting guard and discreetly tucked away the folded envelope in the pocket of his pants.

Interesting. The guard's fingers looked similar to his own. Like Swifty, the man had no fingerprints. He suspected his father had something to do with the fact that all ten of his fingers had been badly burned when he was a child. Those unmarked fingertips had proved more useful to the Grim Reapers over the past two years than he liked to recall.

Trekking toward his car, Swifty tightened his grip on the envelope. He would open it when he reached his vehicle. Then he would see what Gervasio was scheming—and decide on his own course of action. Either way, he refused to contact his father again. Juan Castell had gone absent for the last time.

Author Note

I hope you enjoyed *Addicted: Dark Road One*. When I began writing this story, I was determined to make it as realistic as possible. Some of what you'll read in this series will be based on my own experiences and some, I have researched and reached out to people to ensure everything I wrote was accurate.

There are numerous characters to explore, so as you can imagine there will be a lot of books in this series. While I love hearing your thoughts on them, what I love even more is if you have a story to share. Did you experience something similar? Do you know someone who has gone through this? I'd love to know if this helped you in some way. You can write me at **krysfenner@gmail.com**.

And if you're up for it I'd love a review of *Addicted*. Regardless of what you thought—I'd just enjoy hearing from you.

If you'd like to see what books are coming out next in the series, check my site **www.krysfenner.co/** for updates or sign up for my newsletter.

Thank you so much for reading *Addicted* and for spending time with me.

In gratitude,
Krys Fenner

www.ingramcontent.com/pod-product-compliance
Lightning Source LLC
Chambersburg PA
CBHW071557110726
47908CB00007B/2141